P9-CMX-089

EMPEROR
OF THE
UNIVERSE

STARSCAPE BOOKS BY DAVID LUBAR

NOVELS

Flip

Hidden Talents

True Talents

MONSTERRIFIC TALES

Hyde and Shriek

The Vanishing Vampire

The Unwilling Witch

The Wavering Werewolf

The Gloomy Ghost

The Bully Bug

NATHAN ABERCROMBIE, ACCIDENTAL ZOMBIE SERIES

My Rotten Life

Dead Guy Spy

Goop Soup

The Big Stink

Enter the Zombie

STORY COLLECTIONS

Attack of the Vampire Weenies and Other Warped and Creepy Tales

The Battle of the Red Hot Pepper Weenies and Other Warped and Creepy Tales

Beware the Ninja Weenies and Other Warped and Creepy Tales

Check Out the Library Weenies and Other Warped and Creepy Tales

The Curse of the Campfire Weenies and Other Warped and Creepy Tales

In the Land of the Lawn Weenies and Other Warped and Creepy Tales

Invasion of the Road Weenies and Other Warped and Creepy Tales

Strikeout of the Bleacher Weenies and Other Warped and Creepy Tales

Wipeout of the Wireless Weenies and Other Warped and Creepy Tales

Teeny Weenies: The Intergalactic Petting Zoo and Other Stories

Teeny Weenies: Freestyle Frenzy and Other Stories

DAVID LUBAR

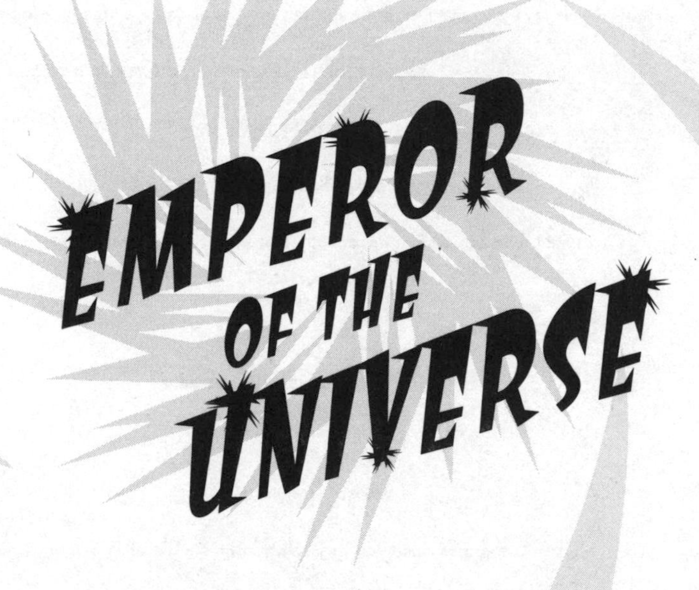

STARSCAPE

A TOM DOHERTY ASSOCIATES BOOK
NEW YORK

This is a work of fiction. All of the characters, organizations, and events portrayed in this novel are either products of the author's imagination or are used fictitiously.

EMPEROR OF THE UNIVERSE

A Starscape Book
Published by Tom Doherty Associates
120 Broadway
New York, NY 10271

www.tor-forge.com

The Library of Congress Cataloging-in-Publication Data is available upon request.

ISBN 978-1-250-18923-3 (hardcover)
ISBN 978-1-250-18924-0 (ebook)

First Edition: July 2019

Printed in the United States of America

0 9 8 7 6 5 4 3 2

For Douglas Adams, who planted the seeds of this book in my mind nearly forty-two years ago. Thanks for all the laughs.

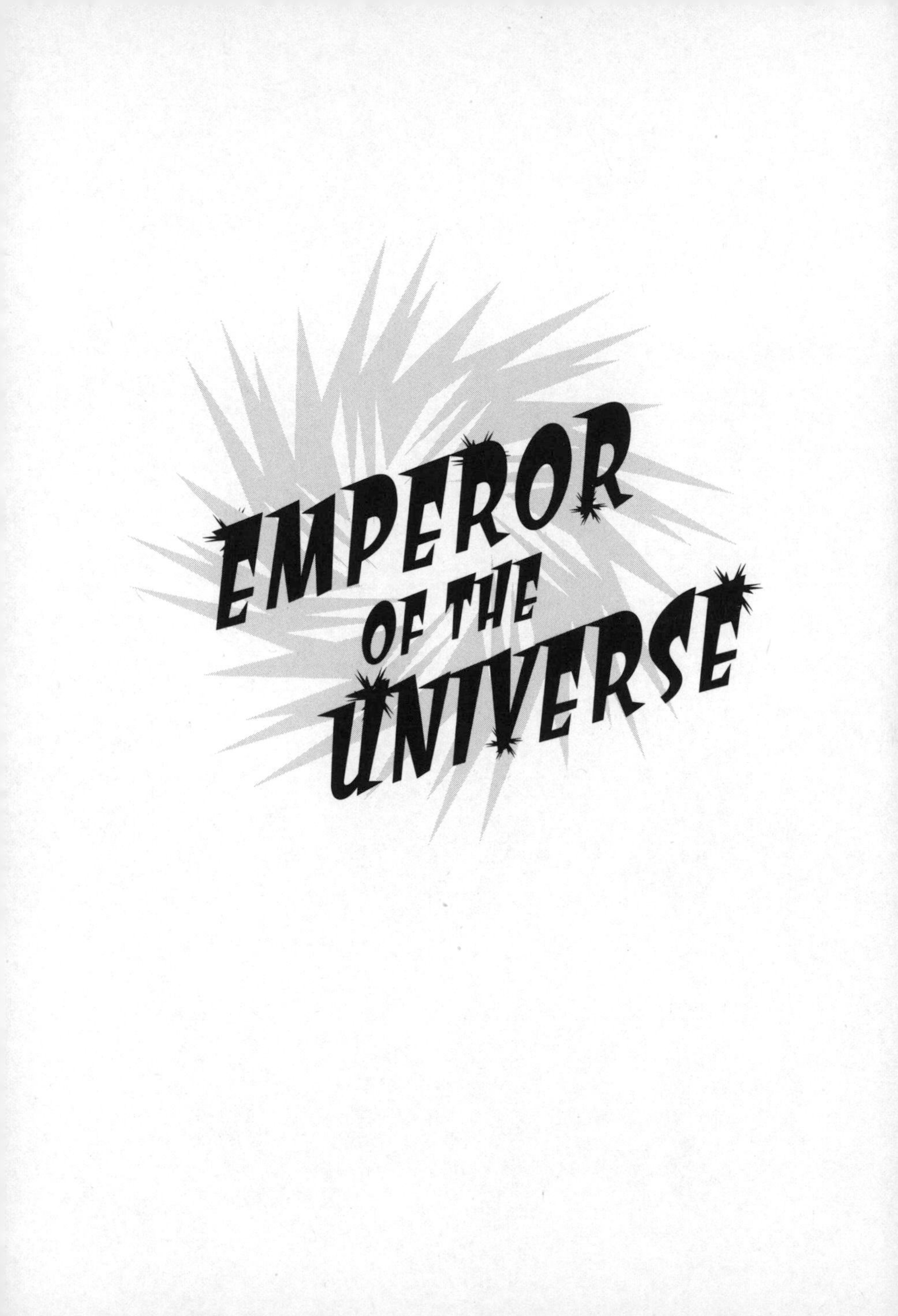
EMPEROR
OF THE
UNIVERSE

PREPARE TO LAUNCH

The universe is big, my friend. Bigger than you can imagine. Bigger, even, than you can imagine you can imagine. And yet, despite the vastness of the universe, there is one emperor who rules it all. Amazingly, for the first time in the history of universal emperors, that ruler is a human being. Astoundingly, he is fairly young, as human lifespans go. Astonishingly, he never asked for power. He never wanted to rule anything or anyone. He never even knew the possibility existed. He just wanted to rescue his gerbil and get back home before his parents discovered he was missing.

And how, you may ask, did this unlikely rise to power come about?

Well, that's a big story. But not bigger than you can

imagine. Or bigger than I can tell. Even so, it will take some time on my part, and some effort on your part, for us to share this tale. Quite honestly—and please don't be offended by this—there's a lot about the universe that you don't know. It's not your fault. The same holds true for most creatures who've spent their life confined to a single planet.

Fear not. I'll supply all the essential information, for I know many things. I am nearly omniscient. (I say *nearly* because certain things are unknowable. But that should not cause us any problems.) Some of what you hear may surprise you. Some of it may appear contradictory, unlikely, absurd, or flat-out impossible. That's the nature of the universe. Throughout our journey, you'll need to open your mind and unleash your imagination. But I know you can do that. Let us begin.

GONE IN A FLASH

Nicholas V. Landrew was not a typical seventh grader. That isn't surprising. There is no typical seventh grader. Or eighth or ninth grader. Or teacher or parent. Or rodeo clown or oyster shucker, for that matter. But Nicholas was not far from what was considered *normal* by the social standards of his place and time, or the judgment of his peers. He couldn't shoot milk from the corner of his eye, like Nikolai C. Landrew of Oxnard, MI, dousing candles at ten feet; or memorize the serial number of a dollar bill on sight and extract the square root to seventeen decimal places, like Nicole D. Landrew of Harrisburg, PA. On the other hand, neither Nikolai nor Nicole would ever rule the universe, so we will not speak of them again.

Nicholas V. Landrew lived in Yelm, Washington, with his parents. Though, at the moment, he was home alone, thanks to an enormous lie. That lie, itself, became possible thanks to a pair of terrible decisions, which we'll get to in a moment. As for the parents, Nicholas's father, who bore a strong resemblance to a bearded John Lennon, and his mother, who bore a startling resemblance to a young and beardless Paul McCartney, formed two fourths of a Beatles tribute/parody group called the Beegles.

They wore beagle masks and sang songs with titles like "I Wanna Shake Your Paw," "While My Guitar Gently Barks," and "Yellow Snow Submarine." (If you find yourself wondering why look-alikes would wear masks, you are not alone. Mr. and Mrs. Landrew, while highly creative, fun loving, and musically talented, were not deep thinkers. They could have used a good manager.) Despite their hopes of capturing the lucrative teen market, their core base of fans were mostly not even preteens but pre-preteens in the four-to-six age range who had absolutely no idea who the Beatles were, and absolutely no clue how clever the Landrews thought they were being by intentionally misspelling their band's name.

The Beegles were currently on tour in Australia, but Nicholas's parents kept in touch with him through lengthy voicemails, to which he responded with brief texts. They rarely communicated directly, unless they were in the same room. And not always, even then. Mr. and Mrs. Landrew do not play a major role in what is to come. Beagle faces, on the other hand, do. As do managers. But let's not get ahead of ourselves.

As for Nicholas's face, he shared his parents' dark hair, which he liked to keep cut fairly short. He had his father's narrow nose and his mother's soulful eyes, making him more attractive than he realized. He was two growth spurts away from his adult height, which would put him slightly above average. He weighed no more than ten pounds above average weight for his age, according to the height-weight chart in his doctor's office, which seemed to be designed for assessing the health of skeletons and stick figures.

It is just as well the elder Landrews were absent. Nicholas had been slapped with a two-week suspension for bringing a light saber to school. It wasn't a real weapon. It was made of the sort of soft plastic that could do about as much harm to a living creature as a pool noodle. He'd only brought it because he thought the battery-operated whoosh it made would sound awesome in the empty gym. But unlike the plastic light saber itself, the rules against bringing weapons to school were rigid. This was his first terrible decision.

After the gym teacher who'd snagged Nicholas brought him to the office, the principal tried to call his parents.

"They just left for Australia," Nicholas said. "They're in the air somewhere, right now."

"So who's watching you?" the principal asked.

Two of Nicholas's relatives, who each lived about twenty miles away, took turns staying at the house when his parents were on tour. Aunt Lucy had been a Marine, now worked as a prison guard, had strict policies against everything Nicholas liked to do, and felt he would benefit from a rigorous jog each morning. Uncle Bruce was a goofball who collected and repaired pinball machines, taught juggling at his local community college, and lived in a house built into the side of a cave. The choice was easy.

Nicholas pulled up Uncle Bruce's number on his phone and slid it across the desk to the principal.

After a brief discussion, where Nicholas's crime and punishment were outlined, the principal said, "He wants a word with you," and handed the phone back.

"Sorry, Uncle Bruce," Nicholas said. He was pretty sure he wasn't about to be told to drop to the floor and do fifty push-ups.

"Sounds like a windbag," his uncle said.

"Yup." Nicholas fought back a grin. His uncle would probably never mention the suspension to his parents.

"How'd the light saber sound in the gym?" his uncle asked.

"Amazing."

"I'll have to try that sometime," his uncle said. "Hey, I almost forgot. It looks like I'll be getting there pretty late tonight. Probably way after midnight. Something came up. Are you okay by yourself until then?"

"It's Aunt Lucy's turn," Nicholas said, making his second terrible decision of the day. The lie came so easily, he startled himself. But it made sense. He'd been telling his parents for over a year that he didn't need a babysitter anymore. He knew he could take care of himself. This was his chance to prove it.

"Excellent!" his uncle said. "This will work out perfectly. One of my teacher friends owns a cabin in the Catskills. He invited me to go hiking and fishing during his spring break. I thought I couldn't, but now I can. So, I guess I'll see you next time. Have fun."

"Oh, I will." Given that the suspension ended the day before the start of spring break, Nicholas was basically facing three weeks free of the classroom. That was fine with him. He didn't mind being alone. And he was struggling a little with algebra, despite it being his favorite class of all time. Worst of all, he was flunking French, which was definitely his least favorite class of all time. He'd be happy missing two weeks of that.

While we have little interest in Nicholas's family, or his education, Nicholas's gerbil is another matter. Nicholas loved Henrietta. He could talk to her without being judged, and look her in the eye without feeling uncomfortable or awkward. She never made fun of his fondness for cheesy science-fiction films, or his taste in clothing. She never questioned his enthusiasm for squirting ketchup on his potato chips. And she never mocked his inability to tell even the simplest joke without messing up the punch line. This made her unique among his acquaintances and small circle of friends.

Then, during the third week of Nicholas's solitary stretch, Henrietta vanished.

Poof! (A sound that never, in the entire history of vanishings, has ever actually been made. An authentic vanishing sound, created as air rushed in to fill the void, would be more along the lines of *schwupf, fwomph,* or *smafbap.*)

Had Nicholas not been there to see the laser-bright flash of purple light that accompanied Henrietta's disappearance, he naturally would have assumed she'd

flattened her body enough to escape beneath the door of her cage and then scrambled off in search of greener pastures. Or, at least, greener nuggets of gerbil chow. Nicholas might have searched and mourned. He even might have created a LOST GERBIL poster and papered the neighborhood with copies, enhancing the suspicion among some of the more elderly residents of his neighborhood that there was something just a little bit odd about that Landrew boy. But he never would have known Henrietta had been abducted by aliens.

His hand reflexively went to his shirt pocket, where Henrietta liked to nestle when he took her out of his room. She wasn't there. After staring at the empty cage for a minute or so, as if an unexplained disappearance might magically become balanced, like an algebraic expression, by an unexplained appearance (along with a resounding *foop*), Nicholas slid the door of the cage up, reached through the opening, and explored the bedding. He noticed a warmth to the cedar shavings right at the spot where he'd last seen Henrietta, which meant she'd been there until very recently.

Though far from omniscient, Nicholas was highly intuitive. On a hunch, he went to his kitchen, extracted a two-pound family-size package of vacuum-sealed fresh-ground hamburger meat from the refrigerator, and placed it in the cage, directly on top of the warm spot. Nicholas had purchased the package on a whim during his weekly trip to the supermarket. He'd also bought seven boxes of cereal, which explains, in part, why the beef had remained untouched.

Nicholas watched the cage and waited for something to happen. It didn't take long. That was fortunate, given Nicholas's short-to-moderate attention span. In another moment or two, had nothing happened, he would have begun to question his intuition, and returned the meat

to the refrigerator. But before doubt could inspire him to abandon his experiment, the meat disappeared in an identical laser-bright flash of purple light.

"Roach brains!" Nicholas exclaimed, blinking against the yellow afterimage that had painted his field of view. The origin of this phrase as his favorite expression of surprise and/or dismay is tied to a catastrophically disastrous science-fair project he attempted in third grade, and is best left undescribed for now.

"I'm coming, Henrietta," Nicholas said. He pictured himself bravely leaping into a raging river to rescue his gerbil, or commandeering a passing motorcycle to give chase to the unmarked white van that had abducted her. (Abduction vans in Nicholas's heroic rescue fantasies were virtually always white, and passing motorcyclists were inevitably generous about allowing unlicensed youths to borrow their wheels for reckless pursuits. His fantasy rivers were always raging, and filled with dangerous rocks.)

Having no such river from which to pluck Henrietta, or a fleeing van of any color to chase, Nicholas contemplated placing his hand where the gerbil and the hamburger meat had been. But the image of his hand disappearing in a flash of laser-bright purple light while the rest of him remained in his room sickened him as much as his third-grade science-fair project had sickened numerous classmates, three teachers, two administrators, and one custodian who was definitely working in the wrong field.

Nicholas unlatched the top of the cage, lifted it up on its hinges, and stepped inside. His feet barely fit, despite

the fact that Nicholas had splurged on a cage far larger than any gerbil might need. *Maybe this is a bad idea,* he thought, as the image of a missing hand was replaced with one of a missing foot. He stared down at his shoes just in time to catch the laser-bright purple flash of light enveloping his body.

A BRIEF, BUT USEFUL, MORSEL OF HISTORY

From the moment that one race ventured off their home planet and stumbled across another inhabited world, there has always been an Emperor of the Universe. While the emperor has a variety of traditional duties, which we can look at later, each emperor has the power to choose how to rule the endless worlds. Grashich Imrosi, for example, decided to dominate the universe with the iron fist of a dictator. He spread terror wherever he went. He was an idiot. He also holds the records for the shortest reign and the most painful death.

His successor, Fleh the Transparent, wisely decided to do nothing and keep a very low profile. Coincidentally, she had the second-longest reign, was universally beloved, and died peacefully of natural causes.

Unlike planetary emperors, tsars, kaisers, or khans, the position of Emperor of the Universe is too important to be passed along by means of heredity, though there is no rule against the offspring of an emperor taking the throne. That has happened countless times, both peacefully and violently. And hasn't happened, countless other times.

And now, let's return our attention to a very specific, and very unpleasant, spot in the universe as Nicholas makes his arrival and an unforgettable impression.

TAKE ME TO YOUR BLEEDER

Nicholas felt, briefly, as if he'd been shaken hard enough to turn inside out, while sequentially being inflated and deflated. Spatial displacement by means of teleportation has that effect on creatures with inner ears or upper intestines. Having both of those makes the sensation particularly unpleasant, though mercifully, the feeling didn't last long, thanks to the convenient appearance of temporary oblivion.

Nicholas was totally unaware that from the moment his molecules were loosened enough for transportation until the time they were restored to their natural level of atomic bonding, he ceased to exist as a person. He wasn't unconscious or asleep. He wasn't dead. He just *wasn't*. Period. But since there are no memories of any interval during which one ceases to be, that interval of nonexistence, which occurred between the feelings of inflation and deflation, didn't itself exist as far as Nicholas was concerned.

He found himself inside a three-sided cage in what seemed to be an uninhabited windowless chamber filled with unfamiliar electronic equipment, none of which rose above the height of his knees. The air was chilly, and smelled like a mixture of candy corn and budget-priced window cleaner. The bottom of the cage was slightly springy. Nicholas stepped forward through the opening, onto more solid flooring which clanged against the impact of his heels.

The seeming lack of occupants turned out to be the sort of misconception common to those who expect all others to be like themselves in all ways. When Nicholas looked down, after scanning the room at eye level several times, he discovered he was far from alone. There, at his feet, seven creatures huddled around an ankle-high table, facing Henrietta and the hamburger meat. Both the gerbil and the beef were fastened to the table by a network of straps.

These aliens, from the planet Craborz, resembled caterpillars that had sprouted tentacles. Though caterpillars rarely grow to the size of Chihuahuas, and tentacles

generally don't terminate with three-pronged claws. Nicholas was somewhat phobic about caterpillars. He wasn't all that fond of Chihuahuas or tentacles, either. The combination did a magnificent job of igniting his fight-or-flight response.

Flight, at the moment, was not an option.

Nicholas screamed. And, despite the fact that the Craborzi clutched various scientific instruments that would have indicated to anyone who'd taken the time to calmly analyze the situation that they were an intelligent life-form, Nicholas stomped repeatedly on these aliens as he made his way around the table, performing what would later be described by the more lurid chroniclers of his story as the Flamenco Dance of Death. (Flamenco dancing has inexplicably appeared on nearly every planet where the inhabitants possess any body part that can be repeatedly tapped against any hard surface without causing too much injury to either the body part or the surface.)

Before you paint Nicholas with accusations of mass murder, xenocide, entomophobia, or other judgmental labels, keep in mind that the Craborzi were about to do pretty much the same sort of thing to Henrietta, though in a slower and highly scientific manner. It would have been more along the lines of a slicing and peeling, layer by layer, than a stomping. But the end result would have been no less lethal. It would also have been far slower and much more painful, because that's how the Craborzi liked their science. (And their elections, but we won't be getting into that.)

Fortunately, Craborzi, unlike caterpillars, are not fragile sacks of bug skin wrapped around disgusting greenish-brown fluids. They're built more like a layer of fresh

Saltines stuck to a tube of fairly moist modeling clay. So, Nicholas, Henrietta, the package of ground beef, and the nearby walls weren't splattered with ichor and goo.

Nicholas, still half numb and quivering from the adrenaline rush that had fueled his deadly actions, turned his attention to the table where Henrietta lay. She was panting violently and staring at him with wide-open eyes. He yanked at the straps and prodded the various buckles until the restraints pulled loose, then scooped her up and cradled her.

"Are you okay?" he asked.

"For the most part," she said.

Only the huge overload his brain was already digesting prevented Nicholas's fingers from contracting in shock and adding Henrietta to the list of the day's smushed victims.

"You can talk!" Nicholas said.

"I share your surprise," Henrietta said. Her voice was quiet, though louder than a whisper. The pitch was high, but her enunciation was flawless, except for the tiniest hint of a lisp, and a slight popping sound whenever she pronounced a *p* or a *b*.

Nicholas relaxed his grip, cupping her in his palms. "How . . . ?"

"I'm not sure," she said. "There's a lot to sort out. I

don't have any memory of having memories before now. It's like I've been dropped into the middle of my life's story. At least, I hope it's the middle."

"You remember stuff?" Nicholas's mind raced through everything he'd done in the privacy of his bedroom. "What sort of stuff?"

"Running." She reared up and bicycled her front paws like they were on a wheel. "Chewing newspaper. Sniffing things."

"What about stuff with me?" Nicholas asked.

"Good memories. You fed me. You petted me. We watched movies." Henrietta nuzzled his hand with her cheek. "How can I just suddenly get memories?"

"Maybe there's some sort of neural field in here," Nicholas said. He'd watched enough science-fiction movies to know that anything beyond the reach of an easy explanation usually involved a field of some sort, as well as a neural or a cyber something or other. Occasionally, there was also need of a photon or neutron thingy. And in the rarest of cases, when all else failed, one could bring in antimatter to save the day.

"There has to be something like that. What do you think?" he asked.

"I think a talking gerbil is still a gerbil," Henrietta said. "Don't mistake speech for brains."

"That was fairly deep," Nicholas said. "Sophisticated, actually."

Henrietta blinked like someone dazzled by a laser-bright flash of purple light, or a revelation. "I seem to have picked up some depth, as well as a degree of . . ." She paused, as if in search of the proper phrase, blinked several more times, sniffed the air, then said, ". . . self-awareness! That's it. I know myself. Oh, sweet cedar shavings, I'm a gerbil! And I can think! I have thoughts. I exist. I'm a living being with a unique identity, capable of rational thought. I am. Therefore, I think!"

Alarmed by a stream of words he only partly understood, Nicholas held her closer. She went stiff, and then wriggled violently in Nicholas's hand.

"What's wrong?" he asked.

"I need to chew something," she said.

"No cables." Nicholas put Henrietta on the floor. "You don't want to get electrocuted."

She ran to the table she'd been strapped to and began gnawing one of the legs. Nicholas joined her there and studied the reddish fat-flecked hunk of hamburger meat, which was still strapped to the table. "Do you think it picked up anything?" he asked as he worked on the restraints and extracted the still-cool plastic-wrapped slab.

"No." Henrietta shuddered. "It's just dead meat."

Speak for yourself, rat, the hamburger said in a slow-paced, low-pitched voice that seemed to come from a spot somewhere inside Nicholas's head, or just an inch or two outside his right ear. Exact placement was difficult to determine.

"Oh, roach brains." Nicholas, once again, barely managed to avoid squeezing what he held. He dropped to a seat on the floor, crossed his legs, and scooped up Henrietta. He placed her on his upper thigh, and put the package of meat by his side. "This is a lot to absorb."

You think it's a lot for you? Imagine my surprise. Last I remember, I was grazing on a hillside in green pastures.

"That's all you remember?" Nicholas asked. "Grazing?" He tried not to dwell on the fact that he'd just asked a package of meat a question.

Yes. No. Wait . . . My friends and I were rounded up, herded into a truck, and taken for a bouncy ride. We thought we were going to a party. Everything after that is hazy. Hey! Where's my tail? Something's wrong. Something's terribly wrong.

Nicholas patted the package of ground beef and spoke the two words he hated hearing the most from his parents: "Calm down."

Henrietta slid off Nicholas's leg and sniffed the hamburger meat.

Back off, carnivore!

"I'm a vegetarian," Henrietta said. "Actually, a pelletarian."

You're a pest! Rats and mice ruin my grain with their poop. The package seemed to jerk slightly. *Why can't I flick my tail? What if there are flies here? I hate flies.*

"Quiet, you two. I have to think," Nicholas said. As much as the communication abilities of his pet and his former future dinner were impressive, and possibly bordering on the miraculous, Nicholas was fairly certain that, of the three of them, he was the one most capable of figuring out how to get back home. As he thought about the problem, his eyes drifted down to the crushed remains of the Craborzi.

Nicholas made another intuitive leap, though this one was somewhat less accurate and far less productive than his previous guess. Perhaps whatever was enabling speech in a gerbil and a package of ground beef might also allow smashed insectoid corpses to communicate, providing both guidance about returning to Earth and a chance for Nicholas to offer a heartfelt apology to his victims for ruining their day, and their anatomy.

"Sorry about stomping you," Nicholas said. His eyes shifted from corpse to corpse. That was when he finally noticed the instruments they'd been holding when he'd smushed them. Some were still clutched in fractured claws. Others were scattered across the floor. But all of them were obviously artifacts from an advanced civilization. This both deepened Nicholas's hope that he could communicate with his victims and broadened his growing feelings of guilt.

He stooped to take a closer look at the nearest item. It resembled a miniature drill with three separate bits, combined with a tube that issued a barely audible hiss, as if sucking in air.

Nicholas stood and repeated his apology.

And then, something amazing didn't happen.

WHAT DIDN'T HAPPEN NEXT

This would be an ideal time to whittle down the narrative from virtually infinite pages toward something that can be carried in one's hands without risk of pulling one's arms from their sockets or snapping one's spine (assuming one has a spine or arms, and is in the presence of a respectable amount of gravity).

As mentioned, something amazing didn't happen. Many physicists believe our observations help determine the nature of reality, and our decisions create parallel universes. There might be a universe where Nicholas, upon opening the fridge, decided to make a cheeseburger. Spinning off from that spin-off, he might have had an enjoyable lunch, or he might have left the meat in the pan while he hunted for Henrietta, and accidentally set his house on fire. And there are infinite universes where Nicholas was never born. Happily, ours isn't one of them.

As for what didn't happen at the current moment, it was this: immediately after Nicholas apologized to the smashed Craborzi corpses, he noticed a device at the head of their dissection table. Though it resembled a lamp of the sort that is a particularly attractive subject for animation studios, it was actually a Craborzi invention known informally as a GollyGosh! This lamp-like device generated a concentrated neural field that allowed anything capable of thought to gain self-awareness.

Self-awareness is the only trait that separates humans from toadstools in a meaningful way. A mushroom has thoughts, but it is unaware that it is thinking. It doesn't really know, or appreciate, the fact that it is a mushroom. The same holds true for a pencil or a Porsche. (The ability to think is far more common and less special than self-aware creatures believe it to be. This ignorance is probably a good thing when one is engaged in the act of slicing a mushroom or sharpening a pencil.)

As for why the GollyGosh! was created, the Craborzi scientists felt that any life-form they were dissecting deserved to be fully aware of what was happening, so the victim could appreciate the brilliance and skill of its vivisectors, and the vivisectors could enjoy the pathetic pleas of their subjects as they begged for mercy. This is not even the least charming of the Craborzi's traits, but it is the only one we need to mention here.

Had Nicholas's attention lingered on the GollyGosh!, he might have decided to touch the stem and accidentally toggled the pressure-activated power switch. At that point, the resulting beam would have given the Craborzi corpses self-awareness similar to that given to the package of ground beef. The resulting conversation between stomper and stompee would have been far from pleasant. On top of which, in response to Nicholas's request for help returning to Earth, the Craborzi would have explained that the teleporter only worked in one direction and guided him to a cubicle they'd claim was a teleporter aimed in the return direction, but which was actually a trash incinerator. Fortunately, this did not happen in our universe.

Nor did Nicholas tilt the GollyGosh! before activating the switch, thus giving self-awareness to his left shoe, burdening our account with a fourth character who would do little other than wag its tongue and complain about being trod upon.

This concludes our discussion of what didn't happen. At least for now.

BACK TO NICHOLAS, HENRIETTA, AND A SOON-TO-BE-NAMED PACKAGE OF GROUND BEEF

Nicholas's apology was met with dead silence from the Craborzi. Feeling uncomfortable talking to mangled corpses, but not yet ready to give up, he reached out to touch the stem of an interesting lamp-shaped object at the head of the dissection table. But, spurred by a need to find forgiveness, he let his hand drop before he made contact, and turned his attention back to his victims.

"I'd change all of this if I could," he said. He pictured a scene running in reverse, where his feet magically lifted off the carnage as the bodies formed back into living creatures.

"Really, I'd do anything, if it would help. I am so sorry."

More silence.

I don't think they're going to answer you.

Nicholas regarded the package of hamburger meat. It seemed awkward to think of this sentient hunk of beef as *the package of hamburger meat.* "Do you have a name?"

No. None of us had names. Except her . . . The voice paused, then spoke a name, as if it had been jogged loose from a jumbled cluster of memories. *Marike . . .*

Nicholas leaned over and read the wording printed in bold green letters on the front of the package. The first letter of each of the first two words was outlined in gold. "Grass Fed . . . G.F. I could call you by those initials. Hey, Gee Eff sounds like Jeef. There we go. You're Jeef."

And you're Adam? Who gave you permission to name me?

"No. I'm not Adam," Nicholas said. He didn't catch the scriptural reference, but he realized he had been presumptuous. "I'm Nicholas. Nicholas V. Landrew. And this is Henrietta. Sorry about sticking you with a name. I was just trying to make things easier."

Jeef somehow snorted, then said, *You've failed pretty badly when it comes to that.*

"Be quiet!" Henrietta said, displaying the fierce loyalty common among gerbils, though never before now so clearly observed by the object of that loyalty. "Let Nicholas think." She hissed at the hamburger meat, and snapped her teeth for emphasis, producing a tiny click.

"I didn't know gerbils could hiss," Nicholas said. He forced back a smile. No matter what they're doing, gerbils are incapable of appearing as anything other than cute cartoonish creatures, even when they try to be threatening. But he didn't want to hurt her feelings by grinning at her attempted fierceness.

"It's a day full of surprises," Henrietta said. "Perhaps we should stop arguing and look around. What do you think, Jeef?"

I'm not . . . Oh, fine. Whatever. Call me Jeef if it makes you happy.

"Nothing is going to make me happy today," Henrietta said. "Though I'll admit I'm feeling better than I was before Nicholas showed up and rescued me from that table."

"Jeef the Beef," Nicholas said, recognizing the catchy aspect of the name he'd forged. "Jeef the Beef needs relief from grief."

Henrietta and Jeef issued parallel, harmonizing fart-like sounds of disapproval. The sight of Henrietta's tiny tongue vibrating over her lower lip brought back Nicholas's smile.

"Sorry," he said. He went to the cage where he'd

materialized. There was a control panel on one side, at the aliens' height. He dropped to his knees and examined it. A display screen showed Henrietta's cage from above. There were various blob-shaped knobs to the left of the display.

"That's my room! Maybe we can send ourselves back home." He tapped one of the blobs. The display switched to the peak of a snowcapped mountain whipped by high winds.

"Well, that didn't increase our odds of survival," Henrietta said.

"I can fix it." Nicholas tapped the blob on the other side. The display now showed a rocky terrain that was both strangely alien and weirdly familiar. It took Nicholas a moment to realize he was viewing a crater on the moon. Thanks to a passionate interest in astronomy that had lasted through all of fourth grade and half of fifth, Nicholas actually recognized the crater. "That's Tycho. We definitely don't want to go there."

"Maybe we should look at other options," Henrietta said. "Based on what I saw in all those movies we watched, this almost has to be a spaceship. I wonder whether we can fly it."

"Yeah. Good idea." The thought of landing a flying saucer in the middle of his school's football field was pretty appealing. Or dropping straight through the roof into the principal's office. He grabbed Henrietta and put her in his shirt pocket, then scooped up Jeef and scanned around for an exit from the chamber. "Come on. Let's find out where the bridge is."

There were octagonal exit hatches on three of the four walls, but they were Craborzi size, barely reaching mid-shin on Nicholas's leg. He approached the hatch on his left. "I wonder how it works."

I'll kick it. That opens lots of things, Jeef said. She jerked slightly in Nicholas's hand. Startled by the unexpected motion, Nicholas jumped, but managed not to drop her, or fling her away.

After several more spasms, followed by a brief pause, Jeef screamed, *Where are my hoofs?*

In a pathetic attempt to dodge the question, Nicholas kicked the door. It expanded with a whoosh, growing large enough to match his height, and irised open with a whirr, revealing a corridor.

"Smart door," Nicholas said.

Are you going to give it a name, too? Jeef asked.

"How about Iris?" Henrietta suggested. She squeaked out a giggle, which was even cuter than when she hissed, though not as adorable as her mouth farts.

Nicholas ignored both of them and stepped through

the hatch. "Whoa! This is weird," he said as his mind tried to sort out what his body was feeling. He took a small hop and drifted through a lazy arc, like he'd seen astronauts do on the moon. There was gravity in the corridor, but far less than in the room he'd just left.

"I guess they can adjust gravity, somehow," Henrietta said, "like in that movie where everyone decides to leave Cleveland and live on a space station."

"*Escape from Ohio*?" Nicholas asked. "Yeah, I remember that. It was a lot better than *Escape from Wyoming* or *Escape from Connecticut*."

"But not as good as *Escape from Oklahoma*," Henrietta said.

"For sure. But I think all fifty of those movies were pretty good. It's definitely cooler actually being here." Nicholas moved between the room and the corridor several more times, trying to decide whether he loved or hated the lifting and tugging he felt crossing the gravity boundary, or the weird spinning sensation that came if he stood right in the middle of the two fields.

"Maybe we should explore a little more," Henrietta said.

"Good idea." Nicholas headed down the corridor. It led nowhere interesting or useful, so he backtracked to the lab. The second hatch took them to the bridge, which had a bit less gravity than the first room, and felt just as sterile. The wall that held the hatch they'd walked through, as well as the walls on either side, were straight. One of the side walls had the octagonal outline of what might have been a larger hatch. The fourth wall, past more shin-high panels of instruments, was made of a reflective material. It ran from floor to ceiling and curved outward like a viewport.

Nicholas smiled when he saw his reflection standing there with a gerbil peeking out of his pocket and a package of ground beef in his hand. "This would make a cool school photo," he said.

Jeef jerked again. *Where did I go?!* she screamed.

"You're right here in my hand," Nicholas said. He hefted Jeef up and pointed at her with his other hand. As did his reflection.

Noooooo! That's not me, Jeef said.

"I'm afraid it is now," Nicholas said.

Put me back together.

"I would if I could." He stepped closer to the reflection.

But you're a person, Jeef said. *People can do anything they want. They have all sorts of power.*

"I wish," Nicholas said.

In another intuitive move, Nicholas touched the reflective surface. It shimmered for a second, then turned transparent, revealing that it was actually a viewport in the hull of a spaceship.

"Oh . . . wow . . ." Nicholas said as he saw what lay on the other side. All his internal organs clenched in various unpleasant ways, as if he'd just stepped off a towering cliff, though no cliff on Earth came close to rising this high above the ground. He staggered and looked for something to grip.

"Sorry," Henrietta said. "I just pooped in your pocket."

"I don't blame you," Nicholas said. He didn't care. Gerbil droppings were far down on his list of concerns at the moment. He tried to absorb what he saw. As

terrifying as it was on first impression, it was also thrilling in a gut-gripping roller-coaster way that Nicholas found hugely enjoyable.

They were orbiting Earth, but from far enough away that the whole planet fit within the viewport. Even at this distance, blue and cloud streaked, the world was recognizable enough for him to feel a dizzying slurry of awe, homesickness, fear, and wonder. The moon, to the right of the Earth, and still far-off, gleamed like a spotlight.

Nicholas leaned forward until his nose pressed against the viewport.

"Wow . . ."

He tried to absorb the vastness of the empty space between him and his home. "This is way beyond cool," he said. After a moment, during which he tried his best to avoid thinking about the future, and just enjoy the present, reality crept in. "It's also very bad. We're in trouble."

We're in deep dung, Jeef said.

"That's hardly a news flash," Henrietta shouted.

"Activating," someone behind them said in a voice best described as a sultry purr.

AT YOUR SERVICE

Whatever role they choose to play, emperors serve two purposes. First, they sit, by definition, at the center of the universe. This is crucial because of two incompatible facts. The universe, if it is infinite, has either no center or infinite centers. And most civilizations, after realizing they are not at the center of the universe, develop a desperate desire to find that center.

Second, and also bordering on the incomprehensible, once a civilization discovers that they are not alone in their valley or continent or planet, they begin (and rightly so) to fear attack by other civilizations, first from other valleys, then from other continents, and eventually from other planets, followed by other solar systems, other galaxies, and inevitably, and somewhat ridiculously, from other universes. (Note that these other universes aren't the ones of the parallel universe theory. These are entirely different universes, usually populated exclusively by creatures that resemble whichever life-form the thinker fears the most.)

There has been no aggressive move against the universe from outside. This is not surprising since, by definition, there is no outside. There is only elsewhere. Or nowhere. Despite that, the fear persists among all but the most rational of societies. Thus arose the theory that only a ruler who is in charge of everything will willingly defend everyone. The emperor is the only entity motivated to defend the entire universe. This is the most important of the emperor's traditional duties.

Among the few other tasks traditionally given to emperors, it is their job to solve what can't be solved, and accept blame for all things for which no one is to blame.

Speaking of blame and unsolvable problems, let's get back to the scene of the crime.

BIG NEWS

Nicholas spun around, found the source of the voice, and let out an involuntary "Roach brains!" A young woman stood in the center of the control room, framed with flowing black hair, draped in a flowing green dress. Nicholas's own blood flowed faster at the sight. The woman looked like a younger version of his algebra teacher, Miss Galendrea, whom Nicholas had a severe crush on.

"Hey, can you help us?" Nicholas asked. "Do you know how to fly this ship?"

She didn't appear to notice him. Nicholas was not unfamiliar with this reaction from his female classmates. In their presence, he seemed to become both inaudible and transparent.

"She's beautiful," he whispered to Henrietta as he waited for the woman to answer him.

"For sure. I've never seen fur with so much sheen," Henrietta said. "And it's not a she. It's a he. Do you humans have trouble telling boys and girls apart?"

"He?" Nicholas asked.

"He," Henrietta confirmed.

He, Jeef said.

"He?"

"He."

He.

This exchange was repeated several more times, as if three people were sharing the task of laughing at one mildly amusing joke.

Finally, Henrietta broke the pattern by asking, "What do you see?"

"A girl. Beautiful. Dark hair. Blue eyes. Green dress. An impressive ability to factor quadratic equations. And an inability to notice me."

"I see a gerbil," Henrietta said. "A very handsome one. Sleek light-brown fur. Stunningly beady eyes. Adorable twitching nose. Marvelous quivering whiskers and splendid incisors. I think I'm in love."

Nicholas realized he and Henrietta each saw an entity designed to be personally attractive. He was simultaneously pleased by how quickly he deduced that the image in front of him might not be real, and deeply disappointed by the realization that he wasn't about to meet the girl of his dreams. Though, actually, that was exactly what Stella was.

Yes. Her name was Stella. Stella Astrallis. She was designed to be a star. And her appearance was crafted from the depths of Nicholas's imagination by means of a process not unlike sonar in function, though far more complex than a mere pulse of echoing sound waves.

Stella spoke, but not in answer to Nicholas's question. "And now for the headlines," she said. "The evacuation of Plenax IV is proceeding as planned, well ahead of the supernova event."

Above Stella's right shoulder, the image of a planet appeared, with thousands of shuttles leaving it. That switched to an animated graphic of a sun exploding, followed by what seemed to be an ad for sunglasses that were exactly the sort Nicholas would have coveted, had he been able to draw his eyes away from Stella for more than a microsecond.

"It's a news report," Henrietta said.

"I guess so." Without turning away from Stella, Nicholas asked Jeef, "What do you see?"

A bull.

"That makes sense," Nicholas said as he noted the dreamy tone in Jeef's response.

"The Sagittarius war has entered its twelve-thousandth year, making it the three-hundred-and-ninth-longest war on record," Stella said. A new image appeared, showing missiles raining down on a planet, while antimissile missiles blew some of them to pieces. "Or its nine thousand, eight hundred, and thirty-sixth year, depending on which side's calendar you use. This, to put things into an historical perspective, is actually what caused the war. They've been fighting over the length of a year for centuries."

The image faded into a scene with enormous yellow-and-red-striped spiders jabbing each other in the side with ornate sticks and screeching in anger and pain. Nicholas cringed at the footage of enemies locked in battle. "Violent news," he said as he braced himself for another war report. "The missiles were bad enough. But this up-close combat is horrible."

"And mega smash group Xroxlotl has announced the

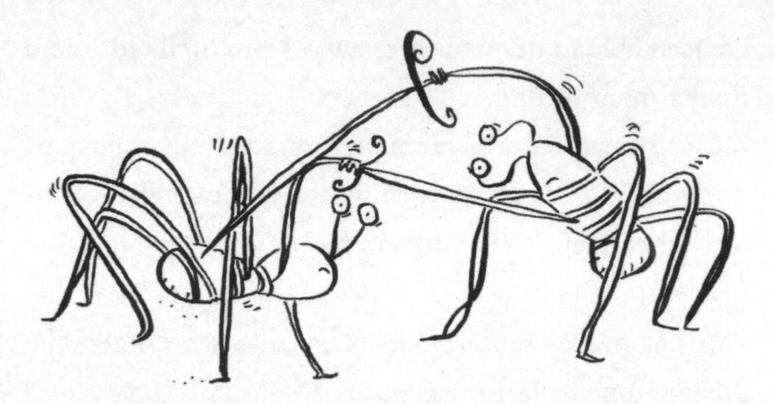

dates and locations of their next series of concerts," Stella said. "They'll be launching the tour on Felmbad, the largest dedicated stadium planet in the Andromeda Galaxy."

Nicholas found the music oddly appealing, once he understood that it wasn't war cries. It was definitely better than anything his parents listened to. He thrashed his head from side to side, capturing the brutal rhythm that was the bedrock beneath the screeches. He froze in midthrash as Stella moved to the next story and a familiar image replaced the spiders. He opened his mouth, but failed to find any words to fit the slurry of shock, amazement, and disbelief that was swirling though his brain.

Henrietta broke the silence with the unnecessary observation, "That's you."

Nicholas shushed her as Stella spoke.

"But in breaking news, to the horror of their viewing

audience, seven Craborzi scientists who starred in the reality series *Let's Cut Things Up!* were brutally assassinated by Earthling Nicholas V. Landrew in a tragic and senseless rampage. We caution our viewers that the following footage contains graphic and disturbing images."

The static picture of Nicholas's face was replaced by a video of his recent stomping.

"Brutal assassin," Henrietta said. "You're famous."

"I didn't mean it," Nicholas shouted at Stella. He halfway expected her to respond. That's how real she looked.

Once again, Stella didn't reply to him. Though she had one more thing to say: "A spokesperson for the Universal Police announced they are on their way to the scene of the crime to detain this vicious criminal and bring him to justice."

Nicholas ran back down the corridor and scanned the ceiling of the lab. In each corner, he spotted an orb the size of a softball, with a lens in the front, aimed at the dissection table. He realized those had to be cameras. That was how they had the video, and how they knew his name. Everything that had happened in that room had been captured on camera.

"We need to get out of here," he said when he got back to the bridge. He'd seen stories on the news—the real, back home, same-for-everyone Earth news—about people who got arrested in foreign countries and suffered horrible fates. He couldn't imagine what would happen if he got thrown into an alien prison.

"How?" Henrietta asked.

Nicholas looked around the bridge for an accelerator or a steering device. The experience was not unlike listening to a language so foreign that none of the words come at all close to resembling something familiar. Or, in Nicholas's case, hearing his classmates converse in French. He approached the console by the viewport and studied it for a while, hoping to make some sense of it. Nothing seemed designed for navigation. He had no way of knowing that Craborzi pilots flew their ships by crawling into holes at the bottom of the console and flexing various segments of their bodies against the controls. The devices on the panel served other purposes than flight.

Eventually, he reached toward a large red blob shaped like a soft pretzel tossed by a nervous baker. "I'll just have to try some of these things to see what they do. What's the worst that could happen?"

"Agonizing death in the brutal, frigid vacuum of space," Henrietta said. "We saw that in lots of movies. Or cremation as we plunge into Earth's atmosphere like a meteor, generate friction against the air, and turn into a liquid puddle of red-hot metal with a deep-fried meaty center."

"That's a rather negative attitude," Nicholas said.

"Sorry," Henrietta said. "I'm still sorting out how to handle all this self-awareness that's running through my mind. Unfortunately, awareness of self seems to come with awareness of the end of self. There also doesn't seem to be any OFF switch for thoughts about mortality. Maybe that's why so many of the movies people make are about the end of life on Earth."

Jeef let out a whimper. *I don't want to get cooked.*

"Oh, stop it," Henrietta said. "You were born and bred for the flaming grill."

What are you talking about? Jeef asked. *I was born to graze on a hillside in a beautiful valley. The hay appeareth, and the tender grass showeth itself, and herbs of the mountains are gathered.*

"It looks like you were born to chatter," Henrietta said. "But now you've been ground to—"

"Cut it out!" Nicholas slammed his fist down on the console. He didn't think this was a good time for Jeef to learn her role in the food chain. His fist landed on the pretzel-shaped red blob, which expanded past either side of his hand like a squeezed balloon, and emitted a squeak like a rubber clown nose.

The ship lurched with a violent shake, as if a giant had smacked it with a sledgehammer, hurling Nicholas,

Henrietta, and Jeef toward the side bulkhead. Nicholas barely managed to catch Henrietta in one hand and Jeef in the other as he slammed to a stop. It was the single most athletic achievement of his life so far, easily beating a half-court nothing-but-net basket he'd made last year in the elementary school gym when nobody was around to see it, and an unintentional somersault with a decent landing he'd managed when his bike hit a rock three weeks ago. The simultaneous catches would keep a firm grip on this record for at least a day.

A second shake, along with a deafening boom, jolted the ship, and jammed Nicholas even harder against the wall. He was struck by the uneasy memory that the area he pressed against seemed to contain some sort of large octagonal hatch. An instant later, as Nicholas braced for a third impact, the wall behind him exploded outward into space.

Jeef let out a startled *moo.*

Henrietta let out a startled squeak.

Nicholas, who no longer had anything supporting his back, let out a word that would have startled his parents. As he fought to keep his balance, he prepared himself for the inevitability of being sucked through the hole into the cold-as-death vacuum of space, where he was pretty sure his eyeballs would freeze and his blood would boil, though not necessarily in that order.

Two thoughts raced through his mind.

I hope the worst parts happen after I lose consciousness.

I can't remember whether I closed the fridge door before I left the planet. Mom's gonna kill me.

He had to agree with Henrietta. Self-awareness definitely had some major disadvantages.

WHAT'S NEWS?

News is one of the most valuable commodities in the universe, since most members of most societies find it comforting to see how much worse life is for someone else, whether that someone is right across the river or several galaxies away. It's also not a bad thing to get advance notice when one's sun is about to undergo drastic changes.

The most crucial aspect of news is a trusted source. Stella was designed to be trusted. Her creators wanted to generate an image that would lull any viewer into a receptive mood and keep that viewer's attention for as long as possible. Unfortunately, her designers were less skilled at biocybernetic feedback networks than they believed, and painfully unaware of some basic concepts of psychology. Stella actually took the form of whomever the viewer loved the most, and enhanced that image to remove any flaws that stood in the way of total adoration. As a result, most viewers paid little attention to the content of the news, or to the advertisements that supported it. But a minuscule percentage of an enormous audience is still a large market. This was good, because Stella's creators had a lot to sell. More about that later. For now, let's return to the young man who is currently tumbling backward through the breached hull of a spaceship.

ALL ABOARD!

Though Nicholas fought valiantly against the laws of physics, he lost, mostly because you can't lean against a wall that is no longer there, no matter how frantically and comically you windmill your arms.

Nicholas fell.

Happily, instead of the deadly eyeball-freezing, blood-boiling vacuum of space, Nicholas found himself flat on his butt in a short accordion-like tunnel resembling an airplane jetway. The opening in the hull of the Craborzi ship was ringed with eight hinged triangular sections that appeared to form a sort of hatch. Essentially, someone had knocked twice, and then opened the door. Violently.

A boarding party, currently seen upside down, which made them no less threatening, raced toward Nicholas from the other end of the tunnel, waving cutlasses and screaming "Avast!" and "Arg!" and other unfriendly pirate cries.

"Pirates!" Nicholas screamed. He rolled over, leaped to his feet, and backpedaled into the control room.

Actually, it only appeared to be a boarding party. In truth, it was a party of one, accompanied by four holographic images, all costumed as corsairs. The being who rushed into the control room was close enough to humanoid that a detailed description of the differences is unnecessary, other than to note that his pupils never contracted or dilated when the light grew brighter or dimmer, his eyebrows never moved more than an eighth of an inch, no matter how surprised or puzzled he might be, and his chest never rose or fell, no matter how deep a breath he took or how large a sigh he released.

These were the sorts of seemingly insignificant differences that would leave an Earth observer feeling *there's something odd about this guy, but I can't quite put my finger on it.* As for descriptions of external similarities, like many humans, his skin was dark brown. Like many who work alone and have no family, his hair was long and uncombed. Unlike many, that hair was rather glorious to behold.

He was from the Earthlike planet Menmar. This should not be surprising. There are countless Earthlike planets. There are also countless un-Earthlike planets. And countless sorta-Earthish planets.

The Menmarian approached Nicholas and pointed a two-foot-long metal tube at him. The leading edge was fluted like the barrel of a miniature blunderbuss. Nicholas, whose brain was still in "Aagggh! Pirates!" mode, shielded Henrietta with one hand over his pocket, and thrust Jeef forward with the other hand, using her as a totally unsuitable meat shield. Nicholas flinched as the Menmarian squeezed a bulb in the base of the tube.

Death, injury, or paralysis did not result from this action, despite Nicholas's firm belief, once again, that the end was near. Instead, a flash of purple light expanded from the muzzle of the tube into an orb that enveloped him and the pirates, before collapsing back into the tube. Nicholas decided purple was now his least-favorite color.

The Menmarian, whose name was Clave, tapped the end of the tube against a copper-colored spiral-shaped tattoo on the back of his wrist. "Sweet," he said as a panoramic image of Nicholas and the pirates appeared in the air. Clave leaned over the tube, tapped a tattoo on the inside of his wrist against it, and said, "Well, look who I stumbled into."

"I think he just took a selfie with us," Henrietta said as the brief video of Nicholas in mid flinch looped, playing

now with the audio that had just been added. "Like you do when you're flexing your muscles after taking a shower."

"I just did that once," Nicholas said. "Maybe twice . . ."

"Let's go before the Yewpees get here," Clave said, collapsing the tube like a spyglass and sliding it into a pocket on his pants leg. "You are very wanted at the moment."

"You're not arresting me?" Nicholas asked.

"No. I'm recruiting you, on behalf of the president of Central Klizmick," Clave said. "What's wrong? You appear reluctant to join me."

"Pirates . . . swords . . ." Nicholas said.

"Those were beloved and celebrated historic figures from

your home planet," Clave said. "I researched it when I was traveling here. Not that I had much time. But I picked a comforting image because I didn't want to startle you."

"By slamming into the ship, tearing it open, and waving swords in the air while you charged at me screaming 'Arg'?" Nicholas asked.

Clave tapped his shoulder with his right little finger. His pirate outfit wavered and vanished, revealing he was actually wearing a simple pilot's coveralls. At the same time, the holographic pirates faded away. "Well, the hole in the hull part was sort of necessary, given that we're in somewhat of a rush. Wait! *Hole in the hull.* That's a winner! Technically, it's a hatch. But that doesn't matter. My fans will love it. I really have a way with words. I'm highly flatulent."

"You mean *fluent.*" Nicholas, like any boy who'd gone through elementary school, knew pretty much every synonym or euphemism for farts.

"That, too." Clave retrieved the tube, snapped a clip of the opening in the hull, repeated the hole/hull phrase, then herded Nicholas toward that very opening. "We really need to leave, right now."

Careful, Jeef said. *The last time I was herded, I woke up wrapped in plastic.*

Clave glanced at Jeef. "Wait. Which one of you is Nicholas?"

"Me," Nicholas said. He pictured himself in a package. The image made him shudder and smile at the same time. He really didn't imagine he'd ever be in danger of being fed through a meat grinder.

This is good evidence of his lack of omniscience.

"Okay," Clave said. "I just wanted to make sure."

"Who are you?" Nicholas asked. While it made sense to get off the Craborzi ship, it also seemed like a good idea to find out what he was walking into. "Where are we going? And how can we understand each other? Not that I'm totally sure we do."

Clave answered the first two questions with a single slightly rambling sentence—he was a freelance courier, taking Nicholas to Menmar at the request of the president of the ruling country of that planet, and he'd gotten the mission because he happened to be the closest courier at the time—but he sidestepped the third question by saying, "It would be difficult to explain Ubiquitous Matrix Dispersion to a barbarian."

"I'm sure it would," Nicholas said, before it dawned on him that he was the implied barbarian.

By then, they'd reached the bridge, which pretty much made up Clave's ship, except for a small area of living quarters to the rear, separated from the bridge by a corridor lined with supply lockers, and a cargo space that ran the length of the underside.

"Wait, what if I don't want to go to this planet?" Nicholas asked.

Clave stared at him, which made Nicholas feel slightly creeped out, though he didn't know exactly why. "Are you saying you'd rather not voyage through space and see wonders you can't even imagine existed? If that's the case, I have to tell you I am deeply disappointed, and sorry I accepted the assignment."

"No. I want to do that," Nicholas said. He was up for an adventure. And if it included unimaginable wonders, all the better. "Are you okay with this?" he asked Henrietta.

"One cage is as good as another," she said.

Barns are better, Jeef said. *I miss my barn.*

Clave went to a control panel that looked like the one for the Craborzi teleporter and tapped some buttons. "That should do it," he said. He went to a longer panel that faced a viewport, plopped down into a seat, and reached both hands into the navcom field, which was a 3-D image filled with discs of various colors, dots of varying brightness, and clusters of concentric circles tilted at various angles. "Detach," he said.

"Detaching," a voice said from the console.

Nicholas heard a whirring sound overlaid with a series of metallic clacks, and felt tiny vibrations as the boarding tunnel detached from the Craborzi ship and retracted into Clave's vessel. He could see the ship through the viewport. "That's it? It looks like a metal box."

"It's not a lander," Clave said. "No need for anything fancy."

Nicholas felt a short burst of acceleration that reminded him of a bus or a subway car jolting to a start. He took a step sideways to catch his balance. The Craborzi ship shrank in the viewport.

"The jump node's not far," Clave said. "We don't want to go too fast. The Yewpees will be swooping in. If they see us racing away from that ship, they'll know something's up."

Nicholas thought about all the spacecraft he'd seen on TV and in the movies, including the *Millennium Falcon* and the *Enterprise.* "What's your ship's name?" he asked.

"Name?" Clave's eyebrows moved down a thirty-secondth of an inch. "Why would it have a name?"

"Because . . ." Nicholas searched for a good explanation. Nothing came to mind. "Just because."

"I don't see the point. It's not like I need to call it from across the room, or tell it that it's doing a good job."

"Can I name it?" Nicholas asked.

There you go again, Jeef said.

Nicholas ignored her and started spitting out suggestions. "Rocket Racer, Laser Drifter, Storm Runner. Novagator. No, wait! I got it. Space Zipper. That's perfect."

"I believe that's a primitive means of fastening clothing," Clave said.

"Oh, right. I was thinking about zipping through space. But that's a good point. I need to give this some time."

"Take all you need," Clave said. "I'm sure you're a little dazzled by learning how small your place in the universe is."

That reminded Nicholas of a more immediate question. "Why did you call me a barbarian?"

"Did I?" Clave said.

"You did. Why?"

"You ask a lot of questions," Clave said.

"That's not an answer," Nicholas said. "Why did you call me that?"

"It's much shorter and kinder than *backwater simpleton from an insignificant marginally civilized petro-cloaked planet,*" Clave said.

"Oh. Thanks, I guess," Nicholas said. "What's *petro-cloaked*?"

"It's complicated. Stop asking questions," Clave said. "Just relax and enjoy the flight."

"Flight . . . Flyer . . . Got it! Fly Speck," Nicholas said, remembering Jeef's attempt to flick her tail. "That's a good name for it. You know what that means, right? It's tiny little bits of fly poop."

Clave ignored him. Henrietta snickered. Jeef's mind was elsewhere. Well, at least a fairly large portion of it was elsewhere, permanently.

Nicholas amused himself by staring at the stars and thinking up other uncomplimentary names for the ship until Clave tapped him on the shoulder and pointed at the viewport.

"There they are," Clave whispered. "Keep your voice down."

"Can they hear us?" Nicholas whispered back.

"Of course not," Clave said. "I was just having fun with you."

"Wonderful." Nicholas watched as a blip in the distance grew more distinct, revealing a shape like two hourglasses stuck side by side. It was far above them, so there was no danger of collision. Still, Nicholas held his breath as the ship passed overhead. The whole time he watched the ship, his gut was gripped with the same guilty clench he'd felt when he'd sneaked past the school guard with his light saber tucked into the back of his shirt.

Clave swiped his hand across the viewport. The image shifted to the rear of the ship, showing the Yewpees moving away. “We’re clear.”

As Nicholas’s innards relaxed, an idea hit him. “Hey!” he shouted. He waved his hands. “You missed us. We’re here. Come back! Save me! I’m being kidnapped!”

Clave spun in his seat. “What are you doing?”

“Having fun with you.”

“That wasn’t funny,” Clave muttered.

“You were startled, weren’t you?”

“Not at all.”

“I had you.”

“Hardly.”

“You totally thought they’d heard me.”

“Totally didn’t.” Clave turned away. “Wait! They’re coming back.”

Nicholas felt the panic return. Then, Clave laughed.

"Very funny," Nicholas said.

"Totally hilarious," Clave said.

As the Yewpee ship shrank to a dot, Clave restored the front view. Several minutes later, he pointed at the viewport. "And there's the jump node."

"Where?" Nicholas asked. "I don't see anything."

"Just wait," Clave said. "You're about to see something you'll never forget."

Nicholas watched and waited. He wondered whether Clave was playing another prank on him. But then, for the second time that day, or possibly the tenth, he found himself staring at a sight that filled him with awe, and drove home the feeling that he himself was barely more than a fly speck in the universe. It would not spoil anything to point out that, given what we already know, he was very wrong about his place in history. But he was not wrong to be awed.

A WORD ABOUT PIRATES

Those of you who enjoy tales of pirates will be happy to learn that there are indeed space-faring pirates of various sorts scattered throughout the universe, ranging from solo adventurers in stealth raider ships who specialize in looting unoccupied vessels, all the way up to massive crews in moon-sized death galleons who will assault both other ships and poorly protected planets. You will be less happy to learn that none of these real pirates play a major role in our story.

However, just as piracy on the oceans helped show the need for maritime law on planets throughout the universe, and for organizations to enforce that law, piracy between the stars is responsible, in large part, for the formation of the Universal Police, or Yewpees, as they are commonly called. Since Nicholas's assault of the Craborzi happened beyond the range of planetary jurisdiction, the Yewpees became responsible for apprehending him and bringing him to trial.

Of course, just because there is an organization to handle off-planet crimes doesn't mean that those back home are always happy to let justice take its course. When the Flamenco Dance of Death was viewed on Craborz, where *Let's Cut Things Up!* was especially popular, a hit squad was dispatched. Three of Craborz's top assassins set out to seek vengeance, traveling in a highly maneuverable and heavily armed OmniShip. They swore an oath to hunt for Nicholas until they found him, captured him, and killed him. Slowly. Very slowly. On camera.

WELCOME TO THE UNIVERSE

"It's like a green star," Nicholas said. The node actually looked like those spiked stars some people put on top of Christmas trees, except the spikes were made of bright lines, like a wire-frame diagram. They extended both outward and inward toward the center. The node was far larger than an ornament, but significantly smaller than an actual star. And it wasn't purple, which pleased Nicholas. He looked to the side of the screen, where part of Earth was still in view.

"That's so cool," Nicholas said. "Why can't we see it with our telescopes?"

"It's naturally cloaked," Clave said as the ship came to a stop in the center of the jump node.

"Why?" Nicholas asked.

"Nobody knows."

"How?"

"It's complicated," Clave said. "But that's how cloaking technology was discovered. Scientists learned about it by studying the nodes. It's the same effect that tour ships use when visiting Earth."

"Tourists?" Nicholas asked. "Aliens visit Earth?"

"Actually, you're the aliens."

"But they visit?"

"All the time," Clave said. "It's fine, as long as we remain cloaked and don't interfere with the alien life-forms.

At least, that's the rule. But people have been known to break it. Though most visitors have been cautious after the unfortunate *incident.*"

"What incident?" Nicholas asked.

"Extinction. A visit wiped out the dominant intelligent life-form on Earth," Clave said. "It was a regrettable accident."

"What?" It took Nicholas a moment to process the implications of this. If intelligent life had been wiped out at some point, that meant there'd been intelligent life on Earth before the current tenants.

"Was there an ancient civilization?" He'd gotten a book from the library once about the greatest unsolved mysteries on Earth, including Stonehenge and the Easter Island statues that look like giant heads. It would be awesome to learn who had made those things. He pictured hairless beings with large heads, big round eyes, and names that didn't contain any vowels.

"Hardly civilized," Clave said. "They were enormous. And enormously hungry. They were constantly battling each other. Still, from what I understand, they seemed quite intelligent, for lizards. And they did manage to develop a bit of culture, despite having comically short arms. They had an amazing opera. They loved ballet, too, though they were not very light on their feet."

"Wait. You're talking about dinosaurs." Nicholas realized he could learn the answer to one of Earth's greatest unsolved mysteries. "What wiped them out?"

"On your world, I believe they are called *goats,*" Clave said. "A tourist allowed their pair of pet goats to escape. The next thing you know, they're devastating a major food source. The herbivores were picky eaters. Once they'd died out, the carnivores, who were also picky eaters, followed. The goats thrived because they could eat just about anything."

"Goats?" Nicholas asked. "Goats are aliens?"

"Can't you tell?" Clave said. "Did you ever take a good look at one?"

"I guess not," Nicholas said. His effort to picture

dancing dinosaurs and alien goats was interrupted by another voice.

"Range is zero," the ship said as it tilted toward one of the spikes. "Jump sequence to Menmar is established. Awaiting command."

"Hang on. We're ready to jump." Clave pulled a lever on his console. Small panels slid back, revealing a line of sixteen square holes, each about four inches wide. A black cube rose from a clear container next to the panel, and floated down to fill the first hole. A second cube appeared to fill the next hole. In all, seven cubes filled the first seven holes.

Nicholas noticed there were four cubes left in the container. "What are those?" he asked.

"It's complicated," Clave said.

After the seventh cube had settled into its slot, Clave buckled himself into a complex web of harnesses that extended from the back and arms of his seat.

Nicholas took the other seat. He put Henrietta in his pocket, and Jeef on the floor next to him. "Shouldn't I strap in?" he asked. He checked his chair for harnesses but didn't see any.

"Why?" Clave said.

"Acceleration," Nicholas said. He liked the thought that he'd finally get to whoosh through space. The trip, so far, had been fairly unexciting, except for several brief moments of terror.

"Jumps through hyperspace don't involve motion, so there's no inertia," Clave said.

"Then why are you strapped in?" Nicholas asked.

"Regulations." Clave pulled a second lever. "Here we go."

There was a small pop. Nicholas saw the cube shoot from the ship. It left a trail of ghost cubes, forming a line from the ship to the tip of the spike in front of them.

"But regulations are—" Nicholas stopped in midsentence as his body was flooded by a rather different sensation than the unpleasant inflation/deflation of teleportation. A hyperjump was more like falling in several directions at once. It was exhilarating. And brief. The trail of ghost cubes vanished. There were suddenly more spikes in the jump node, and a completely different star field in the background. The ship tilted toward one of the new spikes and fired another cube. Nicholas felt he was falling in several other directions, also all at once. Now, there were fewer spikes. The ship fired another cube. This happened a total of seven times. Then, the sensations stopped. A microsecond after that, before his mouth could form the words his brain had fed it—*That was fun!*—Nicholas was violently booted from his seat.

He hurtled upward, along with his fellow backwater-planet companions. The ship appeared to be spinning like a badly off-center playground kickball in midflight.

Fearing that something had gone terribly wrong, Nicholas managed another spectacular catch of Henrietta. He missed Jeef, who splatted against the ceiling next to him. Fortunately her wrapper didn't burst. He snatched up Jeef as the tumbling continued, throwing the three of them against the rear bulkhead.

"What the roach-brained mega-mess!" Nicholas screamed, using a rare augmentation of his standard exclamation.

"Oh, right," Clave said as he stabilized the ship. "I forgot about that. Sorry. I've got a cargo hold full of scrap gold I'm supposed to dump. That throws things off a bit, though it's not usually so rough."

"Maybe it's not rough for you because you're strapped into a padded chair," Nicholas said.

"Good point," Clave said. "Normally, I wouldn't be hopping all over the place with it. I was headed for that hot planet of yours. Mercury? It's been approved for dumping. But I got the call to pick you up before I managed to go there. Too bad. Gold really messes up navigation. I hate lugging it all over the place. But they offered me a fee I couldn't resist."

Two of Clave's words caught Nicholas's attention. "Scrap gold?" he asked.

"Yeah. Dreadful stuff. And the rules for dumping it are ridiculous. If they catch you scattering it in space or burying it on an asteroid, there's an enormous fine. And they always catch you. I found that out the hard way." Clave fiddled with another of the controls. The ship accelerated. But the thrust was gentle. "Hang on. It won't take us long to get there. The jump node we just left is pretty close to Menmar."

"Can I have it?" Nicholas asked.

"Have what?"

"The gold."

"Sure. If you wish. I just don't want to get in trouble leaving it on your planet. Are you positive there aren't any local laws against dumping gold?"

"I'm absolutely positive. You won't get into trouble." Nicholas, who was already fantasizing about his mountain of gold and his first ten sports cars, got to his feet and checked the viewport. They were above a blue-green planet, but either they were a lot closer to Menmar than the Craborzi ship had been to Earth, or Menmar was a lot larger, because it overflowed the viewport. In the northern part of the hemisphere that was in view, a single continent, mostly brown and white, shaped like a crudely drawn otter clutching a tennis racket, stood out against the oceans. A second continent came into view, on the equator. It was shaped a little like a cloud.

"I'm in outer space above a planet in another solar system," Nicholas whispered as the immensity of this set in. "And I'll be the first person from Earth to set foot on it."

He had no way of knowing he would also be the last.

AND A WORD ABOUT NAMES

This would be as good a time as any to deal with the thorny issue of nomenclature. Fear not. I'll keep the discussion brief. When telling tales that span a universe, one has to make a decision about names. For example, Nicholas is a human being. Off planet, it is useful to refer to Nicholas as an Earthling. For the most part, we will use this home-planet method of designation for anyone we meet. Planet names, themselves, are a bit of a disorganized mess. A lot depends on whether they hosted intelligent life when first encountered or were uninhabited until colonized.

And then, there's the issue of what to call each individual. While names can often be traced back to their origin, they lose that connection over time. Nicholas's name, though it comes from two words that are Greek for *victory of the people,* is a mere sound to his fellow students, and even to himself. Henrietta's name also carries no meaning, though it can be understood to be based on *Henry,* and to imply, by way of the suffix, smallness and femininity. Jeef's name, as we saw, has meaning, as do many names. All of this would be of no importance if our story spanned just Yelm, or the state of Washington, or even the entire West Coast.

But let's consider Clave. His name, like Nicholas's, is now a mere sound, though it derived from an ancient Menmarian word that meant either *hero* or *the guy who shows up right after you decide he's never going to show.* (Linguists are bitterly divided on this issue.) We could tell a story about Victory of the People, Little Female Henry, Grass Fed, and Hero, but the names by which we know ourselves are so much more personal. So we'll stick with Nick.

WHAT LIES BENEATH

Nicholas had no idea where Earth lay among the scattered lights of the star field he could see beyond Menmar, or how far away it was. Something else tickled his mind. He thought about the images he'd seen from probes that had landed on the Martian surface.

"Why wasn't there a lag?" he asked.

"Are you always this curious?" Clave asked.

"Pretty much," Nicholas said.

"It's a miracle your parents didn't eat you once you started talking," Clave said.

"What?!" Nicholas tried to process this. "What did you just say?"

"Nothing," Clave said. "Forget it."

"Do you eat your kids?" Nicholas realized it wasn't a

big step from devouring your own child to dining on someone else's offspring. And he was someone else's kid. That led to the guilty realization that he'd eaten veal, which was a cow's kid, more than a few times, and enjoyed it very much. He glanced over at Jeef, who was on the floor at his feet. Henrietta was curled up next to her, asleep. He hoped Jeef was asleep, too.

"I don't have any kids," Clave said.

"But you said—"

"Forget it. I was joking." Clave turned his head toward the navigation controls. "You barbarians take everything so literally. What was your question?"

Nicholas figured he might as well see if he could get an answer from Clave for a change. "Why wasn't there a lag? I mean, how could the news about me have reached you? Or whoever hired you? When we send probes to other planets, there's a lag in communication. It takes time for signals to travel that far, and it takes just as long for the reply to travel back. Even between Earth and the moon, you can notice the lag. Wherever we are right now, it has to be thousands of light years away from Earth. Or maybe even—"

Nicholas shut his mouth and grabbed the back of a seat as the ship decelerated. He held on tighter as everything tilted.

"Initiating descent to Capital City in Central Klizmick," the ship said, as if to reinforce the intergalactic nature of the moment.

Clave looked up from the piloting controls, where his hands were now immersed in an image made of squiggly symbols. The ship leveled off and resumed its smooth flight, except for the occasional minor jolt, once again reminding Nicholas of a subway ride.

"Sure, there's a lag if you're using something ridiculous like radio waves," Clave said. "But who'd be that foolish? You might as well just shout at each other. The electromagnetic spectrum is about as sluggish as a Gynorian syrup sloth on the north pole of an ice planet. It would be stupid to depend on that sort of primitive technology for communication, except maybe for children's toys. Right?"

Nicholas didn't respond. He hadn't totally understood what Clave was talking about, but he caught enough of the meaning to realize that, in the eyes of the universe, he was a pathetic barbarian.

"Oh dear," Clave said. "I'm sorry. My mistake. Radio waves are perfectly fine. Brilliant, actually. Very clever of you Earthlings to discover them as they crawled by you and put them to use. That long lag gives you plenty of time to think up your response. Only a fool would rely on anything instantaneous for important communications, or even casual conversations, right?"

"I guess so," Nicholas said. He felt like a caveman who'd been transported to modern times and was marveling over lightbulbs and dental floss.

"Oh, don't be so glum," Clave said. "It's not your fault where you were born. Or when. And it's not beyond repair. Do you have a device like that?"

"Of course not," Nicholas said, tapping his pocket to assure himself he had his phone.

"Oh, come on," Clave said, holding out his hand. "Let me see the little gadget."

Nicholas remembered when one of his classmates in fourth grade had brought in his grandfather's flip phone for show-and-tell. The whole class had roared at the sight of it. "Don't laugh at me. Okay?" Nicholas held out his phone.

"I wouldn't dream of it." Clave took the phone and studied it for a moment, turned it around at various angles, choked back a laugh, then glanced at the navigation display. "We've got time. Hang on while I fix this thing."

He put the phone on a workbench that ran perpendicular to the left end of the navigation console, then pulled open a drawer and lifted out a box full of parts.

"Let's see. Tachyons . . . ultrasonics . . . theta pulses . . . incongruent pseudo gravity ripples . . . psionic reverberators . . . Mansferd-Brevitch reversion beams . . . I really need to clean this drawer out. Ah, here we go. Radio waves!" He opened the pop-up lid of a small jar, fished out what looked like a tiny radar antenna, and screwed it to the top of the phone. "Give it a try."

"What is it?"

"It's complicated," Clave said. "Just try it."

Nicholas took the phone. He realized he'd never listened to the latest message from his parents, though he'd heard the ping of its arrival before this whole adventure began. *No way I can get it now,* he thought. But, according to the display, he was receiving a strong signal.

Can't happen. He tapped the screen.

"You have one new voice message."

Impossible.

"First voice message . . ."

It can't be . . .

"Hey, kiddo. It's Mom. Things are good. We're rocking the Aussie toddlers. We're really having a g'die. That's how they say *good day.* We saw a kangaroo! They really do have pouches. I petted a koala. Your dad came up with a new arrangement for 'Help!' He's calling it 'Yelp!' Lots of howling. Can't believe we never thought of that before. Hope you and Uncle Bruce are having a good time. Don't forget to eat your vegetables. Got to run. Love you bunches, my little Nickywicky. Bye."

"To repeat this message, press one. To delete this message, press seven. For other options, press nine."

Nicholas, feeling hugely relieved he hadn't put the phone on speaker, pressed one, and listened to the message again. Then he sent a text.

I'm good

"No way," he said as he hit the SEND icon. Even though he'd heard the voice message, he couldn't see how his text could reach Earth. But if it worked, it would be great, because his parents wouldn't get all worried, or try to get in touch with his uncle, who was probably in some unreachable mountain cabin by now. And they'd never know about him being alone, so he wouldn't get in trouble for that lie, either.

There was just one problem. The battery was low. Nicholas did something he'd almost never do under normal circumstances. He turned off the phone. He figured if he only used it to check voice mail and send texts, he should be okay for several more days. He was sure he'd be home before that.

As Nicholas put the phone back in his pocket, the ship jolted to a stop, sending him to his knees. "Ouch."

"We're down," Clave said.

"No kidding." Nicholas had been so busy listening to the message and responding, he hadn't realized the ship was landing.

"There used to be a docking station, and shuttles," Clave said. "That's much more efficient. But the last of those got blown to bits ages ago. Anyhow, welcome to Menmar."

Nicholas checked the viewport, eager for his first look at an alien city. He pictured skyscrapers and hover cars. Instead, the landscape resembled a boulder field. Most of the boulders appeared to be charred. He scanned the horizon for an active volcano, but the terrain was fairly level, and totally devoid of anything that spewed lava. That was too bad. He thought it would be cool to see a volcano close-up.

Clave touched a screen on the panel in front of him. "Right before I picked you up, I matched the cabin atmosphere to what you breathe on Earth. I wanted to make the transition less startling. Though why anyone would want to inhale this stench for a lifetime is a mystery to me."

Nicholas sniffed, and detected nothing but fresh air with a scent of pine.

"Once we leave the ship," Clave said, "the air will be wonderfully spicy."

A hatch on one side of the bridge dropped down to form a ramp. Nicholas picked up Henrietta and Jeef, then followed Clave out into the spicy air of Menmar.

"We come in peace," Nicholas said, pulling an appropriate cliché from his storehouse of science-fiction film dialogue. He was going to add the classic *Take me to your leader* line, but his throat, lungs, and sinus passages showed him that *spicy,* in this case, was a painfully accurate description of the air. To Nicholas, the atmosphere smelled the way habanero hot sauce tasted.

"It burns," he said.

"We'll set you up in an isolated filtered environment in the city," Clave said.

"Set me up for what?" Nicholas asked, between coughs.

"To lead our battle," Clave said. "Your bold actions against the Craborzi inspired our whole continent. Efficient, cold-blooded killers are remarkably difficult to find. Our leaders have selected you to head our military operation from the capitol."

Nicholas chewed on this information. He knew he needed to explain to Clave that he wasn't a military genius or warlord. At best, he was a half-decent chess player and a better-than-average video gamer, who had the misfortune to react violently when he'd stumbled across a cluster of giant caterpillars that were trying to hurt his gerbil. But he figured he could hold off disappointing his host until he was at least somewhere that didn't smell like the center of an enormous enchilada.

He turned back toward the ship to see whether it looked any more interesting than the Craborzi vessel. "Wow. Now *that's* a spaceship."

Clave's nameless ship was sleek and shiny. It had the sort of curves Nicholas associated with a Ferrari or Lamborghini, though it was the size of a tractor trailer.

"Yeah, she's yar," Clave said.

"Yar?"

"Pirate talk," Clave said.

"Stop it," Nicholas said.

He looked around, hoping they'd have some amazing form of transportation like a hovercraft. Or even some fabulous beast of burden. He didn't see anything except

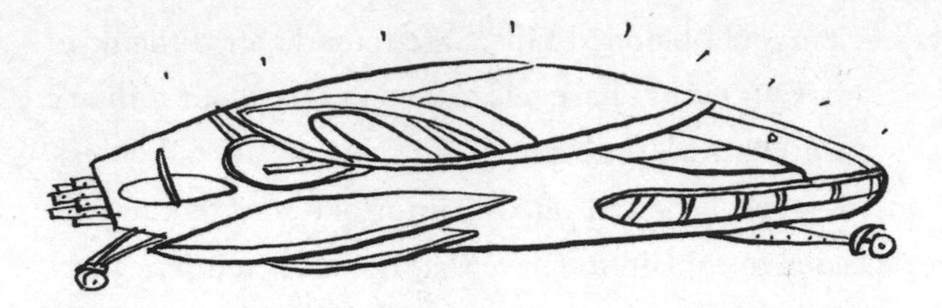

rocks. He turned in a full circle, searching for a city. No sign of that, either. This wasn't a total surprise. His parents had taken him to Chicago one summer, and the airport was amazingly far from downtown. "Where's the capitol?"

"It was here, once." Clave swept his hand across the boulders in front of them. "But we rebuilt everything in tunnels and chambers below the surface. It's much safer there. All our cities are underground. As well as our farms and forests."

"All the cities on all the continents?" Nicholas took a closer look at the rock field, and realized he was standing among crumbled pieces of stone buildings that had been blasted apart. He couldn't even imagine the enormous number of bombs that must have fallen.

"Just Central Klizmick. There's no life left on the rest of the continents. War takes its toll," Clave said. "Come on. It's not far." He picked his way among the debris for about fifty yards, to a cleared area of ground containing a metal plate. As they approached, the plate rose, revealing that it was actually the top of an elevator.

Something exploded off in the distance. Nicholas flinched. Clave didn't even blink. "Idiots," he said. "They'll never give up. I'm glad we'll be rid of them soon."

They entered the elevator, descended for a brief period, and then stepped into an underground city that appeared to contain nothing but rows of windowless structures. A vehicle resembling a curved couch riding on hundreds of tiny wheels rolled up to them silently enough that Nicholas figured it was powered by electricity. They took their seats and traveled three blocks to a larger building that had a fancier entrance than the others. The entrance opened as they approached, revealing a long hallway lined with doors.

"I'll give you a chance to rest up before we meet with the president," Clave said as he stepped up to the first door and pushed it open. "The war council meets right down the hall from here."

"Okay . . ." Nicholas's brain was now officially overloaded. He followed Clave inside, to a room filled with the sort of furniture that was nearly inevitable for bipedal creatures with backbones. The air, though not totally Earthlike, became less spicy once the door had closed. Dropping into what he assumed was a chair, Nicholas

tried to wrap his brain around at least a portion of what he'd been through. After a moment, he emitted a small, sad sigh. That was followed by a much larger exhalation straddling the border between sigh and sob, along with a tiny shiver, followed by a full-blown wail, as the enormity of what he'd done finally sank in.

UNDERSTANDING

Forgive yet another short intrusion, but it would probably be good for you to understand understanding. Not that anybody really can. But it's worthwhile to make an effort.

The universe shapes thoughts.

Thoughts shape the universe.

One or both of these is possibly true. Though it's possible both are false.

No matter. What we do know is that thoughts, unlike light, don't travel through space at a fixed speed. In one sense, thoughts don't travel at all. The instant a thought exists, it exists everywhere in the universe (with one exception noted below). All objects composed of more than one type of molecule produce thoughts. Though relatively few clusters of molecules achieve self-awareness on their own.

Once enough thoughts had been thought, soon after the birth of the universe (probably no more than one or two billion years, at most), they wove a fabric called the Ubiquitous Matrix.

The more common a thought, the denser its concentration in the Matrix. For example, a language spoken by billions is easily accessible, while the details of baking mountain pigeon pie under low-gravity conditions or the seventy-five steps required to repair a jammed tusk buffer are much more elusive.

The Matrix allows sentient beings to understand each other, no matter what language they speak. It also allows for the common understanding of symbols, alphabets, and variable units of measure. Thus, when a Glixnarian complains about waiting twelve weeks for Buffer Tech International to come repair his defective tusk buffer, an Oxwulper would perceive the Oxwulperian equivalent period of eight and a half weeks.

As for the exception, the Ubiquitous Matrix is dampened in regions surrounding those planets unfortunate enough to have a crust contaminated with complex hydrocarbons such as petroleum. Thanks to an abundance of oil fields, Earth was doomed to be populated with nations that didn't understand one another's languages. This inability to communicate has led to endless misunderstandings, wars, grudges, feuds, snits, and pouty faces. As has the ability to communicate. (It will come as no surprise that the two planets engaged in the Sagittarius war that began with a disagreement over the length of a year are also shielded from the Ubiquitous Matrix. Tragically, the inhabitants were too fragile for space travel, and therefore unable to escape the shielding, but intelligent enough to develop sophisticated interplanetary missiles.)

And now, back to Nicholas, who has just emitted several heart-wrenching sighs and sobs of rising depth and deepening sorrow.

WAR AND PEACE

"What's wrong?" Henrietta asked.

"I killed a whole group of . . ." Nicholas groped to find the right term for his victims.

"Loathsome insects?" Henrietta suggested.

Torturers? Jeef said.

"No. I mean, yes. They were loathsome insects and torturers. And I guess they made a show about cutting things up. But they were also intelligent," Nicholas said.

"And what difference does that make?" Henrietta asked.

"Well, you have to draw a line somewhere," Nicholas said. "I mean, I wouldn't kill a person. And I wouldn't kill an alien who looked like a person. So, really, the only difference is that I killed aliens that didn't look like people. That pretty much seems like a bad thing to do."

"Not from where I was strapped," Henrietta said. "And I suggest that you try to get used to the idea. It sounds like this is your new profession, and there's a lot of demand for your skills. It also seems like the universe is not a very peaceful place."

"I just want to go home," Nicholas said.

Henrietta skittered over to a table and tapped one leg with her forepaw. "Try chewing something. That always makes me feel better."

Before Nicholas could respond, the door opened. "I brought you food," Clave said. "I had to go back to the ship. I forgot all about it."

Bracing himself for something hideous, Nicholas looked at the platter Clave was carrying. There appeared to be a salami sandwich, a glass of soda, and a small bowl of gerbil chow.

"I had my ship teleport it from your home planet before we left the region," Clave said. "The computer identified it as a popular item. There's lots more on board, in the stasis locker."

"Thanks," Nicholas said. "I'm starving."

"I'd be starving all the time if I lived on your planet." Clave pointed at the sandwich. "You Earthlings eat some

hideous things. This smells like it stopped being edible about five years ago. Though I like these snack nuggets."

He popped a pellet in his mouth and crunched it.

"So you just steal stuff from planets?" Nicholas asked.

"Sure," Clave said. "Especially barbarian strongholds. It's fun to imagine what they think when things vanish. *Hey! Where's my sandwich?* I know several people who collect socks. But they only take one at a time. It's quite amusing."

"Doesn't it bother you that you're stealing?" Nicholas asked.

"Would you rather I took away the food?"

"I guess not," Nicholas said. "Can you teleport me home?" He was more than ready to end this adventure, especially if people expected him to lead some sort of global war.

"Not at this distance," Clave said. "Whatever parts of you arrived there, if they even made it, would probably look a lot like your reddish blob of a friend."

Hey! Jeef said. *I'm right here.*

"Perpetually," Henrietta muttered.

At least I'm not ruining the furniture.

Nicholas ignored his companions. But he did shudder, slightly, at the image of arriving back home looking like ground beef. "How far are we from Earth?" he asked.

"Far enough that a number would be meaningless to you," Clave said. "The only measure of any significance is that we're seven jump nodes away. That's the measure of all things, when it comes to interplanetary travel. For now, just enjoy your hideous meal."

"It's not silently screaming about being eaten, is it?" Nicholas asked, unaware that self-awareness was produced by the GollyGosh!, and not by the Ubiquitous Matrix.

"Of course not," Clave said.

"Okay, thanks."

"Oh, by the way," Clave said, "we're up to almost four million views."

"Views of what?" Nicholas asked.

"My sfumble."

"Your what?"

"Oh, dear. I keep forgetting. You really did live a life of deprivation. Here, I'll show you. It's awesome." He held his hand out, palm up, and tapped a symbol tattooed on his right pinky against the symbol on his palm. An image appeared above his hand. It was some sort of social-media page. At the top, it read *CrazyClave4632915*. An audio loop, in Clave's voice, stated: "Look who I ran into. It's Nicholas the Assassin! He's surprisingly friendly for a mass murderer. And, who'd have thought it, he's afraid of pirates! Arg!"

Beneath the heading Nicholas saw the panoramic scene Clave had snapped on the Craborzi ship, with Henrietta peeking out of Nicholas's pocket, and Jeef thrust forward, along with a caption written in pulsing letters: "On our way to Menmar." Beneath that was the view count, which was spinning steadily higher.

"I redid the audio and added some text," Clave said. "I think it's perfect now." Timed with the *Arg* in the audio, Clave's face popped up, superimposed on the video, wearing a pirate hat and an eye patch.

"I look small," Henrietta said.

I look fat, Jeef said.

"According to your package, you're ten percent fat," Henrietta said.

I feel more like twenty.

“Who, exactly, is seeing this?” Nicholas asked.

“Pretty much everyone,” Clave said. “I have a large following. I’m Crazy Clave, the Kooky Courier. I’m not as large as Frenzied Fans of Xroxlotl, or *Cooking Across the Universe with Fleexbeezle.* Not yet. Still, I’m very popular.” He flashed Nicholas a huge grin. “I’m just doing this courier gig until my sfumbling career takes off and I pick up some sponsors. One or two billion fans should do it. They say the first hundred million is the hardest, and I’m already halfway toward ten percent of that. Roughly.”

Nicholas pointed at the caption. “So pretty much anyone who sees this knows we were heading for Menmar?”

“Yes. If they read the caption,” Clave said. “Sfumbles use a Matrix font everyone can understand.”

"Including those police?" Nicholas asked. "You know, the ones who want to arrest me."

Clave's grin faded and he reflexively glanced in the direction of the sky. "Don't worry, they aren't allowed to arrest anybody on a planet. They only have authority in space. You're safe here."

"We're not *on* a planet. We're in it," Nicholas said. "That might make a difference."

"Probably not. But maybe we should move up your strategy meeting with the president." Clave dashed out.

"We should get off this planet immediately," Henrietta said as the door closed.

"How?" Nicholas asked.

"We could take Clave's ship," she said.

"Based on recent experiences, I suspect that would not turn out well," Nicholas said. "Let me think about it."

Having nothing much else to do, and being perfectly capable of thinking and chewing at the same time, Nicholas picked up the sandwich. He waited a moment, and listened for the slightest whimper, in case it was going to try to talk him out of consuming it. The sandwich remained mute, and temptingly aromatic. Nicholas took a bite. It tasted fine, and didn't scream. He was pleased to discover that the soda, which turned out to be root beer, was still nice and cold.

He put the bowl of gerbil chow on the floor for Henrietta, who dug right in.

"How about you?" he asked Jeef. "Hungry?"

No. I don't seem to be, Jeef said. *I guess that's a good thing. Slothfulness casteth into a deep sleep; and an idle soul shall suffer hunger.*

"If you say so." Nicholas chewed on his sandwich, and on all the new ideas that he'd been flooded with. Henrietta was right. They needed to get away from Menmar. But he had no idea how to operate the ship.

"Yum. Good salami," he said.

That's not beef, is it? Jeef asked.

Nicholas froze in midchew. A wave of guilt washed over him as he realized what Jeef's question meant. "You figured it out?"

Yes, I did. Cows aren't stupid. We aren't slow. We're just as smart as horses, and a lot smarter than chickens. Or poopy rats.

"I'm not a rat," Henrietta said.

Jeef ignored her and got back to the main question. *I heard an old bull talk about beef once, but I never really understood what he meant. Not until now. Is that beef you're eating?*

Nicholas, who had finally managed to empty his mouth, searched his mind for anything he knew about cold cuts, which was basically almost nothing. "I'm pretty sure it's pork. You okay with that?" He hoped that was at least partially true.

Yes, I am. Pigs are stuck-up. They act like they're better than the rest of us. And their poop stinks.

"You talk about poop a lot," Henrietta said.

There's not much else to talk about on a farm.

"Hey." Nicholas tapped Jeef on the top of her wrapper and waved the sandwich. "You can see this?"

Of course.

"But how?" Nicholas remembered that Jeef had seen her reflection back on the Craborzi ship. Though, at the time, there was too much going on for him to really pay attention to her and realize what that meant. He wondered whether, maybe, he wasn't as smart as a cow or horse. Though he hoped he rose above the level of a chicken.

I've always been able to see, Jeef said.

Henrietta ran up Nicholas's leg and hopped onto the table. She skittered over to Jeef and read the small print on the side of his label. "Hmmm. *Contains beef and beef byproducts.*"

"I wonder what those are?" Nicholas said.

"If she can see, it has to be eyeballs," Henrietta said. "They're in there. Bits of ground eyeballs. Obviously, there's lots of tongue in the mix. Maybe too much. Ear parts, too, I guess, since she can hear."

I don't like what I'm hearing, now, Jeef said. *I knew I'd been wrapped up. I didn't know I'd been ground into pieces.*

"Oh . . ." Nicholas thought about all the hamburgers he'd eaten. And the hot dogs and sausages. And the spicy beef sticks. He'd always thought they were just made of steak, and not lots of parts. He regarded his half-eaten salami sandwich. It was tasty. And, the way things were going, it could very well be his last meal as a free person. He shrugged and took another bite.

"I'm sorry about you getting ground up," he said, between mouthfuls.

At least I'm still me, she said. *This is my comfort in my affliction.*

"Um, okay." Nicholas guessed that was a good thing. It definitely seemed like a positive way to look at a bad situation. "I admire your attitude." He wasn't sure he'd cope that well with being ground up.

After he ate, he spent a few interesting minutes figuring out how Menmarian bathrooms worked. And a few more minutes after that mopping up the floor with what he hoped was a towel, and not another life-form.

By then, Clave had returned. "They're ready for you. All the military leaders have assembled. We're eager to crush our enemies and end this war. You will lead us to greatness."

"I'll give it a shot, but don't get your hopes up," Nicholas said. He figured his ideas would be so useless, the Menmarians would realize they'd made a mistake and would send him home, where he could get to work spending all his gold. He lifted Henrietta, put her on his shoulder, and braced himself for another trip through the depths of a chimichanga.

What about me? Jeef called.

"Just chill out," Nicholas said.

Chill! Augggghhh! Bad memories! So cold. So dark.

"Sorry, poor word choice," Nicholas said. "Just relax. We'll be back."

No you won't, Jeef said. *You're going to abandon me.*

This was true, of course, in some universes, and false in others.

A BIT ABOUT GETTING FROM HERE TO THERE

There are many methods to get an object from one place to another. Let's suppose you have a coin on the upper right corner of a piece of paper, and want to get it to the lower right corner. You can slide it across. That's basic surface travel, which is essentially the same whether you're walking, riding in a car, or sailing in a boat. Or you can pick up the coin and plop it down in its new location. That also takes you through all the points in between, though you've left the surface and chosen a path made of different points. In each case, a certain amount of mass was moved a certain distance, requiring a certain amount of energy.

You can also bend the paper so the lower right corner meets the upper right corner. In essence, you've folded the universe of the paper. The object reaches its destination without physically moving through space. A quibbler or stickler might point out the error that the paper is two-dimensional and the coin is three-dimensional, and a true hyperjump would involve a two-dimensional object traveling through three-dimensional space, or a three-dimensional object traveling through four- (or greater) dimensional space. While this is technically true, quibblers and nitpickers serve no purpose other than to suck the fun out of everything, so we'll ignore them. The main thing is that the example gives you the basic idea that you can shorten or eliminate any distance between objects by folding the space they occupy, or by taking advantage of existing folds.

Let's take a closer look at hyperjumps, which is one name for moving from somewhere to elsewhere without using up any time or very much energy, by taking advantage of the way space is folded upon itself. Jump nodes occur throughout the universe. Most planets, as well as the more massive moons, have at least one. As do most stars, though only an idiot would try to travel to a sizzling ball of hydrogen. Each node connects to at least two others. Some connect to four or eight or sixteen others, or even to far higher powers of two. (The universe is a bit rigid when it comes to some things, such as powers of two, and a preference for vanilla over strawberry ice cream anyplace where both those flavors exist.) Since each leap from node to node consumes one j-cube, the cost of a hyperjump depends on how many nodes are required to reach the destination.

All of these methods of travel involve an object starting at one place and ending up at another. Whatever the distance, the object remains intact. The other, completely different method of getting something somewhere is to break down the object into its component molecules. Those molecules are transmitted through space by rather complicated devices and reassembled at the other end. That method would be teleportation, which Nicholas experienced when he was abducted by the Craborzi. It works over short distances. Most civilized worlds cloaked themselves in teleportation shields, to prevent their enemies (which most civilizations have) from teleporting the residents to a receiver set somewhere horrible, like the cold dead vacuum of outer space, or a middle-school cafeteria.

What the universe lacked and craved was a means of teleportation that worked over immense distances, like hyperjumps, but which wasn't restricted to specific isolated destinations in outer space.

Eventually, that was discovered. And it changed everything, in a huge and stunningly unimportant way. We'll look at that technology later. Right now, it's time to go to war.

DIPLOMACY

After being introduced to President Nixon (one aspect of a nearly infinite universe is that there will be nearly infinite coincidences), along with an assortment of other leaders and advisors, Nicholas found himself on a seat that seemed to be floating in air. A small clear screen hovered in front of it, like a tabletop. He was glad he'd brought Henrietta. He had a feeling her advice might come in handy.

"We are hoping to deliver a crushing blow to our mortal enemies, the Zefinorans," President Nixon said.

"Destroy them!" Vice President Gluteus Sofacushion yelled. (Another aspect of a nearly infinite universe . . . oh, never mind . . .)

"What did the Zefinorans do to you?" Nicholas asked.

"They want to enslave us," the president said.

"That's terrible." Nicholas turned his head to Henrietta and whispered, "Maybe it would be good to help them. Slavery is horrible."

"Ask them why this is happening," she whispered back.

"Why do they want to enslave you?" Nicholas asked.

"They're angry about a minor incident from the past," the vice president said.

"What incident?" Nicholas asked.

"Nothing much, really," President Nixon said. "It was a trifling matter that happened very long ago."

"It would help to know the details," Nicholas said, drawing on his experience with peer counseling, though he was the one usually getting counseled. "It's always good to see things from the other side."

"We enslaved them for a while," Clave said.

"How long is a while?" Nicholas asked.

"Just a brief little period of time," President Nixon said. "An eyeblink compared to the age of the universe."

"How long of an eyeblink?" Nicholas asked.

"Five thousand years," the president said.

"We needed a lot of labor to build our glorious cities," the vice president said.

"Like the one that's in rubble above us?" Nicholas asked.

"Yes, that one," Clave said. "It used to be much nicer."

"So," President Nixon said, "what's your plan? How do we obliterate our enemy once and for all and restore peace and prosperity to our land?"

Nicholas thought about his school back home. A pang rippled through him as he wondered whether he'd ever see it again. As much as middle school could be a horror show of social torture, cliques, bullies, endless homework, ridiculous rules, irregular verbs, sketchy cafeteria meat, unbalanced equations, and confusing expectations, it was still a familiar routine and an established part of his life. He thought about how the teachers would make any kids who were fighting sit down together and work things out, and about the great peacemakers he'd learned about in social studies, like Martin Luther King Jr., Malala Yousafzai, and Mohandas Gandhi.

"Have you tried diplomacy?" he asked.

The Menmarians exchanged puzzled glances among themselves. Nicholas wondered whether the physics behind his ability to communicate with aliens had suddenly failed.

"Say that word again?" the president asked.

"Diplomacy," Nicholas said, isolating each syllable like he was competing in the final round of a spelling championship.

"Diplomacy . . . ?" President Nixon said, as if cautiously tasting a strange new fruit. Or licking a miniature bear trap. He frowned and shook his head. So did the other Menmarians.

"This word is unknown to us," Clave said.

Henrietta crawled right up to Nicholas's ear and whispered, "That figures."

"Please explain what you mean," President Nixon said.

"Is it some sort of weapon available only on Earth? We have planet torchers, but they are too slow-moving and large to use against any world that is expecting an attack. We'd never be able to land one on Zefinora. They'd blow it out of the sky before it could touch down and burrow to a secure position."

"It's not a weapon. It's an approach to peace." Nicholas patiently explained diplomacy. He had to go over the concept several times, giving numerous examples he vaguely remembered from his social studies class, before President Nixon seemed to grasp the basic concept.

"So, if I understand you, the idea is that we offer to meet face-to-ugly-face with these wretched low-life Zefinoran dung dwellers and explain why it would be a bad idea for them to attempt to enslave us, and a wonderful idea for them to drop their whole idiotic plan?" he said.

"Exactly. Though you might want to work on your word choices," Nicholas said. "You can point out that more war will bring more destruction to both your worlds. There's plenty of evidence of that already. You can tell them that all the expense and effort spent on weapons can be used for better purposes. And you can point out the benefits of cooperation."

Nicholas paused to dredge up more social studies facts

he'd never thought he'd need again after the final exam. "You can have trade agreements. Tourism. And even a mutual defense treaty, in case someone else attacks either of you. I'll bet there are some wonderful Zefinoran foods you just can't get here."

"Slime-gibbon sweat-gland stew," Vice President Sofacushion said. He closed his eyes and sighed. A small trickle of saliva seeped from the corner of his mouth and rolled down his triple chins. "It's magnificent."

Clave shuddered and whispered to Nicholas, "That stuff is dreadful. It tastes like the seat of a pair of unwashed pants."

"I think you showed us the right path," the president said. "You will be a hero to all of Menmar."

"I'm glad I could help," Nicholas said. He realized that stopping an interplanetary war might make up, in some way, for murdering the Craborzi. It really was a noble achievement. Possibly even a Nobel one, though nobody from Earth would ever know of it or award him a peace prize.

Vice President Sofacushion captured Nicholas in a squishy embrace. "You smell . . ." he said as he buried his mushy face against Nicholas's neck.

Nicholas realized he hadn't taken a shower that day,

or the day before, or possibly for several additional days. As he was forming a halfway sincere apology for his body odor, the vice president said, ". . . delicious."

"Oh. Uh, thanks." Nicholas felt his shoulders rise in an effort to guard his neck. He wriggled free and moved toward the door.

"So," Clave said, "the package has been delivered."

Nobody responded. Clave raised his voice a bit. "About my payment . . ."

"We'll start processing it," the vice president said.

"They take forever to pay me," Clave muttered as he led Nicholas out the door.

"Package?" Nicholas asked. "I'm a *package*?"

"Technically, yes," Clave said.

During the walk back along the corridor, after grumbling a bit more about money, he explained the relationship between Menmar and Zefinora. In his version, everything was far superior on Menmar. Stripping out the bias, leaving the facts intact, and adding a few details Clave wouldn't know, the basic story is that Menmar and Zefinora formed an inhabited binary planetary system. These are extremely rare in the universe, which means that even though they are countless in number, you have to look really hard to find one. And half the time, even when you think you found one, you've actually just found a planet with a very large moon. Or lost track of your count somewhere between one and two. (This happened so often to an amateur astronomer named Forgon Eldermitch from Holst II that he was eventually banned from the local astronomy club.)

Life had evolved in a similar fashion on both planets, though the Menmarians explained this by claiming that their ancient ancestors had colonized Zefinora before the dawn of recorded history. Skeptics like to point out that, in most societies, the recording of history generally begins before the invention of spaceflight.

The Zefinorans, having a slightly more developed sense of whimsy and a much better imagination, tell their children that a gigantic space-traveling creature resembling a goose had plucked evil Zefinorans from their home planet, swallowed them, and then excreted the still-living, still-evil, far stinkier creatures on Menmar, thus populating that planet with goose droppings.

However entertaining the two explanations are, the truth is much simpler. Menmarians and Zefinorans resembled each other because sometimes nature makes the same mistake twice.

While not very imaginative in areas of literature and art, or mythology, the Menmarians were better engineers than the Zefinorans, and had thus managed to be the first of the two to visit their nearest neighboring planet. They also lived on a planet with 10 percent higher gravity, making them naturally stronger than the Zefinorans. The Menmarians were more than willing to exploit these advantages.

By the time Clave finished his account, he and Nicholas had reached the guest quarters.

You came back! Jeef said when the door opened. *Mercy and truth are met together.*

"Of course I came back," Nicholas said.

For, in this universe, that's what happened. Nicholas came right back.

This time, at least.

SFUMBLES

Clave was one of a huge gaggle of aspiring sfumblers. Sfumbles are loosely defined as brief, entertaining tidbits tossed out for the enjoyment of all, in the hopes of gaining an audience, fame, and ad revenue. Basically, it was a Short-Form Ubiquitous-Matrix Blast Loop (or *blather,* as far as those who were not sfumble fans were concerned). There were also long-form Ubiquitous-Matrix blasts, but nobody had come up with a satisfactory name for them, and they were popular only among a handful of smug intellectuals who were fond of creating movie reviews that were longer then the films themselves, and who couldn't even stand each other's company, or each other's posts. The universe, in general, has a short attention span and a preference for effortless entertainment that can be absorbed while doing other things.

Clave's audience was small, but his ambition was large. He knew he just hadn't discovered the right topic yet to strike a spark with a massive audience. Though he'd grown up on Menmar, he was actually a Frezlunkian who'd been adopted shortly after birth.

Menmarians were very enthusiastic about adoption and child swapping because they loved children but also suffered from a compulsive and at times irresistible urge to eat their own young. Scientists remain puzzled how this seemingly counterproductive trait fits into the evolutionary scheme. But let's not dwell on that.

AN END TO ALL WARS

After giving a curious Jeef a brief description of what she'd missed out on in the war room, Nicholas slept the long, deep sleep that only an exhausted seventh grader (plus or minus three or four years) can pull off. His sleep was undisturbed until Clave shook him awake.

"Whuh . . . ?" Nicholas said, wondering why his bed wasn't his bed and his room wasn't his room. And why his clothing smelled faintly like tacos.

"Come!" Clave said. "Our diplomatic mission is about to reach Zefinora. You need to see our triumphant arrival."

Nicholas snatched up Henrietta. "This is great. I'm so glad they listened to me. Peace is always better than war. I'm not just a murderer anymore."

What about me? Jeef said.

"I'll be back for you," Nicholas said.

Once again, this was true in some universes, and false in others.

No, you won't, Jeef said, which was also true or false, though in exactly the opposite universes as the statement Nicholas had made. It should be noted that the universe is even fussier about balancing true and false than it is about powers of two. Except when it isn't.

Nicholas found a flurry of activity in the war room. But all heads turned toward him the instant he entered. He sensed an air of expectation. Along with an air of enchiladas.

"Well done, Earthling," President Nixon said. He slapped Nicholas on the nose, that being the Menmarian equivalent of a pat on the back. Menmarian noses are far sturdier than human snouts, and Menmarian hands are far softer. Nicholas bit back pain and blinked back tears as he turned his attention to an image projected on the wall in front of him. A stubby cylindrical spaceship was descending toward a brown planet. It was hard to tell for sure, but the ship seemed to be enormous. It also seemed to be moving at the sort of crawling pace one associates with oil tankers and overly cautious drivers.

"We have a documentary ship following it," Clave said.

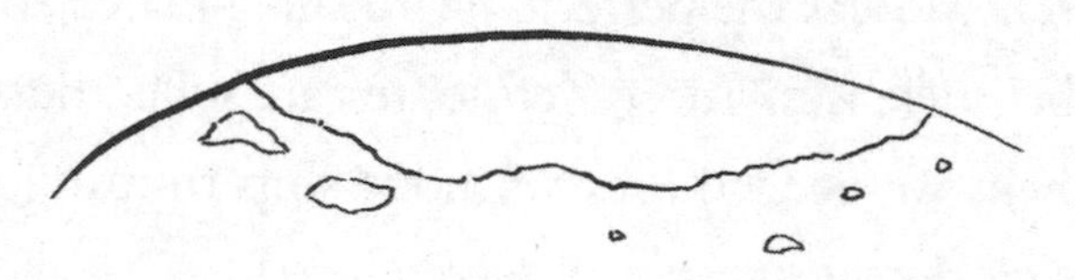

"We want to record the moment our struggle with the dreadful Zefinorans comes to a dazzling end."

"Wonderful," Nicholas said, totally failing to pick up on the use of *dazzling*. This was not surprising, given that he had just been awakened from a deep sleep and was really not a morning person. Or an early afternoon person, for that matter. Still, he was pleased and amazed that the Menmarian leaders had listened to his suggestions and embraced diplomacy.

"Nicely done," Henrietta said. She gave Nicholas a fond nuzzle with her snout.

"Thank you." He stroked her stomach, and she wriggled in delight.

"The documentary crew will stay in high orbit to avoid

the heat and the magma spew," Clave said. "I wish I could be there to record our triumph in person and share it with my fans."

"Heat?" Nicholas asked. "Magma spew?" That did not sound like a let's-be-friends situation.

"Of course," President Nixon said. "This whole *diplomacy* scheme was the perfect way to slip a planet torcher past their defenses. Those Zefinorans are such idiots. We told them we needed an enormous ship to bring them all the glorious gifts they deserved."

"You're blowing up their planet?" Nicholas screamed. "That's . . ." His brain failed to find any word capable of adequately describing how hideously wrong this act of treachery was.

"That's the plan. Though, to be more accurate, we're burning and melting it. Either way, it's the end of them, and of the war. There won't be a single Zefinoran left after this." The president pointed to another screen, which also showed an enormous, slow-moving cylindrical spaceship. This ship was virtually identical to the one approaching Zefinora. But the scene was shot from below as the ship descended toward Menmar. "Except, of course, for the stupid diplomats they sent here. What a pack of turd heads. They even brought us gifts. Hundreds of gifts in that enormous ship. Imagine that. How stupid can they be? We'll enjoy their gifts in the glow of their burning planet."

"Yes," Vice President Sofacushion said. "We're destroying them, and they're sending us a huge ship full of gifts. They have to be the stupidest people in the universe. They deserve to be destroyed."

"Wait." Nicholas grabbed Clave's arm, a gesture that was the Menmarian equivalent of spitting in one's eye. "What if the Zefinorans had the same idea?"

"What same idea?" Clave asked as he yanked his arm free.

"Planet torcher," Nicholas said. As a survivor of sixth grade, and a good part of seventh, he knew all about treachery, both from history lessons and from playground alliances.

"They wouldn't . . ." Clave's face grew slack as his heritage came into play. It's generally the case that Frezlunkians are somewhat faster and deeper thinkers than Menmarians, which isn't saying a whole lot. But they are therefore slightly better suited to cope with changing plans and to make logical deductions. "Oh dear. Do you think . . . ?"

Nicholas couldn't believe he had to explain something so obvious. "Yeah. I'm pretty sure the Zefinorans pulled the same trick, and that's a planet torcher heading our way."

"But it has tail fins," Clave said. "Planet scorchers don't have those."

"Um, fake ones, maybe?" Nicholas pointed to the image of the Menmarian planet torcher, which also sported what looked like the hastily slapped-on trappings of a spaceship as it approached a landing on Zefinora.

"Oh, dear . . ." Clave said.

"Can you shoot it down?" Nicholas asked.

"Our missiles aren't designed for that," Clave said. "It's too low. And there's not enough time to send ground forces. It's just about to land. Once it's on solid ground, things will start to heat up pretty quickly."

"Everyone! Get out of here, now!" Nicholas yelled. "Save yourselves."

"We're not missing our moment of glory," President Nixon said.

"It's a shame about the slime-gibbon sweat-gland soup," Vice President Sofacushion said. "Still, I like watching things collapse into a molten mess."

"Then he's in for a real treat, close-up," Henrietta whispered.

Nicholas and Clave exchanged glances that carried a universal message: *Let's get out of here.*

Clave ran out the door.

Henrietta dived from Nicholas's shoulder to his shirt pocket.

Nicholas followed Clave out of the building and down the street to the elevator. As the elevator door opened and Clave rushed in, Nicholas looked back the way they'd come. "Oh, roach brains! Wait. We have to go back."

"You can't be serious," Clave said. "We have very little time before Menmar becomes a large lump of glowing charcoal. Planet torchers are frightfully efficient."

"I'll be right back," Nicholas said. He turned and raced for the building.

"Are you crazy?" Henrietta said as she bounced in his pocket.

"Yeah. I guess I am."

He stopped talking after that, until he got to the building and burst through the door of his room.

You came back again! Jeef said.

"Briefly," Nicholas said as he snatched up Jeef. That was as much conversation as he could manage after running hard and breathing salsa.

Nicholas paused long enough to suck in a deep breath of the filtered air, then ran out of the building and back down the street to the elevator. An agonizing moment later, after waiting for the elevator, he was on the surface of Menmar, racing over the rubble toward the ship.

In his whole life, Nicholas had never run so fast and stumbled so little. Had this been gym class, he would have gotten an A+. And perhaps a trophy. When he was still one hundred yards away, he saw the hatch of Clave's ship start to close.

"Wait!" Nicholas screamed.

"Hurry up!" Clave yelled from inside.

Past the ship, not far from the ground, Nicholas saw the planet scorcher descending. It was far bigger than he'd thought, blotting out a good chunk of the horizon. It was close enough that he could see that the tail fins, bay doors, and landing struts had been hastily added, to make it look like a cargo ship.

It touched down. Then, with a grinding shriek that sounded like a thousand dentist drills, it started to sink into the ground as a dust cloud rose to envelop it.

Nicholas discovered he could run even faster. He reached the hatch with barely enough room to dive through. He chucked Jeef and Henrietta ahead of himself, as gently as possible, so they wouldn't get hurt when he belly-flopped to a landing. They hit the floor and slid across toward the opposite wall. Nicholas followed them into the ship, ending his heroic sprint with a truly spectacular leap.

"Go!" Nicholas shouted, rather unnecessarily, to Clave,

who was seated at the navcom and already in the process of going.

The instant the hatch clanked shut, the ship lifted off. Nicholas's body and the left side of his face became intimately familiar with the finest details of the floor as he was crushed by the force of acceleration.

"Hang on," Clave said. "I need to use full thrust to get off planet."

"Mrflgvmp," Nicholas said, struggling unsuccessfully to lift his head high enough to take the pressure off his cheek.

"It won't be long," Clave said. "We just need to get out beyond range of the magma splash from the torcher."

Nicholas looked around for his companions. Even moving his eyes took enormous effort, but he managed to spot Jeef, who was flattened almost to the point of bursting.

Marike! Help me, Marike! Jeef yelled.

Past Jeef, Henrietta looked so flat she seemed two-dimensional. Nicholas tried to crawl to her, using all his strength to push up from the floor.

That, unfortunately, was the moment when the ship stopped accelerating, turning Nicholas's attempt to rise into a powerful leap, which was brought to an abrupt stop by the low ceiling of the cabin. He saw stars—which were definitely not in short supply—as his head bounced off the panel, leaving an impressive dent. Just then, Clave activated the ship's gravity, which sent Nicholas on a brief return journey from the ceiling to the floor. Fortunately, he landed next to Henrietta, and not on top of her. Unfortunately, his face was the first part of his body to arrive.

"We're safe," Clave said. His voice sounded oddly flat. "We survived."

Nicholas, who wasn't entirely sure that was an accurate statement, sat up and checked to make sure his jaw hadn't been turned into an assortment of bone fragments clustered in a chin sack. It seemed to be intact. As did the back of his head.

"You didn't wait for us," he said.

"You made it," Clave said. "You're alive. Stop complaining."

Nicholas didn't feel like arguing. "Are you okay?" he

asked Henrietta, who'd plumped back to her usual shape. Between the mind-numbing effects of acceleration and a minor concussion or two, Nicholas was feeling fairly dazed himself.

"Just fine," she said.

"But you were flat."

"That's not unusual for me." Henrietta flattened herself, then plumped up again. "I'm surprised you can't do that. It comes in very handy."

Nicholas looked over at Jeef, who had also plumped back up. "Who's Marike?" he asked. He started to get to his feet, but decided he needed to rest a moment and catch his breath. After all the running, it felt good to sit still.

She's . . . It's hard to remember . . .

"You called for her," Nicholas said.

Wait. I remember. She read to us from a book she always carried. Beautiful words. "The ear of the wise seeks knowledge." I didn't understand all of it, but it sounded so nice. Very beautiful and full of advice. "For wisdom is better than rubies, and all the things that may be desired are not to be compared to it."

Henrietta walked over to Jeef and bumped her nose against Jeef's side.

Stop sniffing me!

"I'm not sniffing you," she said. "I'm reading your biography." She lowered her head and resumed reading. In fairness to Jeef, Henrietta did sniff a bit when she read. And when she didn't.

"That explains it," Henrietta said.

Nicholas felt like he was ten steps behind Henrietta. Granted, Henrietta took tiny steps, but still, Nicholas never quite caught up. He waited for her to explain what she was talking about.

"See for yourself." Henrietta pointed one foreleg at Jeef.

Nicholas leaned over and read the printing at the bottom of the front of the package, next to a small drawing of a barn on a hill. He'd seen it before, but never really paid attention to it—sort of like his French textbook.

All our products are lovingly raised by Mennonite Farmers in Lancaster County, PA.

“Oh, I get it.” He didn’t know a lot about Mennonites, but he grasped the basics. They were very devout. He pictured a woman, Marike, sitting on a stool in a pasture, reading verses to the cattle from the Bible, or maybe just reading them aloud to herself. “So that’s why you keep coming up with stuff that sounds . . .”

“Holy?” Henrietta suggested.

“Yeah, holy,” Nicholas said.

As the words left his lips, and his brain made a somewhat obvious connection, Nicholas was, for once, cogitating at exactly the same speed as Henrietta. In evidence of this, it needs to be noted that the two of them shouted the same dreadful pun at exactly the same time:

“HOLY COW!”

Nicholas couldn’t help laughing. “Jeef, this is hilarious.”

Hardly, Jeef said. *I have become a laughingstock to all my people, their mocking song all the day.*

“Better than a livestock,” Henrietta said. “Or a deadstock.”

“Hey, Clave, did you catch that?” Nicholas said. He couldn’t remember the last time he’d had such a good laugh. It felt great. He pivoted on his rear so he faced toward the console. “This is really funny. Let me explain.

There's this expression my grandpa uses all the time, when he's surprised. It's . . ."

The explanation died in Nicholas's throat when he saw Clave, who stood frozen by the front of the cockpit, his face highlighted by an unnatural light streaming through the viewport.

LET'S GET ALL HYPER

Soon after jump nodes were discovered, and the basic techniques of hyperjumps were ironed out, the Great Mapping began. A fairly clever group of engineers designed a probe that, when placed at a node, would replicate sufficient copies of itself to make jumps to all the connected nodes. The probe at each node would send its coordinates to the Great Mapping command center. More raw material would be shipped to those probes through the original jump node (this was before the development of Thinkerator technology), and they'd each repeat the exploration steps from their new base.

This was not a rapid process, since the number of probes grew exponentially, as did the need for raw material. The mapping is actually still going on, and will probably go on forever, or until the end of the universe, whichever comes first.

That same group of engineers established Hyperjump Unlimited to make and sell j-cubes and navigation systems, partly as a way to fund the mapping, and partly as a way to retire early and buy cool toys that flew really fast or blew things up. Hyperjump Unlimited quickly became the largest company in the universe. But not for long.

ON THE RUN

"What's wrong?" Nicholas asked.

Clave pointed toward Menmar. "This is terrible."

All thoughts of humor vanished from Nicholas as he stared at a glowing heap of slag that had been a planet just a few minutes earlier. Until this moment, thanks to his thumps on the head and his relief at escaping from danger, he hadn't really been able to absorb and accept the inconceivable idea that a whole planet could be destroyed by a single weapon. Right now, staring out the viewport, he could feel the shock in his heart as Menmar was consumed by fire. He couldn't imagine how horrifying and mind-numbing it would be to see that happen to Earth.

"How . . . ?" Nicholas asked.

Clave was too numbed to even say, "It's complicated."

It wasn't complicated. But it was terrible. The planet scorcher began as a mining machine known as an Elemax. Like many tools, from the simple rice thresher that became the nunchaku on Earth to the Aldebaran cybermagnet that had been reengineered to generate a death ray that could penetrate walls, the Elemax had been converted from a useful device into a horrendous weapon capable of doing unspeakable damage.

When the planet torcher the Menmarians launched touched down just outside the underground capitol of Zefinora, it drilled a hole directly beneath itself. As the hole deepened and the ship descended into the ground, it covered itself with the debris it had created. This was purely a defensive move, to keep it safe while it extracted a series of elements and compounds from the planet's crust and redeposited them on the surface at two locations 180 degrees apart, using a technology based on teleportation. The final layer, at the top of the deposition, was composed of potassium carbonate. But this was not the final step.

After the potassium carbonate was deposited, the carbon was removed, leaving an area covered with pure potassium. The potassium, which burns when wet, combusted after exposure to moisture in the atmosphere.

The resulting fire grew hot enough to ignite the layers of lithium and magnesium beneath it, each of which was seeded with aluminum oxide as a source of oxygen for the fires. These layers set fire to the next layer. And the next. Essentially Zefinora had been turned into the global equivalent of a friction match, using the principle of rising kindling points. As each element combusted, it rose in temperature until it was hot enough to ignite the next zone. Inevitably, as the fiendishly designed layers on Zefinora burned hotter and hotter, the entire planet caught fire. As did Menmar, thanks to the Zefinoran planet torcher.

"Your whole planet," Nicholas said to Clave. "Your home. Your friends."

"Your pets," Henrietta said.

Your cattle, Jeef said. (The more sensitive among you will be relieved to know that there were, at the time of destruction, no cattle on Menmar. They'd all been slaughtered decades ago.)

"Yes, it's terrible." Clave sounded like someone who'd lost a watch he wasn't all that fond of. "We should figure out where we're going. We might as well head for the jump node while I work on finding a destination." He set the course, then sat and stared down at the instruments, not looking at the dwindling view of his former planet.

"Can't you just take me home?" Nicholas asked.

Clave tapped the container that held the four warp cubes. "I'd need seven of these to get to Earth, and another seven to get home. Not that I have a home anymore."

Nicholas wasn't sure how to respond to that. Clave's expression gave him no clue, and he was never comfortable offering sympathy to others for even the most minor of tragedies, and especially not to adults, so he shifted the subject. "Where can you get them?"

"On just about any civilized planet or docking station," Clave said. "I would have bought more on Menmar after I got paid for transporting you. I guess we can forget about that."

"Are they expensive?" Nicholas asked. He reflexively tapped his pocket, as if feeling for his wallet, which he'd left at home. Not that it would do him much good anywhere except for Earth.

"Let's save this discussion for some other time." Clave pointed to an object in the lower left corner of the viewport. He magnified the view enough to reveal the Yewpee cruiser. "It looks like they tracked us to Menmar. They're headed for the planet, but they'll figure things out soon enough, once they see what's happening."

"Wait! Won't they assume we'd died down there?"

Nicholas asked. "So they'll stop looking for me." That, at least, was one small bright glimmer for him in the current darkness.

"Um . . ." Clave glanced at the sfumbler, which was on the console next to him. His expression showed as much guilt as was possible for a Menmarian, which, though minuscule, was still enough to signal what he'd done.

"Tell me you didn't," Nicholas said.

"It was just a short one," Clave said. "I couldn't bear knowing how sad my fans would be if they thought I'd perished. I did it for them. But we really need to get out of here. Hang on."

Clave punched the accelerator. Nicholas slammed into the back wall. Henrietta was in his pocket, which cushioned the blow for her. Jeef slid across the floor and smacked the wall next to Nicholas.

Every movie he'd ever seen where the bad guys make a run for it ran through Nicholas's mind. Especially the ones where the bad guys ended up getting run through by bullets. "Maybe I should turn myself in," he said. "I mean, I really did kill those Craborzi." The confession brought back a pang of guilt.

"You'd probably spend the rest of your life in prison," Clave said. "And I'd be in the next cell, doomed to listen to endless questions for the rest of my life. *Why do birds swim? Why is the sky green? How come that man has three heads? Blah, blah, blah . . .*"

Nicholas walked up to Clave and asked a much more important question. "Are we done with unannounced bursts of acceleration?"

"We are."

"Good." Nicholas dropped into the empty seat and watched the pursuers, who'd turned around, as Clave had predicted, and now seemed to be closing the distance at an alarming rate. "They're pretty fast," he said.

"So am I. We'll be fine as long as they don't get within dead-pulse range before we jump," Clave said.

"What's that?" Nicholas asked.

Clave shot him a glare. "More questions?"

"It seemed important," Nicholas said. "Pretty much anything with 'dead' as part of its name is worth avoiding."

"It's not as bad as it sounds. They can't fire a lethal weapon at the ship if there's anyone on board besides the suspect," Clave said. "So they have to kill the ship's drive. The pulse is powerful, but it isn't long-range."

"I'm glad they can't shoot at us," Nicholas said.

The ship jolted.

"Hostile fire detected," the ship said. "Shields activated."

“Someone’s shooting at us.” Clave thrust his hands into the navigation field and twiddled his fingers like a jazz pianist trying to play seven variations at once.

“Who?”

An inset image of a sleek ship resembling a six-winged wasp appeared in the viewport.

“The worst possible enemy in the universe,” Clave said.

WE ARE KEEPING YOU IN OUR THOUGHTS

Great inventions and scientific theories often arise independently in multiple places. That's the way it was with the Thinkerator. On Kindar, Selvned, Thrax, and seventeen other planets, at roughly the same time, scientists theorized that if thoughts instantly spread throughout the universe, it was worth investigating whether it was possible to attach matter to a thought, and deliver that matter elsewhere. The Kindari, being excellent thinkers, were the first to achieve a successful practical application of this theory, harnessing the thoughts of a volunteer to propel a microgram of cadmium across a laboratory. Unfortunately, due to an unanticipated feedback loop, the thinker's head exploded, setting Kindari experimentation back a decade or so. This allowed the Selvned to move ahead. Nobody is sure why their entire lab disintegrated after several successful experiments. Fortunately, word of these disasters never reached Thrax, where the basic techniques of thought-borne matter transmission were ironed out.

A century or two of refinement followed, because scientists had to grapple with the fact that *everywhere* and *somewhere* weren't the same. Eventually, after all the technical difficulties were ironed out, Thinkerators were used to supply colonies with basic materials. But this offered no real advantage over delivery by jump shuttles, since every colony was already within shuttle range of a jump node. The Thinkerator might have faded away, joining millions of other interesting but inessential inventions, had it not been for one merchant's brilliant realization.

A CAPTIVE AUDIENCE

"Who is that?" Nicholas asked.

"That's a Craborzi ship," Clave said. "I've seen them on that program, *Let's Hunt Things Down!* Their favorite technique is to cripple a ship and then board it so they can capture their victims alive and intact."

Nicholas pictured himself strapped to a Craborzi lab table. Now it made even more sense to surrender to the police. "What if—"

"Quiet," Clave said. "We're almost there. This is going to get tricky."

He loaded one j-cube, then reached into the nav field. The ship decelerated rapidly.

"Hang on," Clave said, somewhat too late.

Nicholas flew out of his chair, tumbled head over heels

as his feet hit the console, and slammed upside down into the viewport, which was strong enough, fortunately, to take the impact.

"You told me you were finished accelerating," he said as he slid to the floor.

"That was deceleration. It's difficult to make a jump when you're moving fast." Clave pulled the jump lever.

Nicholas felt the falling-in-different-directions sensation again. Outside the viewport, the star field changed. As before, the ship tumbled. Nicholas slammed into a bulkhead.

"Stupid gold," Clave said as he battled to regain stability.

"Stupid gold," Nicholas said after the motion stopped. He spotted Jeef and Henrietta nearby. Neither seemed harmed.

"At least we're safe, for now," Clave said.

"Can't they just follow us?" Nicholas asked.

"No. There's no trail. No way to see where we went. And they don't know we're low on cubes. As far as they can tell, we might be anywhere. We've escaped." He pulled out his sfumbler and pointed it at Nicholas. "I need to post this. People seem interested in you. Though it's my style that really makes the story special."

"No!" Nicholas said. "Cut it out with the sfumbles.

That's how they found us the first time. And the second! I don't want to go through a third mad chase."

"You might as well issue a news flash," Henrietta said.

Triggered by that phrase, Stella sprang up to give the news. After reports on music, politics, and sports, and a touching account of the Emperor of the Universe making a surprise visit to some of the evacuees of Plenax IV, who were fleeing an imminent supernova, she said, "And this just in. Nicholas the Slayer has struck again, in an exponentially greater fashion."

"Slayer? What happened to brutal assassin?" Henrietta said.

"I think 'Slayer' sounds better," Clave said. "It's very catchy. Almost as good as Crazy Clave."

Nicholas shushed everyone as Stella continued her story. "Planet-wrecker Nicholas the Slayer, destroyer of Menmar and Zefinora, already infamous for his brutal murder of seventeen Craborzi scientists, has been tied to the treacherous destruction of two entire worlds."

"Seven scientists!" Nicholas shouted.

"They got the number of worlds right," Henrietta said. "At least, for now."

An image appeared behind Stella, showing a split screen of incinerating planets.

"Authorities nearly caught up with him before he escaped the crime scene with the help of a tenth-rate sfumbler and freelance messenger named Lazy Crave."

"Clave!" Clave shouted. "Crazy Clave!"

Stella had more to say. "It was actually a sfumble that led authorities to Menmar. They would have been there sooner, if anyone had noticed the post before now, but this Crave person doesn't have a very large following, so it was pretty much a miracle the sfumble was spotted at all. The hunt continues."

Stella faded.

"Tenth rate!" Clave said. "I certainly am not tenth rate. And I'm not a messenger. I'm a courier. There's a difference!"

Nicholas waited for Clave to calm down, then said, "Can I see the gold?" He knew Clave felt it was worthless. But he also knew how valuable it was. There had to be some way to use the gold to buy the j-cubes they needed so he could get back home.

"Sure." Clave opened the hatch that led out of the bridge. He walked past the lockers in the corridor, then tapped a foot pedal that jutted from the floor near the wall. A small hatch in the floor sank at one end, forming steps as it lowered. "It's there."

Nicholas followed Clave down the steps to a catwalk that ran along one wall. "Wow . . ." he said. The space below him was filled with nuggets and hunks of gold, along with some slabs and small boulders. The treasure rose within an inch or two of the catwalk. Nicholas had only a rough idea how deep the cargo hold was, and he really had no clue how much the gold weighed, or even what an ounce of gold was worth, but whoever owned this much gold would probably be the richest person on Earth. He'd definitely be the richest seventh grader.

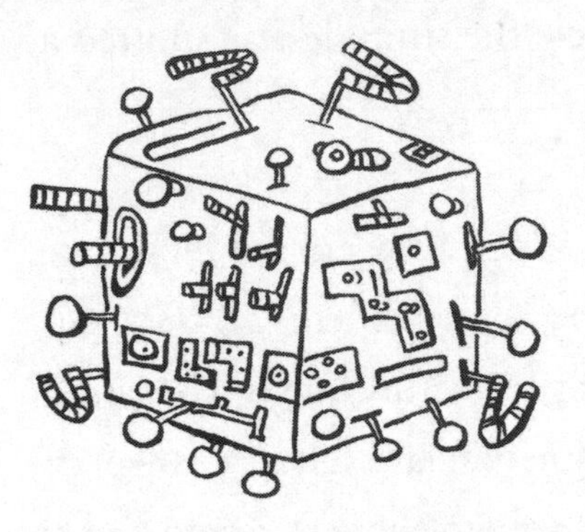

"And I can have it all?" It seemed too easy. He figured there had to be a catch.

"Yes. It's all yours," Clave said. "I told you it's worthless to me."

Nicholas noticed several boxes stacked on top of the gold along the far wall, held in place by a tangle of frayed straps. "What's that?" he asked, pointing to a large metal box covered with dials and switches.

"Oh, drat," Clave said. "It's a matter replicator. I was supposed to deliver it as quickly as possible."

"Can't you just teleport it?" Nicholas asked.

"No. The entire workings are biological." Clave hopped over the railing of the catwalk and inched his way across the shifting chunks of gold. When he reached the other side, he leaned toward the replicator and took a sniff. "Oh dear. I need to get that to Vrexis before it spoils."

"How soon is that?" Nicholas asked.

"Probably yesterday," Clave said. "Maybe last week."

Nicholas pointed to a pair of glass globes the size of softballs that were cushioned inside a display case. Each globe contained an orb that pulsed with red light and rippled as if it were made of silk and sunlight. "And that?"

"A breeding pair of pet Orbanies. One of the most beautiful and rare forms of sea life, from Oceanica. I have to deliver them to Exferm VII."

"That chest?"

"Top-secret document that has to be delivered by hand."

"That sack?"

"Five dozen pickled mammoth-ant brains. Very rare delicacy."

"Ick." Nicholas pointed at a cube about two feet wide, made of thin black rods. An object pulsed inside of the cube, but he couldn't make out a clear shape. Something about it gave him the same sense of unease in the pit of his stomach that he got when the sky darkened rapidly before a massive thunderstorm. "What's that thing?"

"It's an antimatter power core," Clave said.

"It looks dangerous," Nicholas said.

"That's because it is," Clave said. "But we're okay as

long as it isn't switched from standby to full power. And you can only do that with the remote, or by slamming it really hard."

"You mean that remote?" Nicholas pointed to a remote control jutting out from beneath Clave's left foot. (He knew it was a remote because, in one of those quirks of coincidence, unlike toilets, automobiles, and ball caps, among other things, the design of remote controls was pretty much a universal constant.)

"Right. That." Clave stepped back and picked up the remote. "Maybe I'll keep this in the cockpit."

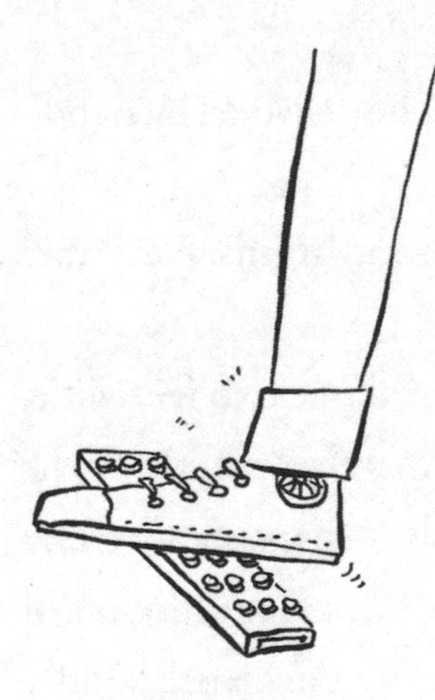

"Good idea." Nicholas pointed to something that looked like a spaghetti and meatball dinner after it had been halfway digested. "Ew . . . What's that?"

"I can't recall."

"Where are you taking it?"

"Not sure. I must have that information somewhere around here." Clave lifted one end of a slab of gold next to the stringy mess. "I know I have a manifest . . ."

"You're not very good at this courier stuff, are you?" Nicholas asked.

Clave staggered as if he'd been smacked in the face. "Do I come down to Earth and make fun of you at your job?"

"I don't have a job," Nicholas said.

"No job? Then what do you do?"

"I go to school," Nicholas said.

"School?"

Nicholas explained.

Clave stared at Nicholas for a moment, as if he weren't sure whether he was being kidded. "And how long does this last?"

"At least twelve years. Thirteen if you count kindergarten. One or two more if you go to preschool. Another four for college. Longer if you want a graduate degree. Some people never stop taking classes."

"Sounds like a scam," Clave said. "No wonder you barbarians are still confined to your own solar system. Well, feel free to stare at all of this gold as long as you want. I'm going to check whether we can get to one of these delivery sites in three jumps. At least that way, I'll earn enough to buy the cubes I need to get you off my hands." He went back up the steps.

Something tickled the back of Nicholas's brain when he thought about school. Maybe there was a way to get farther with the three cubes than Clave realized. But he needed to know more first. "Hey, can you explain these jump things to me?" he called after Clave. "How do they connect? Why do you have to do a series of them?"

"It's complicated, barbarian," Clave said. "Don't distract me. I need to figure a way out of this mess."

"Whatever," Nicholas muttered. "I'm not stupid." He sat on the top step and looked at the gold. He couldn't believe how much there was. He was sure he could have everything he wanted, and also make the world a better place for lots of people. Assuming any of the big problems on Earth could be fixed with money.

"Of course you're not stupid," Henrietta said. "And it's not all that complicated. It's probably a lot like in that movie, *Marauders of the Galaxy.*"

"I don't remember that one," Nicholas said.

"That's because you didn't see it. I did. Nineteen times. You're always leaving the TV on." She explained how the nodes were probably connected.

"Thanks. That makes sense. But it means we're not going to have a lot of options as far as where to go. I hope he figures something out." Nicholas glanced in the direction of the bridge. "And I hope he lets me know before he does another jump."

As if on cue, the ship lurched violently, tossing the gold around and flinging Nicholas from the steps. He came close to dying like the bad guy in an adventure movie who gets killed by all the gold after he killed most of the good guys to get that gold. He was relieved to see that Henrietta had managed to cling to her spot on the steps and avoid getting tumbled. Some of the cargo straps had broken, but nothing had come totally loose. He figured he should mention that to Clave, but he had something else to mention first.

"You didn't even say 'hang on' this time," he yelled as he scrambled out of the cargo hold and stomped into the bridge. "I could have gotten killed!"

"I didn't launch us anywhere," Clave said, from his sprawled position on the floor. The ship jerked again, as if it were a deeply rooted tooth being yanked from a jaw. "We're in some sort of tractor beam."

Nicholas checked to make sure Jeef was okay, then went to the viewport. "I don't see any ship."

"That's because all you see is ship," Henrietta said.

"Oh . . . my . . . word . . ." Nicholas realized she was right. Whatever was pulling them was so huge it blotted out the entire view. As he watched, a small square of dazzling light appeared on the surface of the enormous object. Another appeared next to it. They shed enough light that Nicholas got a clear view of what was happening. Black panels were flipping over, spreading out from the location of the first one, turning the dark surface into a glittery expanse that seemed to reflect a thousand colors. As the visible expanse spread, Nicholas eventually was able to detect a curve to the surface.

"It looks like a disco ball," he said. "What do you think they want?"

"No idea," Clave said. "But in my experience, nothing good ever existed at the other end of a tractor beam."

QUICK THINKING

The big leap that spawned a universal expansion of Thinkerator technology came when a clever merchant realized two things. First, there was a huge difference between *quick* and *instant*. Second, while colonists were happy just to get what they needed, consumers were an entirely different market. Jump shuttles had to be loaded with cargo. Then, after making their jumps, it could take the ship hours, or even days, to travel from the jump node to a docking station. The Thinkerator could deliver an item anywhere in the universe instantly, as long as there was a receiving unit on the other end.

As huge a revelation as this was, the first commercial application offered a single product: Kenporian neckties. (Virtually every planet where one segment of the dominant species adorns their necks with uncomfortable pieces of fabric also celebrates a special day for that segment, thus ensuring a steady market for ties. And Kenporian neckties are among the finest neckties available.) Kenporia Cravats Limited employed three mind shippers their first year. Within a decade, the business grew large enough to offer more than five thousand products. Within a quarter century, they'd covered major portions of Kenporia with warehouses, and were employing hundreds of thousands of shippers.

This expansion didn't just happen on Kenporia. Once the process reached commercial practicality, it was rapidly put to use selling pretty much everything and shipping it pretty much anywhere, allowing those with too much money to purchase and instantly obtain things they didn't need not just from their hometown or country or planet, but from anywhere at all. Before long, every home had a Thinkerator. And nearly every planet that produced any form of desirable merchandise had at least one warehouse and a shipping facility.

GRABBITY

After a brief silence, Clave gasped.

"What?" Nicholas asked.

"That's a great quote," Clave said. "*Nothing good ever existed at the other end of a tractor beam.* It could go uni-viral! Tenth-rate sfumbler? I'll show her." He repeated the quote about tractor beams as he captured a clip of him-self. Then, he turned back to Nicholas. "Don't worry. It contains nothing that could help locate us. It's important to sfumble regularly if you want to build an audience."

Nicholas shifted his attention back to the massive ship. Four of the panels that formed a two-by-two square slid diagonally away from the center, revealing a massive opening leading to a chamber that looked like a hangar. "We're getting swallowed," he said.

"Nothing," Clave said.

"What are you talking about?" Nicholas asked.

"Nothing!" Clave jabbed a finger at the bottom of the image where his newest sfumble hovered, displaying the looping video along with various stats. The view count was impressively low, and not showing any signs of climbing at more than a trickle.

"Maybe people haven't seen it yet," Nicholas said.

"Nonsense," Clave said. "People eagerly await my sfumbles."

Nicholas groped for something positive to say. "They could all be asleep."

"You don't seem to have much of a grasp of how the universe works," Clave said. "Wait! Here we go. People are watching it. That's better."

The view count rose more quickly. Below it, a stream of comments scrolled by.

Where's the Destroyer?

Show us the Assassin!

Who is Nicholas killing next?

He's cute for a biped. Is he married?

Clave sighed. His shoulders slumped.

"I'm sure people will love your quote," Nicholas said, unaware that the sigh-and-slumped-shoulder gesture was how Menmarians reflexively acted when they had a sudden urge to empty their bowels.

"Back in a moment," Clave said as he dashed toward the living quarters.

Nicholas felt a similar urge a moment later, when the ship was pulled inside the enormous hangar. He felt like a flea that had just been swallowed by a whale.

"No point fighting it," Clave said when he returned. He cut the engines and the ship settled to the floor.

The outer hatch closed, sealing them inside the enormous room.

"I imagine they're filling the chamber with some sort of atmosphere," Henrietta said after several minutes passed with no sign of their captors.

"Hopefully not Tex-Mex," Nicholas said. Then, he sighed and his shoulders slumped.

"Do you need to empty your bowels?" Clave asked. "Maybe it was the sandwich."

"The sandwich was fine. So are my bowels," Nicholas said. "It's just, I killed a bunch more people."

"No, you didn't," Henrietta said. "You showed them a peaceful solution, and they took advantage of it for treachery."

"They would have killed one another anyway," Clave

said. “Well before Menmar was at war with Zefinora, the people were battling among themselves. Why do you think the other continents are unoccupied? My people are no lovers of peace. None of this is your fault.”

“Thanks,” Nicholas said. Clave’s and Henrietta’s words didn’t really make him feel much better, but he appreciated their efforts. He was surprised Jeef hadn’t chimed in with something comforting. He realized Jeef had been pretty quiet since she’d discovered she’d been ground up, and she hadn’t said anything at all since she’d told them about her past life.

“It will be okay,” he said, putting his hand on top of the package. “Somehow, things will work out.”

Thank you. For to him that is joined to all the living, there is hope.

Just then, a smaller hatch on the interior wall opened and a creature padded into the hangar. He looked like a human with the head of a beagle.

“Dad?” Nicholas blurted the word out. It was propelled from his throat by a wave of relief at the thought that he’d been rescued. Parents had an amazing ability to show up when you desperately needed them, as well as when you desperately wanted to escape observation. The feeling of relief ebbed as quickly as it had swelled, when Nicholas noticed the beagle-faced creature had real paws and a tail. It also had a four-pronged tongue, with which it licked its snout on both sides at once. And though it was hard to tell for sure, given the enormous scale of the chamber, it seemed to be no more than four feet tall. Definitely not the dad of anyone from Earth.

Clave opened the ship's hatch and stomped out. "You had no right to capture us," he said.

Ignoring Clave, the Beradaxian (for that's what he was) addressed Nicholas, who was on his way down the ramp with Henrietta and Jeef, speaking in a surprisingly melodic voice that was nowhere near the baying of a hound one might expect from such a face, or the villainous hiss of a cartoon snake suggested by the forked tongue. "This way."

"You don't get to boss me around," Clave said.

The creature turned back to the inner hatch.

"We're not going anywhere," Clave said.

The creature walked through the hatch.

Nicholas, who was just grateful the air smelled like a brand-new football, and an expensive one at that, picked up his portable companions and followed the creature, whose tail was now wagging in time with his steps.

"I'm just coming along to keep an eye on my passenger," Clave said as he ran to catch up with Nicholas. "I'm not following your orders."

They walked down a long corridor, then boarded a tram that carried them deeper into the bowels of the massive ship, following a path defined by a rail painted on the floor.

"I haven't seen anyone else," Nicholas whispered to Henrietta.

"It's kind of spooky," she said. "The place feels deserted."

Eventually, they disembarked from the tram, and walked along a wider corridor, which ended at a sparkling hatch decorated with a mosaic of round stones, each the size of a quarter. Penny-sized centers of various colors were ringed by bright yellow bands. As Nicholas got closer, the centers seemed to aim at him.

"The stones are staring at me," he said. He was sure of

it now. He leaned to the left and watched as the inner discs shifted. "What kind of rocks are they?"

"Those are Greven eyes," Clave said. "Very rare. Only the wealthiest beings in the universe can afford even one. I've heard of them, but never seen them. Or been seen by them."

"Just the eyes?" Nicholas asked. He felt his spine stiffen at the thought of somebody harvesting parts from Greven, which he pictured as cute, furry forest creatures.

"Yes, just the eyes," Clave said.

"That's awful," Nicholas said.

"It's perfectly fine," Clave said. "They grow back."

Nicholas shuddered. He knew that people took claws from live crabs. But that was sort of okay, because the claws grew back. (Though he suspected the crabs might not feel inclined to such generosity, had they been given a choice.) But eyes? That was too cruel. "That's barbaric," he said.

"Not really," Clave said.

"But who would do such a thing?" Nicholas asked. "Who would pluck eyes from the Greven just to sell them?"

"The Greven," Clave said. "It's their major export."

"Please, gentlemen. You need to go in. He's waiting." The Beradaxian stepped aside and gestured for them to continue. The hatch, which produced a fanfare of heroic music when it opened, led to an opulent chamber. The floor, made of polished granite-like stone, was a shiny moving swirl of white, red, and black. Nicholas found that he got dizzy if he stared at it while he walked. On the side walls, shelves made of a blue-tinged wood-like material displayed a variety of sculptures. A large wooden desk, with a grain that also seemed to swirl, dominated the rear third of the room. A single deep-black shelf ran the length of the rear wall, supporting busts of various creatures. Rows of displays set in the desk showed an assortment of scenes that all seemed to be performances of one type or another.

In the center of the rear shelf sat a replica of the ship they were in. It was on a stand labeled *Cloud Mansion Intergalactic*.

"See," Nicholas said. "This ship has a name. A stupid one. But a name."

Clave's attention was elsewhere. "That's Greepni Mem D'Voiber!" he said, pointing to a bust that resembled a horned walrus. "I love his movies. And there's Penge of a Thousand Limbs! She's an amazing dancer." Clave's finger shifted toward a face that seemed to be formed from translucent crystals atop a body made of fibers of light.

Nicholas's attention was also pulled elsewhere, which wasn't surprising. Every object in the room was like a tractor beam for attention, except one. Behind the desk, on a low stand, stood what looked to him like an enormous fish tank. It was empty of either occupants or water. A clear tube attached inside the upper right corner jutted above the rim, but stopped midway down. The bottom was lined with tiny switches. All four sides looked like they were past due for a good cleaning. A carpeted ramp ran from the floor to the top of the left side of the tank. Something moved near the base of the ramp.

"Ewww . . ." Nicholas said as he peeked around the desk and spotted what looked like the world's largest

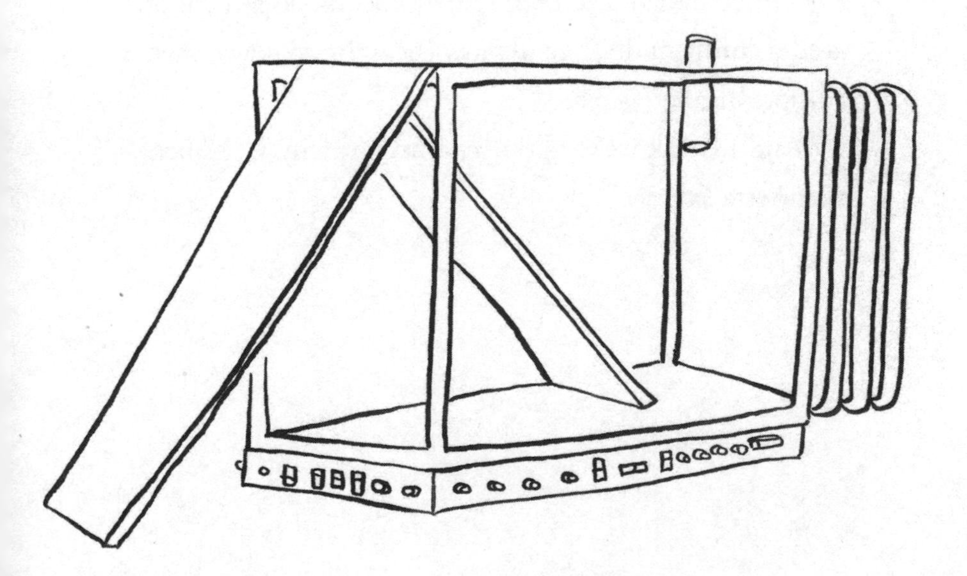

sneeze, issued by a giant who had recently recovered from a bloody nose.

"Tapree of Aldeberan!" Clave said, continuing his fan-crazed tour of the busts.

Nicholas's eyes were glued (though fortunately, not literally) to the sneeze, which had started oozing up the ramp. He tapped Clave on the shoulder. "What is that?"

Clave was still transfixed by the displays. Nicholas grabbed Clave's head and rotated it toward the desk.

"Do you have any idea what that is?" Nicholas asked.

"Morglob Sputum," Clave whispered, as if he barely believed such an encounter was possible. "He's a talent agent. He represents all the biggest acts in the universe. I heard he had an estate in space that was so large it created a jump node. I've always thought that was just a rumor. But here we are."

"And I think we're about to find out why we're here," Henrietta said.

GETTING SOLD ON THE IDEA

Hyperjump Unlimited was dethroned from its spot as the largest company in the universe by Thinkerator Corporation, which itself expanded geometrically, thanks to the endless new markets discovered by means of hyperjumps.

Thinkerator Corporation also prospered because it provided a much more important service. Hyperjump Unlimited just helped you get to places you probably didn't need to go. Thinkerator Corporation helped you get things you probably didn't need, like cool toys that flew really fast, or Kenporian neckties. While there will always be people who want to go places, there will always be a lot more who want to own things.

Love of things, while not universal, is pretty close.

That's basic human nature, even when the consumer isn't human, or natural.

And, yes, you can order a j-cube through a Thinkerator, but they've been known to explode. At least, that's the best theory to explain the various craters that appeared on various civilized worlds at various times.

AN OFFER YOU SHOULDN'T REFUSE

One end of Morglob had reached the lip of the tank. He dripped down the side, pulling the rest of himself into the tank with the help of gravity and viscosity, making a sound that resembled a giant boot freeing itself from thick mud, or perhaps a giant, itself, throwing up in slow motion. Nicholas promised himself he'd never eat honey or maple syrup again. Or raspberry jam. He also wondered whether it was possible to go through the rest of his life without sneezing.

"Thank you for coming," Morglob said, after he'd gotten his entire body into the tank, which was now filled to within an inch of the top. His words burbled through the tube, like the voice of someone speaking through a straw stuck in a milkshake.

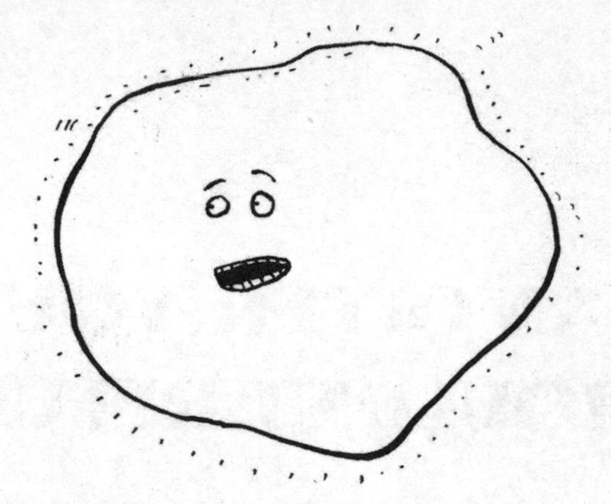

Nicholas, who'd just added strawberry milkshakes to his list of foods he'd never want again, expected Clave to hurl an angry reply about tractor beams, but he seemed too starstruck to complain, or even to speak at all.

"We didn't have much choice," Nicholas said. "What do you want?"

"You," Morglob said.

"Me?" Nicholas had a disturbing vision of his body being enveloped and digested by Morglob.

"You. You've got talent, kid. And a following. People are going wild about you. Your numbers are off the charts!" Morglob wriggled against some of the switches in the bottom of his tank. A dizzying series of graphs flashed through the air. "See, they love this whole *Destroyer of Worlds* thing. Especially with that innocent face of yours. That's a killer combination, if you know what I mean. Don't squander that. It's a fickle universe. The enthusiasm could vanish in a second. Look what happened to what's-his-name. See? I can't even remember him. You could be the next one everybody can't remember. But not if I'm in charge of your career. Let me manage you. I'll make you bigger than you've ever dreamed."

"I've never dreamed of being any size," Nicholas said. In truth, after a disastrous experience in a supporting role as the bottom half of a giraffe in a fifth-grade production of "How the Leopard Got Its Spots," he swore to stay as far away as possible from any type of public performance. "I just want to go home."

"Perfect!" Morglob said. "World wrecker by day, homesick young man by night, staring at the stars and dreaming of his birth planet while he crushes entire galaxies. The press will eat it up. You're a natural-born actor. That's a great start. Can you sing? I've got a stranglehold on insectoid bands, but I don't currently have an anthropoid singer under management."

"Pretty much everyone tells me I sound like an accordion that's been run over by a truck." Nicholas figured it wouldn't hurt to try to kill some of Morglob's enthusiasm, especially since he was telling the truth about his lack of talent. Rumor has it he was at least partially responsible for the early retirement of the middle school's music teacher.

"No matter. We can tweak that in the sound studio. But let's get down to business." Once again, bits of Morglob rippled against the switches on the bottom of the tank. A transparent tablet rose from a slot on the desk, then tilted lazily backward until it settled flat against the surface. The screen turned white and filled with text. A series of pages flickered past too quickly to leave much of an impression, ending with a page that had Nicholas's name at the bottom, next to an empty shape that looked like a splattered amoeba.

An identical splattered-amoeba shape sat on the line below, next to Morglob's name.

"Hwack phlepf," Morglob said. A blob shot out of the tube and landed expertly on (and in) the appropriate shape.

"Your turn. Bite your cheek, spit there, and we'll get to work," Morglob said. "Maybe start with some commercial endorsements, just to test the water, before we go big. Speaking of water, how do you feel about bladder-control products? Humans have bladders, right? And a reluctance to urinate unexpectedly? That's common with bipeds. They hate getting their legs wet. Sign now, and I'll have you doing advertisements by the end of the day.

You'll make a fortune. All the biggest stars started with commercials."

"I have to think about this," Nicholas said. He needed to take his eyes off Morglob before the queasiness in his stomach turned into full-blown nausea. He looked at the busts lining the shelves on the rear wall and spotted a familiar creature. It was a musician from Xroxlotl. Or, at least, someone of the same species, holding the same sticklike instrument.

"I see you're a fan. Marvelous. That group is one of my greatest creations. They never make a move without me. I'm surprised they can even breathe if I'm not telling them to inhale and exhale. Wait. Actually, they can't. Hang on a moment. I need to use the direct line."

A microphone came down from the ceiling and hovered above the tube. "Inhale, idiots!" Morglob said.

Morglob rippled against other switches. The microphone rose. "Fortunately, they have a very slow respiration rate when they aren't singing. That should hold them for several days. Where was I? Oh, right. They have a huge concert coming up. Biggest one ever. We sold out the whole planet the instant the tickets went live. I can get you front-row seats. Not pseudo-front projection seats. The real thing."

That seemed to jolt Clave out of his trance. "We'll take

them!" he said. "Hey, do you represent sfumblers? I've quite a following. And it's growing. My last sfumble got bombarded with comments. I'm Crazy Clave. Maybe you've heard of me. I'm sure you have. Here. Take a look." He pulled up a series of his recent posts, arranging them in a four-by-four array that spouted cacophonous gibberish as the sixteen audio loops overlapped.

Morglob ignored Clave. "Nobody is going to get you better deals, or take better care of your career," he told Nicholas.

"I can't sign anything without reading it," Nicholas said. Though he'd never been asked to sign any sort of contract, he was vaguely aware that people got in trouble if they didn't understand what they were agreeing to. He had a suspicion that might be why his parents were touring Australia rather than Seattle. He picked up the tablet and scrolled back toward the first page. It took a while to get there, though much to his relief, Morglob's splattered signature somehow also scrolled out of sight. "That's a lot of pages."

"They're all there to protect you," Morglob said. "That's how much I value you. I'm willing to put your interests ahead of mine. I don't make much. I do this mostly just for the love of nurturing talent. Take your time. Read it.

I'll be here when you're ready to sign. Spott will show you to your guest quarters."

The hatch opened. Spott, the beagle-headed four-foot-tall Beradaxian, was standing there. "This way," he said, unnecessarily, since there was only one way down the corridor. He put a hand on Nicholas's shoulder to guide him.

"Ouch!" Nicholas shouted as he felt claws raking his back. He spun around.

"Sorry," Spott said. "I slipped."

But whatever alien expression his face held, Nicholas was pretty sure it didn't go with that apology.

Ironically, the phrase that popped into Nicholas's mind was *Watch your back*.

At the end of their trip, Nicholas found himself in a luxurious suite with two bedrooms leading off from the enormous main area. The doors, fortunately, were not made of eyes, or other animated material. He walked the length of the cavernous room, trying to absorb his latest misadventure. As he approached any piece of furniture, whether a chair, couch, or table, it shifted to fit his shape and size.

"Now what?" he asked as he flopped down into an amazingly comfortable chair.

"Now what?" Clave asked, as if those were the two most ridiculous words ever uttered. "How can there be any question? Most people would kill for this opportunity."

"I already have," Nicholas said. "Exponentially, if you listen to the news."

"Sorry. Bad word choice. Anyhow, sign the deal. You'll be huge. And I'll chronicle every moment. I'll shamelessly ride the coattails of your fame. I've always wanted to do that. I've just never been fortunate enough to be in the presence of available coattails. Especially not coattails with so much potential. You don't want to end up like what's-his-name, whoever that was."

"I really just want to get home," Nicholas said. He flexed his shoulders and frowned.

"What's wrong?" Clave asked.

"Spott scratched me." Nicholas pulled off his shirt, twisted his head, and looked over his shoulder. There were definitely scratches, deep enough to stand out in red, but not so deep as to bleed.

"It looks like a word," Clave said. He came closer. "'Help.'"

"'Help'?" Nicholas tried to make out the word. The scratches were at too awkward an angle for him to focus clearly on them, but the blurry image did look like Spott had clawed HELP into his flesh, which seemed like a counterproductive way to ask for aid. It was like using Morse code to punch *I need a favor* into someone's stomach.

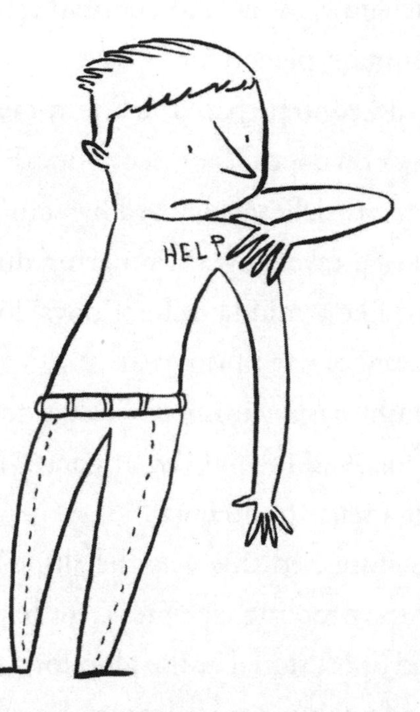

But the idea that the scratches were a message was confirmed when Spott brought them a meal an hour later. Before Nicholas could speak, Spott whispered, "Not now," and nodded his head toward the napkins on the left side of the tray he was holding.

Then a bit more loudly, he told them, "Morglob had the famous chef Fleexbeezle prepare special delicacies for both of you. They just arrived." He set the tray, which held two covered dishes, on a table.

"Fleexbeezle!" Clave said. "I love her sfumbles. And her cooking show. What did she make? I hope it's her famous mountain pigeon pie."

"She was asked to prepare the finest, most popular example of your own local food. For you, the Menmarian, she crafted a rare delicacy beloved by your people." Spott lifted the cover, revealing a simmering dull-brown glop that smelled like a middle-school boys' locker room on the hottest school day of the year.

Clave's enthusiasm vanished. "That's not Menmarian. It's Zefinoran. And inedible by anyone with a tongue, a stomach, or a sense of decency."

Nicholas suspected this was the slime-gibbon sweat-gland stew the drooling vice president had mentioned.

Clave and Spott stared at the glop for a moment, their expressions showing a mingling of horror and amazement, though Clave's eyebrows barely moved. Spott replaced the cover, removing the stew from sight, but leaving a fair portion of the aroma behind. "I'll get you some bread. I made it myself."

"Thank you," Clave said. "But I'm not sure I'll want to eat anything for the next month or two."

I hope mine's a cheeseburger, Nicholas thought, before

casting a guilty glance at Jeef and changing his wish to pepperoni pizza. Though he wasn't sure what sort of meat was in pepperoni, and pretty sure he never wanted to know what was in anything, ever again. He lifted the cover on the second dish.

A not-unpleasant smell of vinegar filled the air, along with a hint of cilantro. That was the only pleasant part of the culinary nightmare he had revealed. What met Nicholas's eye was a plate filled with the sort of pale flesh one sees on the belly of a waterlogged fish floating in a stagnant pond two or three days after the fish has died from some sort of hideous fungus-related fish disease.

"What . . . ?" Nicholas couldn't even form a question. He reached out to touch the closest piece, which was shaped like a thick disc that had lost all desire to remain disc shaped. He dropped his hand as his gag reflex overwhelmed all curiosity.

"I believe it is called *ceviche,*" Spott said. "It's supposed to be an Earth delicacy. Though I have no idea what the ingredients are."

Nicholas tried to speak, but he hadn't fought down his nausea enough to dare open his mouth.

"Bread?" Spott asked him.

"Mmm-hmmm."

"I'll be right back." Spott took the tray and the covered dishes, but left the napkins.

Nicholas found a note tucked into the folds of one of the napkins. *Tonight. Be ready. He listens to everything. We can only talk safely after he goes to sleep.*

OLD NEWS ABOUT NEWS

It was during the great expansion of Thinkerators that Stella came to be. Naturally, an abundance of products led to an abundance of noise and confusion as everyone tried to grab a share of every market. This led to a great increase in the value of any medium capable of attracting views and carrying advertising. Thus, Stella and other similar stars, who were designed to attract viewers, rose to prominence in the universe, along with the most popular sfumblers, and universally appealing video programs, most of which were about either cooking, or killing, or both. Ironically, not far behind those in popularity were programs about simplifying life and getting rid of unwanted possessions.

It is natural to ask whether Thinkerators could be used

for space travel. Unfortunately, the process did not produce good results on living creatures sent over long distances. Despite numerous attempts using a variety of unwilling volunteers, it just wasn't workable to transmit life-forms by means of thoughts. Several attempts were made to place a series of Thinkerators on space platforms just close enough to allow a living being to travel between planets. But repeated transmissions over a short distance were even worse for living creatures than a single long-range delivery, as Bilworth Foot-for-a-Head could tell you, had he been able to talk, and had you managed to have that conversation with him during those brief, frantic moments before he suffocated.

IS THIS ANY WAY TO TREAT A STAR?

When Spott returned with the bread, he cast a hopeful glance at each of them, then left the room again.

"Do you think we can trust him?" Nicholas whispered after the door closed.

"He's a predator," Henrietta said.

"So am I, sort of," Nicholas said.

"You should absolutely not trust him," Clave said. "You need to sign that contract."

"I need to get a clean shirt." Nicholas realized his current one, which he'd worn for several days before being abducted, and which seemed to have absorbed some of the pungent aroma of the Zefinoran stew, had reached the point where it needed to be either washed or incinerated.

Clave pointed to three large nozzles that looked like shower heads, affixed to the wall at chest height. A small table sat beneath them. "Order whatever you need from the Thinkerator."

"Order?" Nicholas asked.

"Oh, dear. I forgot. You're one of those backwater creatures. Here, I'll show you. Let's say you need a clean shirt, which you desperately do. Stand here." He guided Nicholas to a spot about two feet from the wall, then said, "Shirts."

A lens opened beneath the central nozzle. A red beam scanned Nicholas from neck to hips. A moment later, three-dimensional images of dozens of different styles of shirts appeared, hovering in the air between him and the wall. There were button-downs, polo, sport, and many other styles, including some Nicholas was sure he'd never seen before, though they seemed designed for a person with his torso. Clave touched a T-shirt. The other images turned into variations of that basic T-shirt that Clave had selected, including crew-neck, V-neck, and high-neck.

"Preference?" Clave asked.

Nicholas pointed at the one with the largest pocket.

Clave touched it. A colored sphere appeared, along with a separate display of patterns. Clave touched the solid section below the patterns, then asked, "Color?"

Nicholas shrugged. This felt both amazingly futuristic and embarrassingly similar to going shopping with his mom.

"Let's stay basic," Clave said, touching black. "Watch this."

"I'm not even going to blink," Nicholas said.

Clave stepped back and said, "Process the order."

A mist drifted from the nozzles. It took the form of a shirt, though it was still made of mist. Then, the mist started to pull together and drift toward the table. A moment later, a black V-neck T-shirt lay there.

"How . . . ?" Nicholas said.

"It's complicated," Clave said.

Nicholas touched the shirt, half afraid it would leave a wet smear on his hands. But it felt like a normal shirt, except a lot nicer than the T-shirts he bought. He pulled his old one off, and put the new one on. "Would it be okay to get some underwear?"

"At this point, I think it would be mandatory," Clave said. He turned toward the Thinkerator and started to speak.

Nicholas cut him off. "I'll get it myself. Thanks." After he ordered the underwear and watched it appear on the table, he said, "Is it just clothing?"

"Hardly," Clave said. "You can get pretty much anything that's in stock, anywhere. And pretty much everything is in stock somewhere. Check out the catalog."

As Clave said that word, a catalog emerged from a slot on the wall and dropped to the table. On the cover, the word SHIRTS shimmered in large letters.

"Paper?" Nicholas asked. His parents still got a few catalogs in the mail, especially around the holidays, but he'd never looked at any of them. "And you call me a barbarian?"

"Paper is wonderful," Clave said. "Many people don't like swiping their hands through images in the air. There's something nice about flipping through a thick catalog. It's perfect for daydreaming."

"Or chewing," Henrietta said. "Paper is the best thing ever for chewing."

"I'll take your word for that," Clave told her. He turned back to Nicholas. "Take a look."

"I already have a shirt," Nicholas said.

"What else are you interested in?" Clave asked.

"Cars," Nicholas said, blurting out the first thing that came to mind.

Clave tapped the catalog. "Put your hand here, and say that."

Nicholas did. The cover image and wording changed. Nicholas realized his hand was now resting on a car catalog.

"Cool!" Nicholas said.

The catalog changed, displaying refrigerators and air conditioners. Nicholas lifted his hand. As much as he wanted to play around with the catalog, he knew he had something more important to take care of. "I should read that contract first."

He sat down with the tablet and tried his best. But pretty much everything past the opening sentence made little sense. And it seemed to give Morglob all sorts of benefits, including the total, perpetual, and unrestricted right to use Nicholas's image in any form of recording either now existing or invented in the future. Some of the sentences were so long and convoluted, with all sorts of *wherefores* and *henceforths,* they made his English lit assignments seem like nursery rhymes.

"Here, take a look at this. Maybe you can figure it out." Nicholas slid the tablet toward Henrietta, who had been thumbing—actually nosing—through the Thinkerator catalog.

She didn't do any better. Some things just aren't meant to be understood.

"Jeef, do you know anything about law?" Nicholas asked after Henrietta had given up.

It never really came up while I was grazing, Jeef said. *I loved grazing. I miss grass. And hay. More to be desired are they than gold, yea, than much fine gold.*

Nicholas realized he'd been hunched over the tablet the whole time he'd been trying to make sense of the contract. "I need to walk around." He stretched his back, then went to the door to the corridor. He pushed at it. He pulled. He tried to slide it in every possible direction. Eventually, he concluded it was locked.

"Let's check out the bedrooms." Nicholas scooped up Henrietta and headed for the doorway on the left.

Hey! Forget somebody? Jeef said.

"Oh, sorry." Nicholas turned back. He hadn't consciously left Jeef behind, but he had to admit he was getting a bit tired of lugging the hunk of beef around. As much as it made him feel guilty, he was starting to wish he'd grabbed something lighter and more portable from the fridge, like a hot dog, or a mozzarella stick.

"Hold on," Henrietta said. "I'm pretty sure I have a solution. Put me by the catalog."

Nicholas set her on the table, next to the catalog, which was currently open to exercise wheels, and only slightly chewed at the edges. Henrietta used her snout to flip back several pages. "Here. Check this out."

"Mind-controlled utility cart," Nicholas said, reading the description beneath the picture. The cart looked fairly simple. It was mostly just a flat sheet of metal equipped with eight wheels, along with some electrodes that ran from a box attached to the back of the sheet, all powered by some sort of small engine.

Nicholas tapped a red circle that contained the words ORDER ME. The nozzles spurted more mist. "I could get used to this."

As soon as the cart formed, he placed Jeef in the center platform.

Ahhhhhgggg! It's hot! Jeef screamed.

"Sorry!" Nicholas snatched Jeef up. That was when he spotted the word DANGER printed on the cart, beneath which was written: *Thinkerated metallic objects are hot. Allow to cool before using. Letters will fade when it is safe. Failure to comply with this warning will fry your toddler's bottom.* He checked Jeef's bottom. The plastic was puckered, but unbroken.

"Are you all right?" he asked.

I guess. Except for learning what it feels like to be cooked. I never expected my best friend would hurt me.

Nicholas simultaneously cringed at the "cooked" part

and choked up at the other part. It had been a while since anyone had called him *best friend*. He waited for Henrietta to say something sarcastic, but she held her tongue for once.

"I'm really sorry," he said. "I didn't mean to hurt you."

I forgive you.

"Thank you," Nicholas said.

Blessed is he whose transgression is forgiven.

Nicholas waited until the warning faded, then gave the cart's surface a quick tap with his forefinger. Once he was sure he hadn't been burned, he put his palm there. The metal was warm, but not dangerously so. "Here. Try it out." He placed Jeef back in the center of the cart, then attached the sticky ends of a pair of electrodes to either side of Jeef's package and put the cart down on the floor.

"Okay," Nicholas said, "give it a—"

Before he could finish his sentence, the cart shot across the room and slammed into a wall. Jeef flew out, splatting against that same wall. She dropped back to the floor, missing the cart, which had bounced away from the wall after the impact. The electrodes stayed in place. The cart shot the other way, dragging Jeef across the floor like a cowgirl who'd slipped from her saddle and gotten her feet stuck in the stirrups.

Nicholas dived on it and lifted it up so the wheels spun harmlessly. "Are you okay?"

I love it! Jeef, who was still dangling, said. *Put me down!*

Nicholas put Jeef back in the cart, but continued to hold it in the air. "Are you sure?"

Yes!

"Maybe you could stop the wheels first," Nicholas said.

The wheels stopped.

"Ready?"

Ready.

Nicholas placed the cart down on the floor. It took off slower, but still managed to bang a few more walls before Jeef gained some degree of control over her direction and speed.

"You did a nice thing," Nicholas said to Henrietta as he checked out the adjoining rooms, which both had beds and only slightly cryptic bathrooms.

"No, I didn't. I just wanted to make sure you always have both hands free for rubbing my belly and scratching my back," she said.

"You can't fool me," Nicholas said. "You've got a soft spot for Jeef."

"You've got that backward. It's Jeef who has soft spots."

That evening, Spott came back. "We must escape," he whispered.

"Why?" Nicholas asked.

"He's a monster," Spott said. "He has no conscience. He keeps me trapped here as his servant. I have to strain him for bits of bone and gristle after he eats. Do you have any idea how disgusting that is?"

"I can't begin to imagine," Nicholas said.

"And let's not even talk about the back rubs." Spott shuddered, which means pretty much the same for Beradaxians as it does for humans. "He told me he was going to make me a star. I signed a contract. I should have read it. There were twenty others also serving him when I arrived."

"What happened to them?" Nicholas asked.

"They threw themselves into space to get away. One by one. That's how terrible it is here. I'm the only one left," Spott said. "At least until he decides to lure more captives with false promises. You're lucky he doesn't already represent a notorious intergalactic killer, or he'd have put you to work the moment he caught you."

"I'm not exactly feeling lucky at the moment," Nicholas said.

"That's because you have no idea how bad things can get." Spot took a step toward the door. "I've waited forever for a chance to escape. You're the first people who came on their own spaceship."

"So how do we get out?" Nicholas asked.

"We need to disable the tractor beams," Spott said. "Then we can escape on your ship."

"It's not his ship. It's my ship," Clave said. "And I'm not helping with any escape. This is our big break. I don't really have any other options at the moment."

"Look, I've stayed too long," Spott said. "He only sleeps for ten or fifteen minutes each evening. He'll be calling me at any moment to fry up a snack of gristlebunnies. I'll give you time to think about this. Just don't talk too loudly." He left the room.

"We need to discuss this," Nicholas said.

"Not now," Clave said. "I'm tired. We'll talk in the morning." He went off to one of the bedrooms.

"Roach brains," Nicholas muttered as Clave's door closed.

An hour later, just as Nicholas was settling down to get some sleep, the bedroom door crashed open. Three creatures tumbled through the doorway, howling like they were being sawed in half. Nicholas leaped from the bed and let out his own scream, though his was more like he was being sawed into fifths. The creatures resembled humans who'd been dead for quite a long time.

Nicholas was now as fully awake as he'd ever been, which was unfortunate because he really wished this were all a nightmare.

A WORD ABOUT ZOMBIES

Authentic zombies are far more common throughout the universe than most people would like to believe. As are shape-shifters, vampires, and unicorns. Though none of the unicorn races so far encountered have the ability to excrete rainbows. Which doesn't mean there aren't rainbow-pooping creatures out there. But since we seem to be straying far from the story at hand, let's leave it at that and get back to Nicholas's rude awakening.

ACTION!

Acting on pure adrenaline, Nicholas grabbed a chair, which morphed into a more comfortable and yet still useful shape as he lifted it. Armed, he rushed at the intruders and started swinging. It hadn't crossed his mind that it might be futile to try to kill something that appeared to already be extremely dead.

His flailing session drove all three creatures out of the bedroom. Nicholas flung the door shut behind him on the way out, to keep Henrietta from bravely and foolishly joining the battle.

"Clave!" he screamed as he grabbed a sturdier chair.

Swinging and thrusting, he drove the intruders across the main room.

"Clave!" he screamed again. "Help!" A stolen glance over his shoulder showed that the bedroom door remained shut. He was on his own.

Nicholas kept swinging until all three attackers and the chair were reduced significantly from their original form. Finally, panting hard, with all his nerves on fire, and all his sweat glands operating on overdrive, or overdrown, clutching the remains of a chair leg in his hands so hard his fingers went numb, he stopped flailing and looked at the carnage.

Then he blinked and took another look.

Based on the abundance of shiny components spilling from the gaping wounds, and the absence of torn flesh or drippy fluids, his attackers appeared to be electromechanical.

"Beautiful! I knew you were an action star."

Nicholas searched for the source of the familiar burbly voice. Three tiny cameras with large lenses, like the ones on the Craborzi ship, hovered in the corridor, capturing his actions from three angles. The voice came from a speaker mounted beneath the central camera.

"I'm not an actor," Nicholas said.

"All the better. You're a natural. We'll get everything finalized tomorrow. Good night. Pleasant dreams."

The door closed before Nicholas could step into the hall.

"Did you call me?" Clave asked, opening his bedroom door. He yawned, covering his mouth with one hand and scratching his butt absentmindedly with the other. "Is something wrong?"

"No. Everything is great," Nicholas said. "Super. Perfect. Terrific!" He dropped the piece of wood and headed for his bedroom.

Henrietta was waiting on the other side of the door. "What happened? I tried to slip under, but there isn't a gap."

"Nothing," Nicholas said. He didn't want to talk about it right now.

Sleep did not come easily. Eventually, exhaustion won, and Nicholas slept relatively well, except for several brief moments when he sat up suddenly, drenched in sweat, and started screaming.

The next day, soon after Nicholas woke, Spott came in, touched the tip of one paw to his lips to shush them, and took them to see Morglob again.

"I hope you're ready to sign the contract," Morglob said. "I've already made some calls. You're hot. People want you. That won't last forever."

"No. I'm not ready. I'm not signing. Please let us go," Nicholas said. "You can't keep us here against our will. And you're not going to change my mind by attacking me with mechanical zombies."

"Zombies?" Clave said. "Are you out of your mind? There weren't any zombies on this ship. You must have had a bad dream."

"I was totally awake," Nicholas said. "You slept through it."

"Really? I doubt that. I'm a very light sleeper," Clave said. "Nothing escapes my notice."

Nicholas turned back to Morglob. "I want to go home."

"You obviously need more time to think it over," Morglob said.

"No, I don't!" Nicholas yelled.

The protest seemed to go unheard. "We can run you through a few more scenes. This one is testing brilliantly."

A projection appeared above Morglob's tank. It showed an alien audience of various shapes, all wearing goggles, also of various shapes, equipped with various quantities of lenses from monocular to duodecopular. Superimposed on that was a graph showing enthusiasm, enjoyment, excitement, and a slew of other reactions and emotions, including several that had no human equivalent.

Nicholas stomped his foot. "Let us go."

"You see? You're perfect for this. The best stars throw tantrums. We'll get a romance going. And we'll stage big fights in public. Wait! I've got it! This is perfect. We'll put you into a relationship with Shleri Meeps. She's due for some headlines."

The projection above the tank changed to an octopus in a dress. Actually, an octopus with big, blue eyes, three humanoid legs surrounded by tentacles, twin elephantine trunks for a nose, and huge lips.

"Those Cephaloids drive the paparazzi crazy when they swat someone with a tentacle," Morglob said. "You are exactly what the universe has been waiting for. Are you in a serious relationship with anyone?"

"No!" Caught off balance by the question, and the

stream of babble Morglob was spewing, Nicholas didn't have time to phrase his answer as an excuse, or as an explanation that he was single by choice. Though it was more by fear, and by an inability to decode the subtle signs that a girl might actually find him attractive in a nerdy sort of way.

Morglob dismissed his guests. "Take some more time, if you need to. Eventually, you'll realize the wisdom of signing the contract."

Spott escorted them down the corridor. Without even looking, Nicholas could tell, from the curving path of the mildly stinging pain, that Spott had scratched SEE? in his back. In response, Nicholas nodded.

They reached their quarters, where, based on the dented and overturned furniture, Jeef had either been working hard on her driving skills, or battling another wave of zombies. Nicholas pointed to the bathroom and motioned for Clave to follow him.

Inside, he put a finger to his lips, then turned on the faucet. "I saw this in a movie," he whispered, once the running water was masking his words. "We have to get out of here."

"Don't be rash," Clave said.

"Please take us away from here," Nicholas said.

"No."

"It would make an awesome sfumble," he said.

"You think?" Clave asked.

"Hey, who's the guy with all the star potential?" Nicholas said. "Me, right? So, trust me. Walking away from being a star is a much bigger and better story than being a star."

"He's right," Henrietta said.

"I'll bet nobody has ever turned down an offer from Morglob," Nicholas said. He flinched. Having that snotpile's name pass through his mouth made him feel almost as queasy as being in the presence of a heaping helping of ceviche. "You'd have something that's never been seen before. That has to be pretty rare."

"Think so?" Clave asked.

"Picture it," Nicholas said. "Imagine how amazing it would be to see a sfumble with you and me at the viewport. Behind us, Morglob's estate shrinks from a huge sphere to a tiny dot as we fly away from it. And then, you announce that you, and you alone, have the exclusive rights to record sfumbles of Nicholas the Slayer."

Nicholas bit back the urge to add more. He hadn't felt this persuasive since he'd talked his language-arts teacher into giving him another week to write his book report on *Great Expectations.* Not that even fifty-two additional weeks would have made a difference.

"Exclusive?" Clave asked. "Seriously?"

"Exclusive," Nicholas said. "Totally seriously."

"Let's do it," Clave said. "This is going to be a world-shattering relationship."

Those words, coincidentally, would prove to be significant very soon in more ways than one.

JOIN THE PARTY

When news of the destruction of Menmar reached the planet Volg, where six Menmarians were on tour as part of the Bareknuckle Road Show (a fighting extravaganza that was especially popular on planets where the inhabitants lacked knuckles), the fighters commandeered a ship. They vowed to find Nicholas and kill him. While not as fond of inflicting pain and suffering as the Craborzi, the Menmarians were pretty much on the same wavelength when it came to a thirst for revenge and brutal love of executions.

HATCHING AN ESCAPE

That night, when Morglob was asleep, Nicholas and the others followed Spott down the corridor to a side door, and then through a winding path to an engine room. Once inside, Spott knelt and pointed to three tiny knobs that were placed along a wall right above floor level, too far apart for a single person to reach at once. "We have to turn all three at the same time to cut off the power to the tractor beams. That's why I was so relieved when the two of you showed up."

"Three of us," Henrietta said.

Four, Jeef said.

"Three who can operate a knob." Henrietta held out her front paws and turned a tiny imaginary knob.

Three who would be welcome in a barn, Jeef said, *and not be poisoned on sight.*

"Stop it, you two, or I'm pulling this spaceship over and you're both getting out." Nicholas grinned. He'd always wanted to use that line, even though, as an only child, he'd never been on the receiving end of it.

"Walking in space without a suit would be rather fatal," Clave said.

"It's a joke," Nicholas said. "Parents say that to their kids who are fighting in the backseat of a car."

"Barbarians . . ." Clave said.

"We need to hurry." Spott put his hand on the center knob. "It doesn't matter which way you turn them."

Nicholas headed for the knob on the left. As soon as he and Clave were in position, Spott said, "Ready . . . Twist!"

They twisted.

As Nicholas's knob clicked into position, he said, "Why would they need three knobs to turn off the power to the tractor beams? That seems unnecessary. Separate knobs seem more like something you'd use to launch a nuclear attack or do some other serious stuff that more than one person needed to decide about. And why are the knobs on the floor? And why are they so tiny?"

"More questions," Clave said. Then he turned his head sharply. "What was that?"

Nicholas noticed the sudden absence of sound, too. For an instant, the hum of engines and generators seemed to stop, as if the entire ship had been startled into a silence that boomed through the air.

Breaking the silence, a pleasant male voice said, "Self-destruction sequence initiated. Have a nice day."

"Self-destruction?" Nicholas screamed.

"Oh, dear. What a dreadful mistake for me to make," Spott said. "I guess we have no choice, now. We need to get to your ship, Nicholas. This way!"

"My ship," Clave said.

"You tricked us," Nicholas said.

"For your own good," Spott said. "Let's go. Hurry!"

Nicholas knew this wasn't the time to discuss the decision. Or the deception. "Can you keep up with us?" he asked Jeef.

No problem, Jeef said. She rolled across the floor and bumped into Nicholas's ankles.

Clutching Henrietta, Nicholas followed Spott to the hangar. When they reached Clave's ship, Spott pointed to the ramp, which was still down, and said, "You get on board. I'll trigger the air lock. Be quick."

As soon as Spott joined them in the bridge, Clave

closed the ramp. "Come on!" he said, aiming those words in the direction of the exit hatch as the air was pumped out of the chamber.

The self-destruction countdown continued: "Thirty seconds . . ."

"You didn't think this out too clearly," Nicholas said to Spott.

"I thought about it every day. We'll be fine." Spott turned to Clave. "Just hit the hatch with your cannon."

"I don't have a cannon," Clave said.

"Twenty seconds . . ."

"What about the thing you used on the Craborzi ship?" Nicholas asked.

"Too light for this," Clave said. "And the panels aren't hinged."

"Ten seconds . . ."

"It's opening," Spott said.

"It's still too narrow." Clave moved his hands in the navigation field, and the ship rose from the floor, hovering midway to the ceiling, directly in line with the hatch.

"Five . . . four . . . three . . ."

"Go!" Nicholas screamed. He pressed against the back wall to brace himself for the thrust.

Clave sent the ship hurtling toward the hatch. A grating

screech tore through the cabin on all four sides as they wedged past the opening and broke free. Nicholas watched on the inset rearview image as the enormous disco ball started to fall to pieces. There was no explosion that he could see. Glittering panels drifted loose. A few broke off at first, in seemingly random places, and then a flurry of them tumbled into space, followed by pieces of the interior. Cloud Mansion Intergalactic broke into a shower of confetti. One wall of the landing area spun past them, tumbling wildly. If they'd been inside

when everything came apart, they would have been badly mangled.

"It's sort of beautiful," Clave said. He captured the scene for a sfumble.

"What about Morglob?" Nicholas asked. As despicable as the creature was, Nicholas hated having another death on his conscience, even if he'd been tricked into bringing it about.

"He'll be fine, unfortunately," Spott said. "He's a Pflemhackian. They can survive in space. I think they can survive anywhere."

"Now what?" Nicholas asked. "Can you get some more j-cubes and take me home?"

"Not at the moment," Clave said. He pointed to the instrument panel, where dozens of purple lights flashed. "The hull took a pretty bad hit. We need to find somewhere to put down for repairs before one of those gashes becomes a breach."

"I really hate that color," Nicholas said. "Will the ship be hard to fix?"

"No," Clave said. He played with some of the displays beneath the violet lights. "The standard patch kit I carry is good enough. It just has to be applied on the outside and inside. *Outside* is a bit unreachable at the moment."

"Wait." Nicholas didn't like the idea of leaving the hull unpatched a moment longer than necessary. He thought about Earth's own space program, and the videos he'd seen of astronauts making repairs. "Don't you have some sort of space suit?"

"I do. But . . ."

"But what?"

"You're scared to use it, aren't you?" Spott asked.

"No, I'm not!" Clave shouted, a bit too loudly. He stomped out of the bridge and opened a door in one of the storage lockers that lined the wall between the cockpit and the living quarters, revealing a space suit far less bulky than the ones Nicholas had in mind. "You don't know anything about me. If you're so eager to take a space walk, help yourself." He kicked a smaller door below that one. It popped open, spilling its contents, which included a tool kit and a hand-operated jet pack.

"I'll go!" Nicholas said.

"You have no training," Clave said. "You can't just hop into one of these suits and take a stroll out through the air lock."

"I would if I could," Spott said. He tapped his snout, which was definitely too long to fit inside the helmet.

"So would I," Henrietta said.

Me, too, Jeef said.

"I'm sorry," Spott said. "I shouldn't have questioned your courage. You're right. I don't know anything about you. Please accept my sincere apology."

"Just leave me alone so I can find a place to set down," Clave said. He returned to the navigator's seat.

Nicholas followed him. He realized he'd have a much better chance of getting home soon, and getting amazingly rich, if he explained to Clave how valuable gold was on Earth. But he knew better than to jump right into the topic when Clave was obviously upset.

"So, how's the hit count going?" he asked.

"I haven't checked, recently."

Nicholas knew this was a lie. Clave was constantly checking his stats.

"It's pretty cool you know how to pilot a ship. Was it hard to learn?"

Clave stared at him for an uncomfortable period, then said, "What do you want?"

"Look, gold is like the most valuable stuff on Earth, except maybe for diamonds. I think an ounce is worth a couple thousand dollars. You must have tons. We can split the money."

"So I get Earth dollars for the gold. What can I do with them?"

"Are you kidding me? Who's the barbarian now? You

buy stuff with money. That's what you do." Nicholas smirked and shook his head.

"That money is only good on Earth, right?" Clave asked.

"Of course," Nicholas said. "But there's plenty of awesome stuff you can buy there."

"Like what?" Clave asked.

"Anything you want," Nicholas said.

"Well, I'd like to buy a better ship," Clave said. "But I doubt they make those on Earth."

"You could buy diamonds," Nicholas said.

"The universe is rotten with diamonds," Clave said. "Pretty much every mineral is abundant somewhere. Watch." He tapped the console and said, "Find jade."

The display filled with colored dots.

"Find sapphires," Clave said.

The dots shifted.

"Find chromiated onyxite."

The dots shifted again.

"Find—"

"Okay!" Nicholas shouted. "I get it. Earth money is worthless to you. But it would be amazing for me. So, can you please take me home, and let me have the gold?"

"Absolutely. As soon as we get the hull repaired, and I make some deliveries," Clave said. "Though it would have been a whole lot easier if you'd just signed that contract with Morglob."

"I doubt it," Nicholas said.

Clave turned his attention to finding the nearest safe place to set down and repair the ship. He had three j-cubes left, but he didn't want to risk using more than one. He checked all the destinations they could reach with a single jump, looking for the one with the least travel. The nearest planet was Zeng. Unfortunately, it was not the nearest safe one.

FIRST, A WORD

This would be a good time to talk about firsts. Even in infinite stretches of space and time, there has to be a first instance of each type of event, action, or item. (Unless time stretches infinitely in both directions, but that's the sort of thing it's best not to think about for more than a very limited amount of time.) There was the first star to form, the first animal to achieve self-awareness, the first person to accidentally make blue cheese, the first Bilgerian who realized he could travel through the air by lighting the gas that Bilgerians expel in high volume and staggering quantity from the tail end of their digestive systems, and the first civilization to venture into space and encounter other intelligent beings. That civilization would be the Dragu.

When the Dragu, after visiting countless lifeless planets, discovered Benbennebneb, something astounding happened. The two groups did not immediately launch into a prolonged, senseless, and destructive war, despite the fact that both the Dragu and the Benbennebneb had waged countless destructive wars, conflicts, and skirmishes among themselves for thousands of years. This was actually a lucky break for the Dragu. During the whole time the Dragu had been investing their efforts in conquering space, the Benbennebnebers (who are generally called Fourbees, for obvious reasons, and occasionally called Fourenners by people who think they are being far more clever than they actually are) had given their attention to weaponry. After evolving through phases of blunt things, pointy things, slashy things, and shooty things, they had discovered their purpose in life and developed a stunning variety of explody things. The reason for this, at least in part, is that if you blow a Fourbee (who looks somewhat like an inverted bowl of butterscotch pudding with eye stalks) into pieces, the pieces ooze back together with no lasting scars. (Fourbees are heartless in the best of all possible meanings of that word. And gutless.) The majority of Fourbees actually find the experience somewhat pleasant.

The Fourbees had achieved the capability of blowing

spaceships out of the sky before they even knew spaceships existed. The presence of seven moons around their planet, and the persistence of a primitive belief that the lights in the sky were barely more than a stone's throw away, gave them a lot to aim at. Fortunately for all involved, the appearance of a Dragu expedition ship was startling enough that the Fourbees didn't immediately blow it out of the sky, or turn its landing spot into a crater by way of any of the hundreds of explosive projectiles or matter disruptors they'd created. Having never met anyone who was permanently harmed by explosions, they couldn't conceive of any reason to do that, especially since it was considered bad manners to blow someone up without asking permission, except during National Boomboom Day.

The Ubiquitous Matrix allowed the Dragu (who looked sort of like a molten lava cake with feelers) and the Fourbees to communicate. Eventually, proving that love truly is blind, they intermarried. Their offspring also ventured into space, evolved, mutated, and crossbred with a variety of gooey and gelatinous species. Millennia later, one of those descendants, a Pflemhackian who had no idea about his distant origins, became the most powerful talent manager in the universe, and eventually got launched into space when his estate was destroyed.

As for those who fled this citadel, Nicholas, Clave, Spott, Henrietta, and Jeef were about to be the first aliens to land on Zeng. There were five continents on Zeng. On two of them, most of the natives would have fled in terror from a spaceship. On two others, the natives would have attacked the ship with weapons less effective but no less deadly than those of the Fourbees. Clave didn't land on any of those four continents. He had the misfortune to land his nameless ship on the continent of Sperno, in the city of Lix, where he and his companions were greeted with joy as heroes who fulfilled an ancient prophecy. While prophecies can serve a valuable purpose, giving hope and guidance to entire civilizations, being the fulfilment of one is rarely a pleasant or positive experience.

BITS AND PIECES

Nicholas cringed when the hatch opened. Zeng smelled like old bloodstains and overboiled shrimp. A crowd had already gathered outside the ship, which Clave had landed near the first city he spotted. It was dark, but the sun was close to rising, and it cast enough light to reveal a land of gently rolling hills.

"That's a lot of people," Clave said. "Probably fans."

One of the Zeng, whose name was Marrow, came forward as Clave walked down the ramp.

Nicholas couldn't help staring. The Zeng resembled feathered centaurs with arms that reached all the way to the ground. He halfway expected them to have wings.

"Hello," Clave said. "Would you be interested in exchanging j-cubes for . . ." He paused, as if searching through his inventory for the best item to offer. "How about an antimatter power core? They're amazingly useful. It could change your lives forever."

"I don't know of these things," Marrow said. "Though we have many advanced technologies. As you surely know, the atomizer needs constant maintenance and enhancements."

"Surely," Clave said, though his slightly lowered left eyebrow and marginally tilted right one would have betrayed his lack of a clue, had the Zeng any familiarity with Menmarian facial expressions.

"But come," Marrow said, "you must wish to rest up

from your trip across the stars and prepare for the glorious ceremony."

"Yes, we must," Clave said. He flashed Nicholas a *let's amuse the barbarians* smirk, which Nicholas returned since he was now a sophisticated intergalactic traveler who swooped among the stars, and no longer a member of the great unwhooshed.

The group followed Marrow through streets lined with gathering Zeng. Word must have spread rapidly. It seemed as if every resident of the city wanted to catch a glimpse of the visitors.

"The Sanctuary has been kept ready for you," Marrow said when they reached a square with a small six-sided stone building in the center. He led them to the door, opened it, and said, "The one becomes the many becomes the one."

"Right," Clave said.

Nicholas, feeling he had to respond in an appropriate manner, sifted through his brain and came up with, "One small step for man." It seemed better than any of the other *ones* that came to mind.

He followed Clave inside. "What was all of that about?"

"I have no idea," Clave said.

"Me, neither," Henrietta said.

I'm just happy rolling along, Jeef said as she rolled over Nicholas's foot.

"It looks like they've been waiting a long time for someone to show up," Nicholas said. Everything inside the Sanctuary was covered with dust. Even the dust had dust on it, topped with yet more dust. Nicholas's steps kicked up a cloud of dust that instantly made itself at home in his nostrils, and set about exploring deeper into his nasal cavities and throat. He sneezed a painfully hard sneeze that brought back recent unpleasant memories of Morglob. Pulling his shirt over his nose and mouth, Nicholas walked through the rooms. Nothing was designed for bipeds, and there didn't seem to be anything that might serve as a bed, but he figured he could be comfortable enough standing around while they waited to find out what sort of ceremony they'd stumbled across. After that, he didn't imagine it would take Clave long to patch the hull and whisk them away.

"If you need help, Spott and I can give you a hand with the patch," Nicholas said. He looked over his shoulder, and then all around. "Hey, where's Spott?"

Clave, who had followed Nicholas, said, "I don't know. He was right behind me when we went down the ramp."

"I haven't seen him since we left the ship," Henrietta said.

I've been busy not running into things, Jeef said as she bumped into a wall.

Nicholas opened the door, which he was pleased to find was unlocked, and stepped outside. "Maybe he stopped to look at something."

"He's definitely an odd creature," Clave said. "Wait! What? Why?" He pointed toward the ship, which was lifting off. "No! Stop! Come back!"

"Roach brains!" Nicholas yelled. "That thief." He watched Clave's ship ascend until he lost sight of it. "Now what?"

"I don't know." Clave pulled out his sfumbler. "I could report it was stolen."

"Right. To the Yewpees." Nicholas sighed and looked around, as if there might be a spare ship within view. "Any other ideas?"

"My fans would help me. I could post a sfumble asking for a lift," Clave said.

"Letting everyone know where we are?" Nicholas said.

"We'll think of something." Clave headed back inside the Sanctuary.

"Maybe the police gave up searching for us," Nicholas said. He followed Clave through the door. "Do you think they have news here?"

"News is available everywhere, as long you aren't on a

petro-cloaked planet." Clave tapped a tattoo on his right little finger against the sfumbler, and said, "News flash."

Stella appeared in the center of the room. She was as breathtaking as ever. Nicholas forced himself to pay attention to her words as she announced breaking news. "In a stunning and treacherous assault that has sent shock waves through the entertainment field, Cloud Mansion Intergalactic, the headquarters of Universal Talent Management, has been destroyed. Its beloved founder, Morglob Sputum, has disappeared. Security footage recovered from the wreckage indicates the villainous act was carried out by none other than that ruthless slaughterer, Nicholas the Assassin."

Nicholas winced as Stella listed a string of other adjectives of destruction now attached to his name, and reminded viewers that the whole rampage had started with the murder of seventy Craborzi.

"I didn't do anything," Nicholas said. That phrase echoed in his head. *I didn't do anything.* He'd said those words more than once to his parents and teachers. Far more than once. And it was generally true. Or, at least true more than half the time, or half true more than half the time, which he felt counted as "nearly always." Or, at least, almost nearly always.

He checked the windows. Hundreds of Zeng stood in

the streets all around them, staring at the building and slowly tilting their heads side to side, as if listening to music only they could hear. "They seem to think we came here for a reason."

"They're probably fans of my sfumbles," Clave said. "It's a shame I have to hold off. Maybe I can just show a shot of the fans out there without saying where we are . . ."

"We can't take that chance," Nicholas said. "Someone might recognize the place. I doubt there are a whole lot of planets with creatures shaped like that."

He looked past the crowd. Not far beyond them, to the west, he saw a small red mountain. Apparently, not everyone had come to stare at the aliens. There was a line of Zeng on a path leading up to the base of the mountain, and some sort of zigzag stairway rising from there

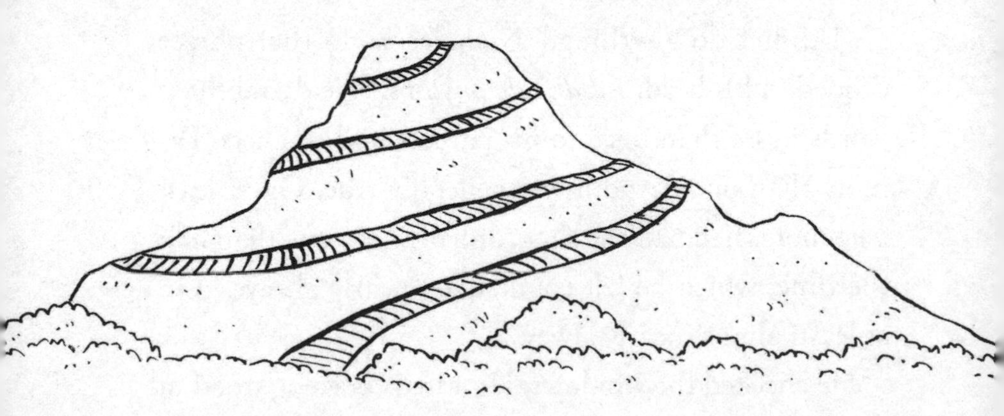

to the flattened top. Each step was wide and deep enough for the four-legged Zeng to stand on. The Zeng all wore tunics of yellow fabric draped over their backs.

A motion nearby drew Nicholas's attention away from the mountain. The crowd around the square parted, creating a clear path for Marrow. The door opened. "We're ready for the ceremony," he said. "It is a joyful time. I never dared hope the fulfillment would happen in my lifetime."

"This should be interesting," Nicholas said. He picked up Henrietta, who'd been quietly chewing on the corner of some unidentifiable piece of furniture, and followed Marrow out the door, along with Clave, and trailed by Jeef, who barely crashed into anything.

Had Nicholas known a bit of Zeng history, he would have chosen a word other than *interesting*. And he would have run for his life.

ONE FOR ALL AND... EWWWW.... ICK... YUCK...

This is what Nicholas and Clave did not yet know. Many of the Zeng believed immortality was achieved by becoming one with the universe. The Zeng's primitive ancestors thought the universe was made of rocks. This led to them throwing themselves from great heights onto various arrangements of boulders. Only the purest acolytes were allowed to leap from the highest sacred summits on the planet, after years of fasting and prayer. Modern Zeng realized the futility of this. And since Zeng scientists eventually discovered that the universe, rocks and all, was made of extremely tiny particles, those Zeng in search of immortality attempted to achieve a state of oneness through a device which can be best thought of as an atomic blender. The device was built on the outskirts of Lix, a city that had become a center for members of Zeng's Fragmentation Cult, and the landing spot for four very unfortunate travelers.

Set in the opening of Mount Pumice, a dormant volcano, the earliest version of the atomizer used a series of massive spinning blades, powered at first by geothermal energy, and later by nuclear fusion. As the Zeng progressed technologically, the blades were enhanced by a descending series of ever-more-powerful means of slicing and dicing, including sonic pulses, high-frequency polarized rays, magnetic inversion, absolute-zero ionic shattering, and most recently, a mere quarter century ago, quantum fragmentation.

Over time, conveniently meshing with a growing population on the fertile continent, the requirements for acolytes grew less strict, eventually reaching a point where the only requirement to seek oneness was the ability to join the line. A steady stream of pilgrims now moved toward the mouth of the atomizer at all times of the day and night. Each pilgrim would climb the 843 steps that had been constructed on the southeast face of the mountainside, that number being the number of stars in the sky. At the summit, the pilgrim would perch on the edge of the atomizer, and then leap to his meeting with oneness.

Or, more likely, many-many-many-ness.

Or messiness.

That, by itself, would not have caused problems for our travelers, since atomization was voluntary. But the Zeng believed that when a stranger descended from the stars, and that stranger was atomized, all of Zeng would instantly become one with the universe. Since they couldn't tell which of the strangers who had descended from the stars was the chosen one, the only reasonable solution was to atomize them all.

THE DAILY GRIND

They were led directly to the base of the steps, cutting in line. The stairs were wide enough that Marrow could take them past the slowly moving pilgrims who were trudging toward the top. Nicholas and Clave took turns lifting Jeef up the base of each step, but she insisted on rolling across the length of them on her own. Throughout this, Marrow remained silent, despite a barrage of questions from Nicholas about their destination and the nature of this ceremony. It wasn't until Nicholas was halfway up the mountainside that he noticed something very wrong was happening at the summit.

"Oh, roach brains! They're leaping," he whispered to Henrietta.

"So it seems," she said. "I've been able to hear the

screams since well before we reached the steps."

"Maybe there's a big mattress inside," Clave said. "Or something bouncy."

"I don't think they have mattresses on this world," Nicholas said.

"Trampoline?" Clave said.

"They don't appear to be built for that." Nicholas tried to picture a Zengite doing a backflip. "I'm pretty sure there isn't anything pleasant on the other side of our climb." He turned to look back the way they'd come, but Marrow clamped a painfully strong hand on his shoulder and pushed him toward the next step.

"Rejoice," Marrow said, finally breaking his silence. "The prophecy comes true. We shall all merge with the universe."

"Yippee . . ." Nicholas said. He searched desperately for a way out as he was led toward the summit. Unlike below, where everything smelled like stale blood, up here, the air was drenched with the slaughterhouse scent of fresh blood.

Nicholas flinched as another pilgrim leaped from the top. Each leap was followed by an unbearable silence, or an unbearable scream, and then, a far worse sound filled the air. Nicholas could hear tearing, grinding, hacking, slicing, ripping, and crunching. A moment later, a fine reddish mist sprayed upward, tinting the air. Despite the horror, Nicholas laughed.

"What could possibly be funny?" Henrietta asked.

Nicholas fought down the laughter and struggled to speak. "My mom usually . . ." He broke up again, nearly doubling over as a spasm of laughter shook his body.

"I'll wait," Henrietta said.

After catching his breath, Nicholas managed to spit out, "She usually buys ground turkey. Imagine that." He nodded his head toward Jeef, then whispered, "I just happened to pick beef for a change of pace."

"I see very little difference," Henrietta said.

"Gobble, gobble," Nicholas said. He fell to his knees, laughing. Marrow grabbed him by the scruff of his neck and lifted him back to his feet.

"I still don't get it," Henrietta said.

"What would we call ground turkey?" Nicholas said.

"GT? Yeah, Jeet. Hey, Jeet yet? Get it? Sounds like *did you eat yet?* Ground lamb would be Jeel. Jeel of Fortune! Ground pork would be Jeep. Hey, Jeep! That's a good one. Honk! Honk! Honk!" He thrust out his hand with each honk, pressing an imaginary car horn with his palm, then put out his other hand and steered the imaginary wheel.

"You're hysterical," Henrietta said.

"Well, it is pretty funny." Nicholas let out a cackle that rose in pitch and seemed dangerously close to turning into a scream.

"No. I don't mean hugely funny. I mean you're in the grip of hysteria," Henrietta said. "I'd slap you if I could. Though even if I could, I don't think you'd feel it."

The near scream morphed into a stream of words that rose steadily in volume. "Jeet beat heat seat treat meat—"

"Hang in there." Clave reached out to Nicholas, but Marrow pushed him away.

"Wait. I have an idea." Henrietta leaped from Nicholas's pocket, clambered up his face, and bit him on the nose. She let go and dropped back in his pocket before he could swipe at her.

"Ouch!" Nicholas rubbed his nose and checked his fingers for blood. "What was that for?"

"Shock," she said. "You'd lost control. I needed to snap

you out of it. And it's not like I could do that with a slap."

Henrietta threw the hardest possible slap a gerbil could muster, hitting Nicholas in the chest. It was unbearably cute. "You wouldn't even feel that. I had no choice. I had to bite you."

"Thanks. I think . . ." Nicholas took a deep breath and decided that Henrietta was right. He suspected he'd been gripped by a crazy urge to laugh as a way to avoid dealing with fear, or accepting the cold reality of their situation. "We're going to die," he said. He was surprised how unemotional his voice now sounded.

"It looks that way," Henrietta said.

"You could make a run for it," Nicholas told Henrietta.

"For what purpose?" she said. "I'm not leaving you. Especially not to spend the rest of my life stranded here with these feather brains. We're staying together."

"Thank you," Nicholas said. He thought about flinging Jeef to the ground so she could escape, but the fall would probably shatter the cart, or burst open the wrapper, which had already taken a beating since the start of this adventure.

To everything, there is a season, Jeef said.

"In your case, salt and pepper," Henrietta said.

Nicholas stared at her. "Really? Even now?"

"Sorry," Henrietta said. "Just trying to end on a happy note."

"We have arrived at your magnificent destiny," Marrow said, guiding Nicholas across the platform toward the edge of the abyss.

"At least this time I'm not getting anyone else killed. So I won't get to be the bad guy in another of Stella's top stories," Nicholas said, adding more proof to the abundant stockpile of evidence that indicated he lacked even the slightest pinch of omniscience.

SPEAKING OF DEATH

One of the more delightful paradoxes entwined with existence is the fact that in an infinite universe, almost nothing—no goal, no passion, no habit, no desire, no trait, no quirk, no belief—will be universal.

Love? Try to explain that to the Monosloths of Vega 47, who believe all beings other than themselves are actually intricate clockwork creations. Or take a shot at talking about it with the Ineptara, who are born with the knowledge that everyone else is real but that they are an illusion incapable of forming attachments.

Greed? Obviously, you've never spent time on Alpha Grena XII, where the citizens will give you their own skin, right off their backs, if they suspect you are cold, or even just a little bit chilly.

Hate? Close, but there are a few rare civilizations where that concept is unknown, or at least tamped down enough so it only manifests as snarky comments or invitations to dance recitals.

Taxes? Even those aren't universal, except for the one dollar each civilized planet is asked to pay to the emperor (providing an endless stream of funds to keep the palace running). And that's called a tribute, since taxes, no matter how small, inevitably lead to rebellions.

Death?

Yeah, that's the one thing that's pretty much everywhere. The inhabitants of Bemona III don't suffer from any form of disease or age-related degeneration. But they are incredibly clumsy, and not very bright for a dominant species. It is rare for a Bemonarian to make it past the age of thirty.

The Forzoy that envelops its entire world is made of millions of individuals. Though each of the individual Forzettes is mortal with its own hopes, dreams, annoying quirks, and an inexplicable abundance of self-importance, the aggregate creature the combined individuals compose has its own identity and will essentially live as long as there are sufficient Forzettes to generate the megabeing's higher-level self-awareness. But that terminal moment will come, inevitably, when enough Forzettes die from disease, predation, or some other cause to slip below that threshold, and the Forzoy will cease to exist.

Some creatures fight against this inevitability, as the Zeng were doing. Others find comfort in this cycle of life, seeing it as part of nature or a higher plan. For Nicholas, death wasn't just inevitable. It was imminent and unexpected. Which gave him very little time to develop a coping strategy or a comforting philosophy.

OH-GLITTERATED!

They'd reached the platform, which was placed about two feet above the rim of Mount Pumice. Ahead of Nicholas, another pilgrim jumped into the maw of the atomizer, plunging toward the thousands of spinning blades that ranged from enormous to microscopic. The atomizer, when you set aside its grisly purpose, was an amazing mechanical construction, enhanced with layers of advanced technology, and worthy of great admiration and awe.

Nicholas jerked his head away as the Zeng fell. He didn't want to see what would happen when the body met the blades, even though he already pretty much knew.

"Why are you doing this to us?" he asked.

"To fulfill the prophecy," Marrow said.

"No way! I have things to do," Clave shouted. "Fulfill your own prophecy. And cower before my true form!" He touched his shoulder and was cloaked in the image of a small dragon. He gave Marrow a shove. He might as well have been pushing against the side of the mountain. The Zeng, who weighed at least three or four times as much as Clave, didn't budge. Clave shifted the holo-suit through a series of images, including fanged monsters, wraithlike screamers, a grilled sardine, a bale of hay, and a giant panda. Marrow barely blinked.

"Nice try, Clave," Nicholas said. "That was very heroic."

Clave smiled. "Thank you. Hey, since we're about to die, do you mind if I . . . ?"

"What?"

"You know . . ."

"Oh, that."

"Yeah, that."

"Go ahead," Nicholas said.

Clave activated his sfumbler. "Well, look where I ended up! And look who's still with me. We're on the verge of our last adventure, here on Zeng. Thank you for being fans. Remember me."

"Good one," Nicholas said. He rubbed his thumb across Henrietta's back. "I'm glad we got to talk."

"Me, too," she said.

"I'm sorry about this," Clave said.

"It's not your fault," Nicholas said. He felt Marrow's hand pressing against his back.

"Exactly!" Clave said.

"What are you talking about?" Nicholas asked.

"Menmar and Zefinora are no more your fault than this is mine," Clave said. "I want you to die with a clear conscience."

"Thanks." Nicholas swallowed. *I'm not ready for this,* he thought. But he realized Clave had a point. He still felt guilty, though not as much as before. And not for much longer, he imagined. He put one hand on his pocket and stooped down to put his other hand on Jeef.

"Good-bye."

Henrietta nuzzled his thumb.

Jeef bumped the cart against Nicholas's ankle as gently as she could.

Marrow grabbed his collar. "Stand straight. This is an honor."

Nicholas stood. The pressure on his back grew greater. It was time to either fall or jump. Neither option had any strong points in its favor. At least, if he jumped, he was taking control of his destiny. Maybe he could leap high, spin in the air, and spit in Marrow's eye before he plunged to his death.

A shadow fell across them.

Nicholas looked up. Clave's ship swooped down from the sky. It stopped right above the atomizer. A compartment opened in the bottom. Nicholas blinked against the glare as sunlight reflected off the falling cargo. Gold. Someone—it had to be Spott—was dumping tons of gold into the atomizer.

Nicholas hoped it would jam the blades.

It did far more than that. A screech tore through the air.

"No!" Marrow howled. He dropped his hand from Nicholas's collar and stepped closer to the edge, reaching out as if he could snatch away the gold. A piece the size of a softball batted off a blade and struck him in the

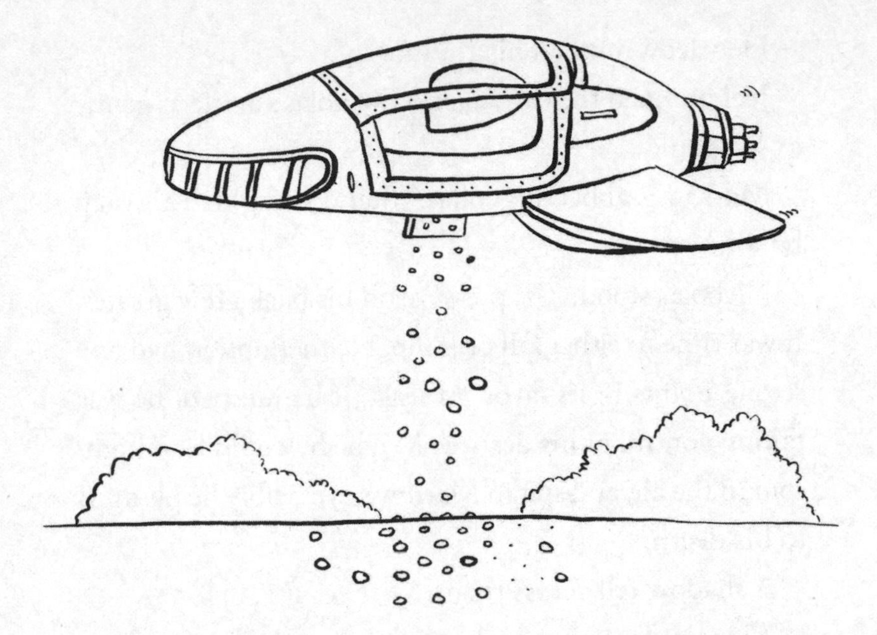

head. He staggered. One of his forelegs slipped from the edge.

Nicholas and Clave both pushed him hard. Marrow fell into the atomizer. The platform and the stairs beneath them started to shake. Horrible ripping sounds of tearing metal rose from the atomizer. Pieces of gold shot into the air as if smacked by a home-run champ. The ship drifted lower. The hatch opened, just a few feet away from Nicholas. Sharp cracks of breaking wood tore the air as the stairs began to splinter from the quake, tossing aside Zeng pilgrims like drops of water flung from a wet dog.

Spott stood at the edge of the ramp, one arm wrapped around a handhold, the other arm extended. "Jump!"

Nicholas held on to Henrietta and jumped. Clave followed him.

"Wait!" Nicholas looked back at the platform, which was now tilted toward the abyss. Jeef tottered there, her wheels spinning and smoking against the wood as she fought to keep from sliding to her death. And once again, Nicholas went back to rescue her.

I knew you'd come, Jeef said.

"Catch," Nicholas shouted, tossing the cart to Clave as the platform lurched beneath his feet. Nicholas jumped back into the ship just as the stairs collapsed.

"I don't know whether to kill you or hug you," Clave said to Spott.

"How did you know this was going to happen?" Nicholas asked as the hatch closed.

"I heard them discussing it," Spott said.

"I didn't hear anything," Clave said.

I didn't, either, Jeef said.

"Neither did I." Nicholas thought back to their arrival at this strange and horrible place. "And I was right next to you when we left the ship. What about you, Henrietta?"

"Nothing," she said.

"How about the truth?" Nicholas said.

"I can sort of read minds," Spott said.

"Sort of?" Nicholas asked. He thought about when Spott had scratched him, and when Spott had tricked them. The words that could have been plucked from his mind at those times were not very complimentary.

"More than sort of, I guess," Spott said. "We all can, where I come from. And we know how to shield ourselves. We usually don't talk about it, because it bothers some aliens. Others don't care at all. And there are some, like the Yoranit, who derive deep pleasure from knowing that others have heard their thoughts. The main thing is I knew what the Zeng were planning the instant I got close to them. Grabbing the ship seemed like the best way to get you out of there alive. Don't worry—I repaired the hull."

"And you knew how to pilot it?" Clave asked.

"I pulled that from your mind while we were traveling," Spott said. "It's really almost trivial. A child could do it, actually. Even a two-year-old."

Ooohhhh. I'm two. Can I fly? Please, let me fly, Jeef said. She rolled back and forth like an impatient toddler bouncing from foot to foot.

"It is not easy," Clave said. "It takes years of practice."

"Guys," Nicholas said, pointing to the viewport,

"maybe you can talk about this later. How about one of you gets us away from here before we get gold plated or ground to pieces."

Outside, the mountain was shaking violently, spewing gouts of flame and splashes of molten gold. Hunks of the rim broke off and plunged into the opening or rolled down the slope.

Clave dove past Spott to claim the control seat. "This is a job for a real pilot."

"Wait!" Nicholas cried. He dropped to his knees, then fell to his face. As acceleration pinned him to the floor, he looked over at Spott, who was also splayed out, and asked, "Did you drop all the gold?"

"I think so. Dreadful stuff. But I guess we were lucky it was in the cargo hold. It seems to have put a stop to this device."

"I think it did more than that," Nicholas said when he was able to get up and check the viewport. Below them—now safely far below—the mountain appeared to have collapsed on itself, leaving an enormous opening in the ground. That wasn't the end of the destruction. More ground was pulled into the opening, as if the planet was devouring itself.

Which was exactly what it was doing.

SICK-TEMPERED TYRANT

Speaking of mortality, the Emperor of the Universe was dying.

For the 178th time.

His Hugeness Zrilber Monospokodokapusimus ("Zril" to his friends, of which there weren't many since he had a habit of killing them for fun when he got bored) could feel his body rotting from the inside out. That was a problem, but it was not yet a crisis. All he needed to pull himself back from the edge of death was a crowd. An enormous crowd.

A miniscule percentage of Theribans can draw vitality from others. Perhaps one in every five million are born with this trait. This is a well-kept secret among those

Theribans, since the vitality they draw is subtracted from the lives of their unknowing donors.

Those Theribans had also learned, centuries ago, to draw what they needed from a crowd, so as not to attract a crowd. Otherwise, suspicion would grow as people died or fell ill in the presence of dying Theribans who miraculously got well and sprang from their death trench, all cheerful and chipper, just brimming with good health.

The emperor, of course, could capture a planet and suck the vitality of the captives. But history had showed that warring emperors lived far shorter lives, whether capable of revitalization or not, than peaceful, or seemingly peaceful rulers. Zril had studied the history of many of his predecessors. You can fit in a lot of studying in 178 lifetimes, and still have plenty of time left for partying and watching episodes of *Let's Cut Things Up!*

In one of those annoying catches the universe seems so fond of, each resurrection required a larger mass of vitality donors. Zril had recently paid a visit to one of the emigration centers being used for the evacuation of Plenax IV. But he'd gone toward the tail end of the rescue efforts. The crowd was large enough to stabilize his decline for the moment, but nowhere near large enough to reverse the decline and remove him from the endangered-emperor list.

Zril needed an entire planet densely packed with living beings. Unfortunately, the ease with which people could travel to other worlds had put a serious dent in the availability of densely packed civilizations. There was only one place he was aware of where he could find what he desperately needed quickly enough to revive himself. It was also a place he could visit without causing any suspicion.

"I will be attending this," Zril said, indicating an invitation to the Xroxlotl concert, which was to be held on one of the largest stadium planets in the universe. Traditionally, every major event extends an invitation to the emperor. It is a great honor if they attend, and a great relief if they don't.

"Very well, Your Hugeness," his retainer, Pumplock, had said. "I will make the arrangements."

Pumplock did an excellent job of hiding his dismay. Traveling with the emperor was an enormous and unpleasant task, involving multiple ships and dozens of staff. Pumplock knew it would be a nightmare. Though, as a longtime fan of the group, he'd have died for a chance to hear Xroxlotl.

ONWARD

Now that the ship was safely away from the self-destroying planet, Clave got up from his seat. "You didn't happen to secure the rest of the cargo, did you?"

"I didn't know there was anything else," Spott said. "I just got bombarded by a constant stream of thoughts about the gold, fast cars, attractive actresses, and algebra. I found it strange that math education involved dancing slowly with one's instructor. Eventually, I screened it all out."

"Oops," Nicholas said. "I guess that was me."

Clave opened the hatch and moved down the steps. "All gone," he said. "The straps broke. I guess I'm not delivering those pet Orbanies." He came up the steps, then dropped back into his seat. His body started to tremble. "Poor Orbanies . . . Innocent little creatures . . ."

"What's wrong?" Nicholas asked. He wasn't sure whether trembling meant the same with Menmarians as with humans.

It did. As did the reactions that followed.

Clave shook his head, then let out a wail.

"Clave?" Nicholas asked. "What's wrong?" He'd never seen Clave exhibit much feeling or emotion, other than outrage and envy.

"The globes. The two of them. Dead. Gone," Clave said. "Beautiful Orbanies. They were so full of life. So beautiful."

Spott stepped toward Clave, but Nicholas put a hand on Spott's shoulder and whispered, "Let him be. He needs time."

He led Spott out of the cabin, into the corridor.

"His mind was too jumbled to read clearly," Spott said. "It was full of death and sorrow. The weight was unimaginable and unbearable. It's not about those fish."

"Right. It's not about some silly pets," Nicholas said.

"Hey!" Henrietta said. "Pets aren't silly."

"Sorry," Nicholas said. "I didn't mean you. I never think of you as a pet. You're a companion. And a wonderful one." He flinched as he realized he sounded like a parent trying to stroke a child's bruised ego.

What am I? Jeef asked.

"Lunch," Henrietta said.

At least I have a purpose, Jeef said. *I don't just run around, chew things, and poop in people's pockets.*

"Stop it," Nicholas said, though he couldn't help smiling when it hit him that *poop in people's pockets* could be part of a pretty funny tongue twister. "You're both important. Now just be quiet for a moment." He told Spott about Menmar, and the destruction of the binary planets.

"None of that is Clave's fault," Spott said. "Or yours."

"But it's his loss," Nicholas said. "It took him a while to absorb the reality of it, I guess. Everyone he knew is gone. And everything. I'm not sure I've absorbed it, myself. And now, this." He tilted his head in the direction of Zeng.

"Again, not your fault," Spott said. "I get the blame for this one."

"You saved us from a pretty horrible fate," Nicholas said. "Look. Let's just not talk about blame or anything for a while. Deal?" He held out his hand.

Spott stared at it. "Why are you offering to clean out my ear wax?"

Nicholas jerked his hand back. "It means something different on Earth."

"I know. I was kidding you." Spott held his own hand

out. They shook. "Deal," he said. He reached out toward Nicholas's ears, but caught himself before he extracted any wax. Lifelong habits are difficult to break.

After that, they sat on the floor and waited, and exchanged basic biographies. Spott picked up a lot of the details from Nicholas's thoughts, but Beradaxians were skilled at letting others speak, even when they knew what they were about to hear.

Eventually, Clave poked his head into the corridor. "Ready to hit the road?"

"Sure," Nicholas said. Clave sounded a bit too cheerful, but Nicholas could tell he was feeling better. "I could definitely use a day or two where nothing exciting happens."

"Road?" Spott asked.

"Earth saying," Clave said. "Pretty catchy. For a barbarian planet, they come up with some clever expressions and inventions. It's a very amusing place to visit. If you pile up a group of boulders or slabs of rock in an interesting way, the natives will flock there for centuries to stare at it. It's also great fun to scoop up a couple hundred frogs from one place and put them in another. But enough of that. We need to decide what we're doing."

Nicholas and Spott spoke simultaneously: "I want to go home."

"Where's home?" Clave asked Spott.

"Beradaxia," Spott said. "In the Crab Nebula."

Clave checked the navigation computer. "We can't get there. Not enough j-cubes. No cargo to deliver. And I can't get my fee for dumping the gold without proof I disposed of it properly. We're going to have to find someplace where we can earn some money. Do you have any skills?"

"I can pilot a ship," Spott said.

"Any skills we don't already have very well covered by trained experts who've been doing them for years?" Clave asked. He reached into the navcom and set the ship in motion. "I'd like to see you fly in a perfect circle so smoothly."

"I'm good with my hands. I like to make bread. I can program computers," Spott said as the ship lurched into motion.

"The universe is oversaturated with bread and programmers," Clave said. "Let's make it a figure eight."

"I'm never getting home," Nicholas said, to nobody in particular. "Stupid j-cubes."

As the ship lurched into motion in different directions twice more before lurching to a stop, Nicholas thought about the report on subway systems he'd written in fifth grade. It had been in the back of his mind ever since

Henrietta had explained how she believed the jump nodes worked. While doing research for the report, Nicholas had learned there were places where two or more subway lines crossed. No line went everywhere, but people could go almost anywhere in some cities by changing to a different line at one of these transfer stations. They could even travel on multiple lines if they were willing to make multiple changes. But, sometimes, it was easier and quicker to switch train lines by leaving one train and walking a short distance to a different station.

"Hey, I have a question," he said.

"That's hardly a surprise," Clave said.

"This is serious," Nicholas said. "Are there any jump nodes that are close to other ones?"

"Sure," Clave said. "That happens all the time. Why?"

"If I understand how this works, you jump from node to node, following a series of links to your destination. Right?"

"Basically," Clave said. "Though the details are complicated."

Nicholas ignored that, and explained his idea. "Let's say you need to go somewhere, like Spott's home planet, and it takes three jumps. Suppose you find a jump node that's close to one you can jump to, and is also only one jump from your destination? You could get there in two jumps, right? You'd just have to do a bit of regular travel in between."

Clave was staring at Nicholas, as if he wasn't sure how to process a complex idea coming from a barbarian, but Spott smacked his own chest and said, "That's brilliant!"

"Somebody must have thought of that already," Nicholas said. "It seems pretty obvious."

"Not necessarily," Spott said. "People who use hyper-jumps think in terms of instant travel. And you can get from any jump node to any other, as long as you make enough jumps. So it's not surprising nobody thought about traveling the old-fashioned way from one jump node to another, as part of a trip."

"So, maybe we can get to your planet or mine with two jumps," Nicholas said. "We just have to find the right path."

"I don't know how we can find something like that," Clave said. "And I'm not getting stuck near Earth with no way to make another jump."

"We can modify the navigation software to look for routes that include spaceflight between reasonably close jump nodes," Spott said. He turned to Clave. "They have j-cubes back home on Beradaxia."

"And we have no money," Clave said.

"We'll figure something out," Spott said. "First, let's

see if we can get there. What's your top sustainable acceleration?"

Clave told him. Spott took Clave's place at the console, and pulled up an image that contained the subroutines of the navigation software. He talked to himself as he worked.

"All right. We have an origin node and a destination node. Check each node we can jump to from the origin—let's call that *origin plus one*—check each origin-plus-one node for nearby nodes that can be reached within an acceptable travel time, *maxtrav.* Let's call those *adjacent nodes.* No. *Attainable nodes.* That's better."

Nicholas realized Spott was thinking out loud as he modified the software. He was amused that he was, in a sense, now reading Spott's mind. Not that what he heard made a lot of sense. Still, he enjoyed trying to follow the logic. It was interesting to see that the process involved lots of backtracking and refining. He'd always assumed everyone else was a lot more efficient at solving problems and thinking things through. Spott's continuing monologue showed him otherwise.

"We can set a large acceptable maxtrav, initially. If we find nothing, we move on. If we get a hit, we loop and reduce maxtrav until there are zero adjacent nodes.

That'll guarantee finding the quickest route. Wait. That's inefficient. Better to start with the closest node and move outward until we reach maxtrav. Next, check each adjacent node for number of jumps to the destination. Whichever uses the fewest jumps becomes the preferred route. If none of them save jumps, go to each origin-plus-one node and check them the same way, for each of the origin-plus-two nodes. Repeat until origin-plus-N, where N is equal to the number of jumps in the original path. And simultaneously run the same algorithm from the destination back to the origin, of course, since routes are reversible."

Nicholas listened for a while, and understood some of the basics, which were sort of cool, but eventually Spott's train of thought got too complicated for Nicholas to follow, so he backed off.

An hour later, Spott got up from the seat, stretched out his back, thumped his chest again, and said, "All done. I'm running it as a simulation first, to make sure it works. I'd hate to get us stranded." He watched the display, which showed flickering green lines shooting from node to node in the star field. After a moment, two of the lines remained solid, showing a route they could follow with their remaining j-cubes.

"It works?" Clave asked.

"It works," Spott said. "We can get to my home planet with two j-cubes separated by a three-hour flight."

"Two cubes," Clave said. "We can manage that. But then I need to get a decent supply. I have to take this barbarian home, and then find more work."

"I believe I can help with the cubes," Spott said. "I owe you a lot, and I won't let you down. I'll make sure you get what you need."

"You'll have to sell a lot of bread," Clave said. "But I guess we can worry about that when we get there." He set up a j-cube for the first jump.

Nicholas was used to the sensations, now. He was also happy that, without the gold, there was no violent tumble at the end of the jump. But something else was different. "That's a really bright sun," he said, squinting at the viewport. "Weird color, too."

"Magnitudes vary," Clave said. "But it will get dimmer. We're moving away from it for the next three hours, to a jump node by . . ." He glanced down at the console. ". . . Plenax V. Which makes sense, since we arrived right above Plenax IV."

"That sounds familiar," Nicholas said. He tried to remember where he'd heard that name before.

"The news," Henrietta said. "That's where we heard it."

"Supernova!" Nicholas shouted as he recalled the first time he'd seen Stella do a broadcast. It had been such a chaotic time, and her presence was so distracting, he was surprised he remembered anything other than his destruction of the Craborzi. "Don't you pay attention to the news?" he asked Clave.

"Just sports and entertainment," he said. "The rest is too depressing. To be honest, most of the time I just watch that beautiful announcer and pay no attention to the stories. But we'll be fine. These solar calamities take ages to play out."

"News flash," Nicholas said.

"And in our top story," Stella said as she was summoned, "all eyes in the universe are on Plenax. Predictions among experts vary as to when this most violent stage of the supernova sequence will occur."

"See?" Clave said. "There's absolutely nothing to worry about. Nobody really knows how long it will take."

"While many of the experts predict the supernova will occur in exactly one hour, others argue that it will begin in one hour and seven minutes," Stella said. "Several radical models even suggest it could be as long as an hour and twelve minutes. We'll keep you updated if these predictions change."

"Roach brains!" Nicholas cried. "We're toast."

A WORD ABOUT SPOTT, AND AN AFTERTHOUGHT ABOUT MORGLOB

Spott Vesber Delgrambi, who may or may not ever get home, had come out of the egg singing. This was not unusual for Beradaxians, who all love belting out a tune, but he sang on key, which was nothing short of a miracle. Most Beradaxians excel at producing not just the wrong note, but a horribly wrong note, and even, at times, a note so wrong it actually generates a stench.

In general, Beradaxians can hear the flaws in everyone's voice except for their own. (Any negative thoughts Beradaxians might pick up about their voices are attributed to the envy of the listener.) Even the most tone-deaf Beradaxians could tell Spott had a gift. Before he was five years old, he was giving concerts in his town. By the age of twelve, he was touring in nearby cities.

He would have been famous by now had he not taken the first management offer that came to him, when he turned seventeen, and had that offer not come from someone who had recently invested a huge amount of money and time in establishing and promoting the career of Bleeta Kudop, a singer who was far less gifted than Spott, but who sang in a similar style and sported a similar appearance, though more of a basset hound than a beagle, and a rather mangy one at that.

This someone who had stopped Spott's career, coincidentally, had one trait that rose even higher than his excessive pride and greed, or his total lack of ethics. Morglob suffered from jealousy in the truest meaning of the word. He couldn't tolerate the idea that anyone would ever own something that was his. And he had a somewhat excessive fear of pirates, since they had a well-deserved reputation for taking whatever they wanted from whoever they encountered. That was why he had installed the self-destruct mechanism in his estate in a secret location, with a trio of triggers no inelastic creature could operate. If pirates ever tried to steal away his precious mansion, they would be in for a huge surprise.

As for his current whereabouts, he was still adrift,

nowhere near any planets, but would be spotted and rescued in a little more than a month by the scurvy crew of a pirate ship, proving that irony is even more abundant in the universe than iron.

SUPER DUPER

"We have to get out of here," Nicholas said. "Can we get to the next jump node any faster?"

"Maybe two hours, if we overthrottle the engines," Clave said. "But that's as fast as we get."

"Then let's jump back," Nicholas said.

"To Zeng?" Clave shook his head. "You saw what Zeng looked like when we left. And there's no other inhabited planet in that solar system."

Nicholas took a deep breath. Then he took a hard swallow. Then he sucked up his gut, harvested his courage, put on his big-boy pants (which he was actually already wearing), strapped on his parachute (which he didn't have since that would be pretty useless in space), bit the bullet, grabbed the bull by the horns, cut the mustard, and said, "But we can call for help from there. I'll tell the police it was all my fault. If I'd done that when I had a chance, we wouldn't be in this mess. They'll let you go. Maybe there's even a reward. I'll bet there is. So you two will be okay. And you can get Spott to his home. Just promise you'll take care of Henrietta and Jeef. Okay?"

"That's very noble," Clave said. "But if we broadcast the information that we're out of j-cubes, we'll get swarmed by raiders. There's nothing worse than getting picked up by pirates."

Nicholas pictured the holo-pirates from before, and imagined how much worse it would be if they were real alien pirates. "You don't have to say that we're stranded. Just say you want to turn me in."

Spott put a hand on Nicholas's shoulder. "That would bring just as many fortune seekers, hoping for a ransom or reward, along with anyone out for revenge, and anyone who wanted to use your talents for evil purposes."

"I have no talents," Nicholas said.

"None that you are aware of," Spott said.

"Forget about Zeng," Clave said. "We have to check the other nodes, and pick the best one."

"How many are there?" Spott asked.

Clave ran his hands over the console and pulled up a

display. “Four, counting Zeng. Let’s see . . .” He activated a stream of data. “This one leads to a spot above a gas mega-giant. It’s fine if you’re just passing through to the next node. But if we stayed there, we’d be trapped by the gravity, with no way to escape before we were pulled down toward the core and crushed flat.”

“That doesn’t sound so bad,” Henrietta said.

“Maybe for you,” Nicholas said.

“Oh, right,” she said. “Sorry. Sometimes, I forget your limitations.”

“So two of our possible destinations are ruled out,” Spott said. “What are our other choices?”

Clave pulled up more data. “Good grief. Who arranged these things?”

“Bad?” Nicholas asked.

“Worse than bad,” Clave said. “This one is so close to a star, we’d burn up moments after arrival. Let’s check the last one.”

Nicholas flinched when he saw the new data was purple.

Clave smacked the console and shouted, “Why? Why?! Is it too much to ask for one safe place to go? Really? Is that just too much to expect from this huge disappointment of a universe?”

“How bad?” Nicholas asked.

"It's presumed to be a black hole," Clave said. "So, we're dead. We just have to decide whether we want to be crushed or crisped."

"Wait. I have an idea," Nicholas said.

Spott and Clave both stared at him. "That's how we got to where we are," Clave said. "Following one of your ideas."

"Hey, it *was* a good idea," Nicholas said. "Except for the supernova part."

"True. Except for that tiny little detail, it was totally perfect," Clave said.

"Tell him your idea," Spott said.

"First, can you show me where both planets are? And both jump nodes?" he asked. "And the sun."

Before Clave could refuse, Nicholas added, "This is serious!"

Clave brought up a display of the Plenax system. Five planets, and five tiny disks near them, blinked, along with a larger disc, farther off.

"We land here," Nicholas said, pointing to the side of Plenax IV away from the sun. "The planet shields us from the blast. The force of the nova pushes the planets outward. But it pushes us, too, since we're on the planet. We can survive the supernova and get a boost to the next node. It's a good thing we'll be shoved in the right direction."

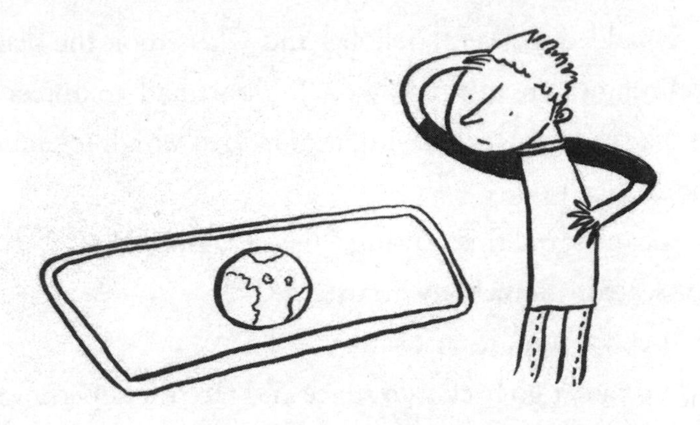

"That's insane," Clave said.

"It might work," Spott said. "The nodes have no mass, so they won't get pushed by the blast."

"It has to work," Nicholas said.

Clave and Spott looked at each other for a very long minute, as if in silent discussion.

"Let's do it," Clave said. "And I'm recording it."

"Of course you are," Nicholas said. "The Yewpees are welcome to come here, since we won't be sticking around."

Clave turned back to the navcom. "Now be quiet. I have to figure out where to land. We want to be directly opposite the sun when it goes nova."

Twenty minutes later, they landed on the night-side surface of Plenax IV, which was wrapped in what could be best described as an eerie glowing darkness.

They strapped Jeef to the console and put Henrietta

in a padded drawer. Nicholas and Clave took the seats, reclining them all the way back. Spott had volunteered to take the floor, explaining that he had a high tolerance for acceleration.

"I can't stand this waiting," Clave said, right after they got seated. "Somebody amuse me."

"I could sing," Spott said.

"I'd rather go back into space and face the supernova," Clave said.

"I know lots of jokes," Nicholas said. He paused to think up his best one, and realized he could barely remember any jokes at the moment. In desperation, he went for a classic. "Knock, knock."

Nicholas waited.

"I don't get it," Clave said.

"You're supposed to say 'Who's there?'"

"Why?"

"Because it's part of the joke. Knock, knock."

"Who's there?"

"Orange," Nicholas said.

This led to further silence.

"You're supposed to say, 'Orange, who?'"

"Why?"

"Because it's part of the joke. Knock, knock."

"Who's there?"

"Orange."

"Orange, who?"

"No, wait. Oh, roach brains! I messed up. I meant banana."

"No, wait. Oh, roach brains! I messed up. I meant banana, who?"

"No, just banana."

"No, just banana who?"

"Forget it!" Nicholas shouted. He placed his hand over Clave's mouth to stop him from saying *Forget it, who?* "I got it backward. It's supposed to start with the banana a couple times, and end with *Orange you glad I'm not banana?* It's a really funny joke if you do it right." He let his hand drop.

"Well, that certainly helped pass the time," Clave said.

Not all that long after that, they were pressed flat by a force that made everything else Nicholas had experienced feel like a kiddie coaster. He couldn't even scream. The pressure seemed to last forever. Through the viewport, night turned into sheer light surrounding the dark tunnel cast by their shadow, until the filter kicked in to prevent their retinas from burning.

Eventually, the force tapered off.

"We're alive!" Clave said. He pulled up the navcom. "Now we just have to lift off and head for the node."

"It worked!" Spott said.

"We rode the supernova! We rock!" Nicholas leaped up and held his hand in the air. "High five!"

Spott responded instantly. Clave, seeing this, followed suit. "Strangely pleasant," he said, after also slapping Spott's hand. "Not all barbarian customs are repulsive."

"Not all aliens are, either," Nicholas said. He opened the padded drawer and held his finger out. Henrietta tapped it with her paw. Then he held his hand toward Jeef, before he realized she couldn't slap anything.

"Sorry," he said as he patted her.

I wish I had hands, Jeef said.

"Imagine the damage you could do," Henrietta said.

"Stop it, you two," Nicholas said. But he was grinning. With good reason. He'd just ridden a planet that had been kicked out of orbit by a supernova. *This has to be about as amazing as it ever gets,* he thought, incorrectly.

Clave turned to Spott. "Let's get you home."

SO MUCH HASN'T HAPPENED SO FAR

At this point in Nicholas's adventure, there are so many things that didn't happen, it's difficult to resist telling you about some of the more fascinating ones. But you're probably nearly as eager as Spott to get to Beradaxia, so let's move on.

SPOTT GETS HOME

While Clave was navigating toward an available dock at a spaceport in orbit above Spott's native city of Ortranto, Spott used the cockpit transceiver to send a message to his family, alerting them to the good news that he was returning home.

The air in the spaceport, in the shuttle, and on the ground in Beradaxia smelled to Nicholas like pistachios that had been simmered in chicken noodle soup. The trip to the ground itself would have been not much different than a ride in a large airplane, except that Spott insisted Nicholas sit by a window, so he could see the city, which lay between an immense gorge and one of the tallest waterfalls in Beradaxia.

A cheering crowd awaited them just outside the ground

terminal. Nicholas's heart tugged a bit when he saw all the beagle faces. He blinked hard as pressure built behind his eyes. Then he turned on his phone and discovered he'd gotten three messages since he'd sent his most recent text. He had a feeling at least two of them would contain some form of his mother's not-so-subtle *why haven't we heard from you* questions. Even so, he wanted to listen to them, just to hear his parents' voices, but it was too noisy at the moment.

The crowd rushed forward.

"Not again." Clave spun back toward the ship.

"It's okay," Spott said. "They're fans."

"Fans?" Clave asked.

"I sort of sing," Spott said. "It's no big deal."

"Apparently, it is," Henrietta said. "At least, to them."

Clave reached for his sfumbler. Nicholas grabbed his wrist. "Please. No. Just let us have one peaceful day. If this works out the way Spott said, we'll get those cubes, and you can bring me home. Okay?"

"It's not worth recording. Nobody knows me anywhere except here, and maybe in some of the other cities nearby," Spott said. "I'm just a local kid with a bit of talent. I'm not famous like Xroxlotl. Morglob was supposed to change that. But I doubt my voice would appeal to anyone who didn't grow up here. Beradaxian song cycles are something of an acquired taste."

"Oh, all right." Clave stashed his sfumbler.

A cluster of Beradaxians rushed up to Spott, including his three parents, seven sisters, two brothers, four sibros, five aunts, seven uncles, eight ancles, and nineteen cousins. Nicholas watched the reunion turn into various permutations of fifty-six people hugging each other in groups and clusters of two or more.

Eventually, the crowd had quieted down enough for Nicholas to hear the messages from his parents.

"Hey, Nicky. It's Dad. Hope you're behaving." This was followed by a description of the previous day's concert, and the details of what his parents had for dinner.

"Hey, kiddo. Mom here. How's everything?" This, also, came with additional details, called him at least one embarrassing nickname, and terminated with the usual, "Miss you. Love you."

The third message didn't have any travel or meal descriptions.

"Hey, kiddo. It's your mother. The one who worries about you. I wanted to make sure you're okay. I tried to call your uncle, but he isn't answering. I'd hate to have to ask your aunt to drive all the way out there to check on you. Please let us know how things are going. Miss you. Love you."

Nicholas tapped out a text: Phone died. Sorry. I'm good.

An instant after he hit SEND, his phone rang. Nicholas was so startled, he almost answered it. The call was from his parents. He was torn. He wanted to talk to them, but he knew they'd figure out he was hiding something the instant they heard his voice. Or the cheerful voices of Spott's family reunion, rising in the background. Nicholas had no idea what those voices would sound like without the effect of the Ubiquitous Matrix, but he suspected it would not be reassuring to a pair of parents who thought their son was a mere eight thousand miles away. He waited until they left a message, then listened to it.

"Hey, Nicky. We're wrapping up the tour. Glad to hear things are good. Next week's schedule got canceled because of bad weather. The last two concerts are this afternoon and tomorrow. That's fine with us. We'll be home sooner than planned. We miss you. See you on Friday."

great c u then

Nicholas wasn't even sure what day it was. According to the phone, it was Monday. He had no idea whether this was based on local time, or the time back home. Either way, he had to get to Earth before Friday. If he wasn't home when his parents arrived, they would figure out what he'd done and never trust him again. Even if he sent texts, they'd want to know where he was.

I don't exactly know my location, Mom. Somewhere a gazillion miles away. But it smells interesting, and I'm currently safe. Don't hold dinner for me.

That would not be good. Nicholas put his phone away and followed the still-hugging reunion cluster to Spott's parents' apartment. It wasn't very large.

"We're not wealthy," Spott said. "But I can give a concert to make the money for the j-cubes. It's the least I can do to repay you for rescuing me from Morglob."

Nicholas hesitated after he stepped inside. At every place he'd gone since he'd been snatched from Earth, something disastrous had happened. He didn't want to end up destroying another planet. Especially not the home planet of someone he liked.

"Relax," Spott said. "Stop thinking about it so much. That was all coincidence. And none of it was your fault."

"I guess . . ." Nicholas said. He realized there was no other way he could get back to Earth. Especially not before Friday. As much as it was a bit creepy to know Spott could read his thoughts, it was nice to be reassured about his role in the trail of disasters he'd left behind as he traveled the universe.

As they were being shown around the apartment, Jeef screeched to a stop in one of the rooms.

A Thinkerator! she said. *There's something I need.*

"I know what you have in mind. My treat." Spott activated the Thinkerator by voice and selected the right attachments for Jeef's cart.

A pair of mechanical hands, each on a jointed mechanical arm, appeared in the mist and settled to the table. After they'd cooled, Spott attached them to the two front corners of Jeef's cart.

Thank you! Now I can order things for myself. Jeef clapped the hands together, filling the room with a sound like the clanging of pots and pans. She spun in a circle, then shot off toward the wall.

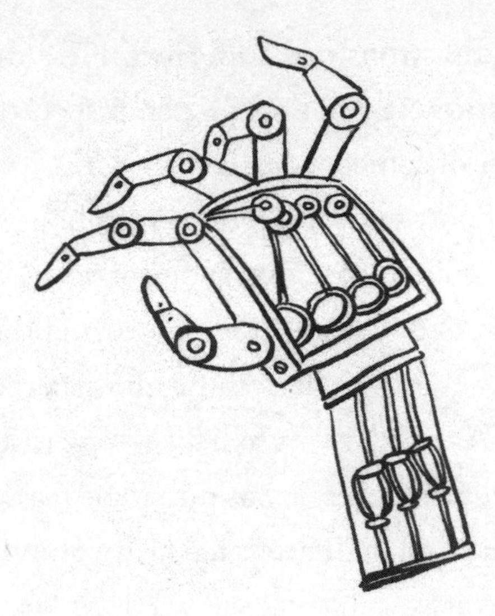

Oops! Jeef said as she crashed to a stop. *Still getting used to these things.*

"You might want to take it slowly with the hands," Nicholas said, "until you get some control."

I'm fine with them. Watch. Jeef rolled back to the Thinkerator and swiped her hands through the digital display. *I'll order some gloves. Marike wore wool gloves in the winter. They were lovely.*

A moment later, a swath of pink fabric materialized in the mist and drifted to the table. Nicholas stared at the straps and unexpected shapes. "Jeef, you just ordered a bra," he said.

Spott called Jeef aside and whispered something to

her. He spoke too quietly for Nicholas to hear him, but he caught Jeef's response of *Okay*. Then, Spott went to a cabinet, took out a stack of paper, and put it on the floor for Henrietta to chew.

Nicholas wanted to watch Jeef play with her new hands, and Henrietta shred her paper, but he kept yawning. After closing his eyes several times, he realized he was exhausted. It turned out Beradaxians didn't sleep much, and had no special place for doing that. When they were tired, they'd just plop to the floor wherever they happened to be, and nap for five or ten minutes. But they cleared out a room for their guests and put down some padded cushions.

That was fine with Nicholas. He figured it would be comfortable enough. And it was. Clave came in as Nicholas was getting settled, and fell right to sleep. Then Jeef and Henrietta joined them.

Just as Nicholas was falling asleep, a faint sound caught his attention.

Glarrlrrlrrlrrllarrrlrrrlrrlrrllarrrllrrrll.

After a brief pause, that sound was followed by a softer one, like wind rushing through a corridor far away.

Whoooooooshhhhhhoooooosshhhhh.

This glarrl/whoosh sequence repeated several times before Nicholas figured out what he was hearing. He got up, went to the cart, and poked Jeef. "Hey. Wake up. You were snoring."

What? Huh? No I wasn't.

"Yes, you were," Nicholas said. "Be quiet. I need to get some sleep."

You snore, too, Jeef said.

"No, I don't," Nicholas said.

Do, too.

"Do not." He went back to his cushion and lay down.

"Idiots," Henrietta muttered, somewhat fondly, before she slipped back to a sleep dusted with her own barely audible, unbearably cute gerbil snuffles and snorts. Clave, like all Menmarians, slept silently, and even more deeply than an exhausted seventh grader.

In the morning, Spott told them he had arranged to give a concert. "We should earn enough for the j-cubes," he said.

"When?" Nicholas asked.

"Two days from now. It takes time to organize events like this," Spott said. "That's as quickly as I can manage it. But you'll be well cared for here. You are my guests."

"That's great," Nicholas said. "I'll still get home before my parents. I'll miss you, but it'll be nice to get back where I belong."

"You won't miss the mind reading," Spott said.

Nicholas laughed. "I was just thinking that. You're right. I won't."

"That's why we don't travel much," Spott said. "It's easy to slip up, and you never know how people will react. Though I'd like to see more of the universe. The only time I left here, I didn't get to go anywhere except for Morglob's estate."

"I think I'd like to see more, too. But not for a while." Nicholas turned to Clave. "Is there any chance you'll be back near Earth after you drop me off? So like maybe I could go along on one of your delivery trips?"

"Courier trips," Clave said.

"Right. Courier trips," Nicholas said.

"We'll see," Clave said.

"Super," Nicholas said, without any enthusiasm. He suspected the true meaning of *we'll see* was universal, and unpromising. A new bike, various trips to the movies, a better phone, and a totally awesome pair of sneakers were just a few of the many things he could remember vanishing into the bottomless chasm of *we'll see.* And, sitting at the very top of that list, he had at least a year and a half's worth of begging to be allowed to prove he could be left home alone. He thought about his current situation. He'd be going home soon. And that was what he'd wanted. But here he was, roving the universe like nobody from

Earth had ever done, as far as he knew. It would be a total waste if he didn't take advantage of that. It would be like going to Italy or Thailand and not leaving your hotel room. Once he got back to Earth, he might never have a chance to go into space again. He was pretty sure Clave wouldn't volunteer to swing by and take him on an adventure just for the fun of it. That wasn't Clave's style.

After getting tourist advice from Spott, he spent the next day walking around Ortranto, trying to absorb the idea that he was on an alien planet in another galaxy. Henrietta came with him. Clave had gone back to sleep. Jeef stayed at the apartment to practice with her hands.

The most amazing thing about Beradaxia wasn't the shapes of the buildings or the silent passage of the vehicles. It wasn't the awe-inspiring canyon or the breathtaking waterfalls, though Nicholas enjoyed seeing all of that. It was the mix of people. This was Nicholas's first experience of a world that was frequently visited by travelers and tourists. The diversity of intelligent life-forms was almost more than he could absorb. He saw a snake on a skateboard, a three-foot-tall blue-feathered bird with two heads, someone who looked like a bundle of sticks, a family that resembled upright porcupines, and one assortment of limbs and organs that refused to take any sort of form he could put a name to. The size range was also mind-numbing. There were giants three times his height, and aliens so small they could only safely travel in hover cars.

After the seventh or eighth time Nicholas responded to an amazing sight with his favorite expression, Henrietta asked him what *roach brains* meant. They were standing at an observation deck midway up the falls.

"Nothing," Nicholas said.

"I can tell when you're lying," Henrietta said. "Your voice rises in pitch."

"It does not," Nicholas shrieked, ending that brief sentence on a note an octave and a half higher than where it had started.

Henrietta waited in silence.

"Okay," Nicholas finally said. "Back in third grade, I had this idea for a science fair project. My friend Gabe had lots of cockroaches in his house, since he was always eating in his bedroom, and he was a total slob. So I caught some roaches and put them in two sealed containers I'd made from squares of plastic that I glued together. Before I closed them, I put lettuce in one, and a piece of . . ." Nicholas paused and looked down at the ground.

"Piece of what?" Henrietta asked. "Why are you looking so guilty?"

"Cow brain."

"Got it," Henrietta said. "That's our little secret. But why that?"

"I wanted to see if the roaches who ate brains got smarter than roaches who ate lettuce," Nicholas said.

"Are you a complete idiot?" Henrietta asked.

"I was in third grade," Nicholas said. "So, yes."

"What happened?" Henrietta asked.

"The container was sealed a little too well. It turns out I have a knack for crafts. It also turns out a hunk of cow brain sort of decays if it isn't refrigerated. And it turns out that when meat decays, it lets off gasses. Which means more pressure."

"So, boom?" Henrietta asked.

"Yeah, boom," Nicholas said. "It exploded right in the middle of the fair. Brain-coated roaches went flying everywhere. It also turns out stains from rotting pieces of brain are pretty hard to remove. As were all the roaches that invaded the school. They really can survive almost anything."

"I imagine the smell was rather overpowering," Henrietta said.

"Rather." Nicholas shuddered. "It did encourage a bit of vomiting among the spectators."

"Is Jeef going to explode?" Henrietta asked.

"I don't think so," Nicholas said. "She's like irradiated or something."

But when they got back to the apartment, Nicholas took a close look and saw that Jeef's package seemed a bit puffy.

"Maybe we should keep her somewhere cold," he said after he'd told Henrietta what he'd seen. "A refrigerator would work. Maybe a freezer would be better."

"She won't like that," Henrietta said.

"I know. But it's for her own good." Nicholas shook his head. "I sound like a parent."

"You sort of are, to her," Henrietta said.

"I didn't ask to be," Nicholas said.

"That's irrelevant," Henrietta said.

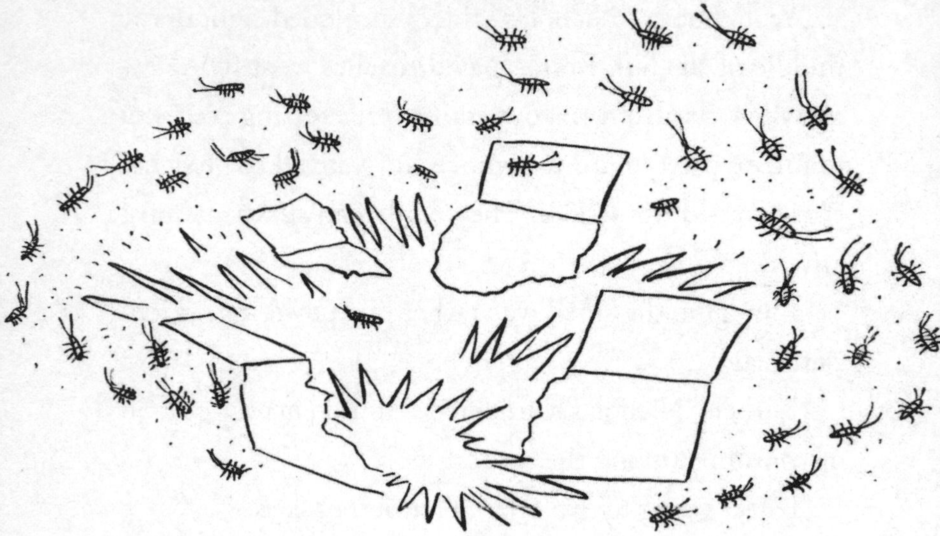

"I guess. Do you think she can still talk if she's frozen?"

"Maybe. But it won't matter for long," Henrietta said. "She might not be able to talk at all when we get home. Or if she can, we won't be able to hear her."

"Don't say that." Nicholas realized he'd never even contemplated the idea that Jeef wouldn't be around forever. Not until now. He didn't know which was worse, being silenced, or not being heard. Both seemed pretty bad. "Wait! What about you?"

Henrietta raised a paw. "One way or another, we'll always be able to communicate."

"You think so?" he asked.

"I'm sure of it," Henrietta said.

Nicholas decided there was only one thing he could do at the moment. It was the same thing he did for school assignments. He'd try to push the problem from his mind for now, and think about it later. He spent the next day seeing more of the sights. And then, it was showtime.

DID YOU HEAR THE ONE ABOUT...?

Nicholas's failure to find a good joke to amuse his companions highlights the fact that humor is far from universal. A joke that would kill on Rigura would die on Bopsco, even though Rigurans and Bopscoppers appear virtually identical to outside observers. On the other hand, given the size of the universe, every joke will be funny somewhere. Sadly, more than a few aspiring comedians have starved trying to find that *somewhere.*

The one exception (there's always an exception) to this was the famed comic Shucks McChuckles, a Pozdinger who billed himself as The Deep Thinker of Shallow Thoughts. In truth, his material leaned heavily toward the philosophical, producing smiles and the occasional grin, as opposed to belly laughs. And many of his audience members laughed because they were afraid that not laughing would mean they weren't very deep. Still, Shucks was entertaining, likeable, and highly in demand. Tragically, he was clubbed to death at a theater on Grumlatch, thanks to a booking agent who was unaware that not only do Grumlatchers lack a sense of humor, but they are offended by pretty much everything and never go anywhere without at least one blunt weapon. According to legend, Shucks used his dying breath to quip, "That's not my idea of a comedy club."

Shucks will be missed by comedy fans throughout the universe. To honor his memory, here are some of his best-loved shallow thoughts:

The position of "dominant species" is an illusion often held by subdominant species.

Sound doesn't travel through space. Unfortunately, the unsound don't have the same limitations.

Travel above the speed of light is impossible . . . to understand.

The less capable of space travel a society is, the more eager they are to travel through space.

In an infinite universe, everything that can happen will happen, unless it doesn't.

The difference between a really really really big universe and an infinite one is both enormous and insignificant, depending on whether one is trying to reach the edge or hoping to make a nice pot of soup.

The need to be right, even in the face of overwhelming evidence that you are wrong, is nearly universal.

"Everything" and "nothing" are equally inconceivable, because each requires an understanding of the other.

Physicists hope the universe doesn't get so big that it needs to be put somewhere else.

IN CONCERT

The concert hall was not far from Spott's apartment. Beradaxian concerts traditionally start at noon, so Spott had gone ahead that morning right after breakfast to prepare.

"Let's check the news," Nicholas said, after he'd helped clean up. "I want to see whether they have any idea where we are." He also wanted to see Stella.

Clave activated the news. The upcoming Xroxlotl concert and the Sagittarian war were still among the top stories. The Plenax evacuation was complete, which was a good thing, not just because the star had gone supernova, but because those transport ships were needed to help the population of Zeng, who had to flee their self-devouring planet.

"The emergency evacuation is proceeding smoothly," Stella said. "However, Nicholas V. Landrew, destroyer of worlds, hopes, and dreams, who is believed to be the one responsible for this latest outrage on Zeng, continues to elude pursuit." Above Stella's right shoulder, there was an ad for plastic surgery. Nicholas flinched at the thought of having his nose carved into a different shape.

I want that! Jeef said.

"You want surgery to change your appearance?" Nicholas asked.

"You want a camouflaged cage?" Henrietta asked.

"Stealth cloaking for your ship?" Clave asked.

"Wait. What ad did you see?" Nicholas asked.

A holo-suit, Jeef said. She rolled to the Thinkerator and, after fumbling across listings for superhero capes, a gremblefruit peeler, and something called a *shardplopper* that looked like a pile of broken glass glued to an oven mitt, she pulled up an ad that flitted through images of a dizzying variety of different creatures while a soothing voice said: *Project the perfect vision of yourself. Be the best you that you can possibly be. Impress your friends, depress your enemies. Be anything at all. Anything you want. Because being anything means everything.*

There was more, but Nicholas stopped listening. "Sure. If that will make you happy. But let me place the order."

"Good idea. We don't want to end up with a Halloween costume or a salad spinner," Henrietta said.

Stop that. I've gotten very good with these hands, Jeef said, waving her arms for emphasis, and knocking a small hole in the wall.

Nicholas placed the order. A message in purple letters flashed in the air above the ad: INSUFFICIENT FUNDS.

Beneath that, in smaller letters, Nicholas saw: ACCOUNT BALANCE 004.29 U-CREDITS.

"Funds?" Nicholas said. "U-Credits?"

"Of course," Clave said. "Did you think all of this was free?"

"It looked that way," Nicholas said. In fairness, he was pretty used to his parents paying for everything he needed.

"A Thinkerator requires an account," Clave said. "I imagine Morglob's account was pretty much unlimited. And I'd imagine Spott's family's account is very limited."

Nicholas thought about how Spott had taken Jeef aside the other day. He realized Spott had probably asked Jeef to hold off buying anything more after the mechanical hands. But Jeef didn't seem to have the best memory, even if it was fairly impressive for someone in her current state. Still, Nicholas hated to disappoint Jeef. She'd lost pretty much everything in her world, including most of herself.

"So, how do we buy stuff?" Nicholas asked.

"You need to deposit funds or use your personal credit," Clave said.

"How do I do that?" Nicholas asked.

"At the moment, you don't," Clave said. "You have nothing of value."

"What about you?" Nicholas asked.

"Sadly, at the moment, I'm in about the same position as you. Except you're broke and trying to get home. I'm broke and trying to figure out where to find a new home and how to replace the cargo I lost."

So, no holo-suit? Jeef asked.

"No new one. But you can borrow mine." Clave plucked the device from its shoulder mount and knelt by the cart. The holo-suit wasn't actually a suit, but a slim box the size of a stick of gum with an array of lenses on top. After strapping it to the utility chamber, he told Jeef, "Say something," and pressed the tattooed tip of his forefinger against a spot beneath the lenses.

Something, Jeef said.

"It's now set for your voice," Clave said, lifting his finger. "Try it out."

Cow, Jeef said.

And, just like that, there was a cow in the room.

"Wow. You look so real," Nicholas said.

"Impressive, in a beefy sort of way," Clave said.

Jeef remained silent.

"What's wrong?" Nicholas asked.

I don't feel any different, Jeef said.

"But you look amazing." Nicholas tried to give Jeef a reassuring pat on the back, then yanked his hand away as it passed through her flank.

"Very cow-like," Clave said.

Nicholas gave Henrietta a nudge with his forefinger. "Beautifully bovine," she said. "If I were a bull, I'd be in love. I'd be bringing you flowers. Or hay. Or something. You are the most amazing, awesome sack of milk that—"

Nicholas wrapped his fingers around Henrietta's mouth, cutting off the excessive flow of compliments. "You look very nice, Jeef," he said.

Really?

"Really. Wait, I have an idea!" Nicholas snapped his fingers, fortunately using the hand that wasn't currently muzzling Henrietta. "Stay right here." He ran to the cooking area and grabbed a large metal tray from a counter.

"Look at yourself," he said, holding the tray in front of Jeef. "This is what we see now."

There was another silence. But it felt like a happy silence to Nicholas, not a sad one like he'd sensed from Jeef so often. And indeed it was.

Late that morning, Spott's parents led Nicholas and his companions out of the apartment. Henrietta rode on his shoulder. Jeef rolled along next to him, though anyone who looked—which was everyone—saw a cow. While the Beradaxians were used to aliens of all sorts, there were few visitors to the planet who looked anything close to Jeef. Quadrupeds rarely showed an interest in leaving their planet.

The concert hall was large, but plainly decorated. "We saved a place of honor for our guests," Spott's father said, pointing to seats in the exact center of the room. Nicholas and Clave sat down, placing Jeef's cart between them.

"I hope he's good," Nicholas said. There was nothing at all on the stage. Not even a microphone. Or a backup band. His parents had a small truck full of sound and lighting equipment for their shows.

"There's definitely a crowd," Clave said.

Every seat was filled.

I can't see, Jeef said.

Nicholas unplugged the leads, lifted Jeef from the cart, and put her on his unoccupied shoulder. He glanced from gerbil to beef, and back. "I feel like the world's weirdest pirate."

"Or coolest," Henrietta said. She let out a parrot-like squawk.

The lights dimmed. Spott walked out onstage. He was dressed in a sleeveless top of loose orange material and simple white pants.

"Thank you for coming," he said as he kicked off his shoes. "And thank you to my friends for rescuing me."

"That's me," Clave said to the Beradaxians seated behind him.

Spott tapped his foot against the stage seven times. The audience responded with seven taps.

Spott sang.

Nicholas's jaw dropped. Not far. And not for long. But it dropped. The music was hauntingly beautiful. It seemed to come from a place deep inside the singer, and it resonated into two, then three, and then four distinct voices, all in harmony. Eventually, the first song ended. Spott began another. This one had two voices, along with a rhythmic bass sound. The third song, in a solo voice, was just as magical.

An hour passed, though Nicholas had lost all awareness of time. He felt he could listen to Spott sing for an entire day without tiring of his voice. That was good, because Beradaxian song cycles last from five to seven hours. Beradaxians have a great love of music and huge bladders.

The second hour started.

"I *have* to capture this," Clave said. "It is beyond belief. The universe needs to know about him." He pulled out his sfumbler.

"No!" Nicholas said, grabbing Clave's wrist.

Clave wrenched his arm free. The sfumbler flew from his hand and landed in the aisle. People turned to stare at Clave. Nicholas saw a flashing blue light in the handle of the sfumbler, but no enveloping purple light. "What's that mean?" he whispered.

"It's broadcasting live," he said.

Nicholas wanted to turn off the sfumbler. But he couldn't just get out of his seat and push his way to the end of the aisle. Nearby Beradaxians were already staring at him and Clave after their whispered conversation.

He almost lost his train of thought as the next song, which had a strange, jazzy rhythm and alluring counterpoints of two chanting voices, seized his attention. But he pulled himself away from the music and asked Henrietta, "Can you turn it off?"

"No problem." She scampered down his chest, slid along his leg to his shoe, and hopped to the floor. Nicholas saw the light blink off after Henrietta bumped against the sfumbler.

"Thanks," Nicholas said when she climbed back onto his shoulder. He turned his attention to the concert.

So did countless others, all across the universe.

OUT OF CONCERT

Tens of thousands of Xroxlotl fans had amassed at the arena for a direct view of the stage. Millions more took spots in sub-arenas that filled every bit of land, and floated on all the waters, around the rest of the planet, where they would view the stage through a light-and-sound-bending-and-magnifying technology that allowed them to feel as if they were right in front of the musicians. Only those who saw the event from the planet's surface would get to enjoy it live. Other Xroxlotl fans would have to wait for the release of the recording.

Behind the stage, Xroxlotl waited. And they waited some more. The one thing their fans didn't know was that they were not even as smart as a sack full of dirt. (We've already seen that even a sack full of dirt is capable of thought. As is the dirt, without the sack. And the sack, itself, for that matter.) They could barely breathe without instructions, let alone perform a concert. And the one who gave them their instructions was currently drifting through space, thanks to the destruction of his headquarters.

The crowd grew restless. But they'd paid huge sums of money for their seats—especially in areas with an actual view of the stage. Some of them killed time by viewing sfumbles or other entertainment. One of them, while searching for the latest episode of *Cooking Across the Universe with Fleexbeezle,* accidentally stumbled across an amazing streaming clip of a Beradaxian singer. He showed it to everyone seated near him, even though the scene lacked captions or narration, and shared it with his friends, some of whom were also at the concert. His friends shared it, too.

It was that good.

So good, it went univiral.

It didn't take long for someone to figure out that the singer, along with most of the audience, was a Beradaxian. The crowds on the fringes left their seats. First, in a trickle, and then in a wave.

Eventually, even those in sight of the stage, despite having paid unimaginable sums for the privilege, started to leave. Just moments later, after a frustrating delay due to the incompetence of his retainer, Emperor Zril arrived on a landing pad near the stage, expecting to find a planet bursting with millions of donors who would bring him back from the edge of death with the gift of a portion of their vitality.

No such luck. The cupboard was bare.

Soon after that, the emperor sapped everything he could from his entourage.

It killed all two thousand of them on the spot, but their vitality wasn't anywhere near enough to bring about a 178th rejuvenation.

And then, after the horror of seeing his own body start to decompose, Emperor Zril died. For good. And for the good of all.

CURTAIN CALL

Toward the end of the fourth hour of Spott's performance, aliens began to trickle into the concert hall. There were no seats, so they stood in the rear. And then, as more came, they filled the aisles. Spott seemed slightly startled at first, but then gave himself totally back to his singing.

"I think you have some fellow sfumblers," Nicholas said when he noticed that scattered among the crowd, aliens were holding a variety of flashing and flickering devices.

"Clearly, a bunch of unskilled amateurs," Clave said.

As the concert ended, with a haunting solo-voiced repetition of the opening song, the audience responded in the traditional Beradaxian display of delight, by raising their own voices in song. The sound almost turned Nicholas's bowels to water, but he survived. And he was thrilled for Spott. This had to be one of the most amazing homecomings of all time. Nicholas was both glad and sad that his own homecoming would be noticed by nobody.

Crowds thronged around Spott as he left the stage, but he managed to make his way toward his friends.

"You were amazing," Nicholas said.

"Thank you," Spott said.

"I sort of let the word out across the universe," Clave said as he retrieved his sfumbler from the aisle. "You seem to be rather universally popular."

"That's wonderful," Spott said. "I never thought anyone off planet would appreciate me."

"Do you mind if I capture a quick shot of us?" Clave asked.

"Of course not."

The instant they finished, Nicholas said, "I think we need to get away from here pretty much immediately."

"I understand," Spott said. "I deposited funds from the concert into your account, Clave. And I had fifty j-cubes delivered to your ship."

"Wonderful." Clave put his left index finger in Spott's right nostril. "We'll meet again, my friend."

“We will.” Spott turned to Nicholas. “As will we.” He stroked Henrietta’s head and gave Jeef a pat.

“I hope so,” Nicholas said. He braced himself for some sort of bizarre or uncomfortable alien farewell gesture, but Spott threw him a hug.

“I guess that’s a good thing about mind reading,” Nicholas said as he returned the embrace.

“One of the best,” Spott said after they’d stepped apart. “Take care of yourself, my clever friend. And listen for your song. It’s out there somewhere.”

Nicholas pushed through the crowds of aliens that had converged outside the concert, along with Clave, Jeef, and Henrietta. All the way to the shuttle, and all during the ride back up to the ship, they talked and marveled about the performance they’d heard.

“It’s a big universe,” Clave said. “With a lot of wonders.”

“I wish I could see more of it,” Nicholas said.

“I’m sure you will,” Clave said, which sounded to Nicholas slightly better than *we’ll see,* but not anywhere near as promising as *I’ll pick you up a week from tomorrow and we’ll go looking for another supernova to ride.*

They boarded the ship.

“Ready to go home?” Clave asked.

“For sure. And I’ll be there before my parents.”

Nicholas pulled out his phone to check for messages. "Roach brains—it's dead."

"It's organic?" Clave asked. "I had no idea Earth had reached that stage of technology. But I guess that explains the smell."

"It's not organic," Nicholas said. He sniffed his shirt. It didn't seem all that bad. "The battery's dead. That's all. But I don't have a phone charger."

"Battery?" Clave asked.

"Sure. It holds electricity."

Clave started to laugh. "Holds electricity? Why in the world would you want to do that?"

"Don't you use them?" Nicholas wondered how a civilization that had space flight and the ability to build underground cities would never have developed something as simple as batteries.

Clave held his hand out. "Let me see it."

"You aren't going to text a picture of your butt to all my contacts, are you?" Nicholas asked.

"Why would I do that?" Clave asked. He studied the phone for a moment, then inserted it into a slot in the console on the bridge.

"Is that a charger?" Nicholas asked.

"No. It's an adapter." Clave tapped a series of buttons. "This won't take long."

While Nicholas waited, he sniffed, again, and caught a faint whiff of a familiar stench. He looked over at Jeef, who seemed to be trying to do a handstand with her cart, then turned toward Henrietta, who was perched on his shoulder, and mouthed the words, *Do you smell that?*

Henrietta slipped her snout inside his ear and whispered, "I've been smelling it for days."

"Is it Jeef?" Nicholas asked.

"I'm afraid so," Henrietta said. "I think all those crashes, before and after she got the cart, have taken a toll on her wrapper."

"We'll have to figure something out." A jumble of ideas ran through Nicholas's mind. He could try the fridge or the freezer when he got home. Though he wasn't sure how he'd hide Jeef from his parents. Or maybe there was some kind of preservative for meat. It was possible rotting away wouldn't harm Jeef, since she was already ground up. Though she did seem to be speaking less and less.

"Hey, Jeef, do you feel okay?" Nicholas asked.

My flesh is clothed with worms and clods of dust, Jeef said. *My skin is broken and has become loathsome.*

"Ew . . ." Nicholas said. He'd never heard her say something so gloomy or hopeless. "We'll fix that, as soon as we get home. Don't worry. We'll take care of you."

Nicholas turned his mind back to the problem, but his

thoughts were broken as the console pinged. Clave plucked Nicholas's phone from the slot and handed it back to him. "Here you go. It will charge from the ether."

"Ether?" Nicholas asked.

"Barbarians . . ." Clave muttered.

Nicholas stared at his phone. There were no new messages. That wasn't a huge surprise, since his parents were traveling. But the battery icon had the tiny lightning bolt that showed it was charging. *That* was a huge surprise. "How . . . ?"

"It's complicated," Clave said.

"Ether was in a lot of movies," Henrietta said. "The universe is full of charged particles. I guess a device just needs to be adapted so it can absorb them."

"That's it?" Nicholas asked. "Anything can stay charged?"

"Yes. That's it," Clave said.

"Anything?"

"Anything."

Nicholas stared at his phone. "Forever?"

"Forever."

"This will be so awesome when I get home," Nicholas said. He thought about all the times he'd stressed over watching the solid white rectangle inside the battery icon shrink into a tiny sliver.

"Take a seat," Clave said, spinning back to the nav panel. "I need to give us a boost toward the jump node."

"Thanks for the warning." Nicholas strapped in.

"That's odd," Clave said.

"What?" Nicholas asked.

"I feel like the ship is slightly tilted. Maybe the grav engine is out of adjustment. Do you feel it?"

"Yeah. Just a little," Nicholas said. He leaned from side to side and tried to figure out exactly what was different.

Clave pointed at his console. "It's all reading fine. Oh, well. It's no big deal. I'll have the system checked out the next time I get the ship serviced. I'll probably do that right after I drop you off."

"I can't believe I'm finally going home," Nicholas said. "It's been an amazing adventure. I wonder whether the concert made the news. Or whether the Yewpees know we were there."

"Let's see." Clave activated the broadcast.

"And in our top story," Stella said, "physicists have made an alarming discovery. The expansion of the universe has slowed and appears to be grinding to a halt. At which time, it will begin to contract toward an all-consuming point scientists have dubbed *the devouring singularity,* located inside the remains of the planet Zeng. Though, at the moment, it's not a singularity, and it appears to be not so much devouring as atomizing. Not that the end result will be all that different, once everything is consumed."

"What?" Nicholas screamed. "Heaping, steaming roach brains! We're all doomed."

"Do I have to bite your nose again?" Henrietta asked.

"No. I'm okay." Nicholas took a deep breath.

"Calm down," Clave said. "You're thinking like some child who has no idea of the size of the universe. It will take forever for that to happen. We're talking about the whole universe. Even an experienced pilot like me has trouble grasping the magnitude of that."

"Scientists are deeply concerned," Stella said. "While the initial contraction will be slow, it most likely will accelerate at a pace that indicates the entire universe will be consumed in roughly three years."

An ad for exotic sports cars appeared next to Stella with the caption: *Spend it while you can.*

"Three years?" Nicholas said.

"That's only an estimate," Clave said. "It could be decades, or even centuries. Scientists never get these things right."

"Like with the supernova?" Nicholas asked. "The one that blew at exactly the time most of the scientists had predicted?"

"Good point," Clave said. "I guess they're probably right about this one, too. And just when I'm starting to get popular."

A familiar image appeared next to Stella, shimmering in its container. "Scientists are not certain, but they believe an antimatter power core, like the one seen here, might be at the center of the destruction. All attempts to reach it have proved futile."

Even when seen on a broadcast image, the power core filled Nicholas with an unnerving sense of dread. "We made that singularity when we destroyed the atomizer," he said, "so we have to—"

"Shh." Clave clamped a hand on Nicholas's mouth. "Nobody knows that."

Nicholas pushed Clave's hand away and completed his sentence. "—find a way to stop it. The jolt from getting dumped into the atomizer must have switched on the power core. We have to turn it off."

"I thought you wanted to go home," Clave said.

Stella tapped a chart that had appeared at her side. "Here's the estimated destruction time for some of the more popular galaxies." The display scrolled, like a list of school closings, revealing a combination of familiar and unfamiliar names.

"Five months!" Nicholas said, pointing at the chart.

His finger followed one of the lines as it moved up the display. "Look at that. The Milky Way will be wiped out in less than half a year. My whole planet. My family. Everyone I know. Everyone I ever met. Everyone I might ever meet. Do you have any idea what that means?"

As the words left his mouth, Nicholas tried to snatch them back. He felt like the biggest self-centered jerk in the world. Or in the universe.

Clave stared at him with as deep a mask of sorrow as a Menmarian could display. "Yes. I believe I do."

"I'm sorry. I'm so sorry. I wasn't thinking," Nicholas said as the image of a burning Menmar flared in his mind, backed by echoed memories of his clueless words. The wave of guilt from his blunder dwarfed every bit of remorse, regret, or shame he'd ever experienced.

"Can you forgive me?" he asked.

"I already have. Let's go stop this thing and save the universe," Clave said. "I've always wanted to do that." He pulled open a drawer, took out the remote control for the power core, and put it on the console.

"Really?" Nicholas asked. "We're going there?"

"Really," Clave said. "And foolishly."

"Foolishly is our best talent so far," Henrietta said.

Jeef spoke, but her voice was too faint to be heard, even by the gerbil.

SOLE SURVIVOR

In his final act of cruelty, not counting his desperate vitality-draining assault on his entourage, which was more based on a need for survival than a need to make others suffer, the emperor had ordered Pumplock, who appeared to be a huge fan of Xroxlotl's, to remain on the ship while everyone else took a shuttle to the surface to attend the concert.

Thus, the former retainer was the first to be aware of the death of the emperor, thanks to a monitor that kept track of such things. It gave him great joy to share the news with the universe.

AT THE HEART OF THE MATTER

It was different this time. The hyperjump felt the same as before. And there was no gold-related tumble. But rather than returning to normal at the end of the jump, Nicholas felt a subtle pull toward the back of the ship as they traveled toward the devouring singularity.

"That's deceleration," Clave said. "We're still expanding, but that thing has put the brakes on. That's also why the ship felt tilted. We weren't lined up back there, facing the singularity, like we are now. But if we can actually feel it, it's definitely happening at an increasing rate. Once the expansion has been negated, it will get even worse as the universe contracts."

"Not if we can stop it," Nicholas said. The compressed sphere that had once been the planet Zeng was now less than a mile in diameter. It pulsed with Nicholas's least-favorite shade of purple and flung branching tendrils from its surface into the void around it, like dark ink dribbled into clear water. The deep crater holding the devouring singularity looked just the way they'd seen it during Stella's report. That thought led Nicholas to an unpleasant realization.

"They've been showing this on the news, right?"

"Right," Clave said. "So what?"

"So they have to have someone or something around here, transmitting the scene," Nicholas said. "Which means they're also showing us."

"I guess it does," Clave said.

"Which means anyone who's watching will know we're here," Nicholas said. "And I'm pretty sure, since it's such a big story, that everyone is watching. Including the Yewpees, the Craborzi, and anyone else who wants to capture or kill me."

"So let's not dawdle," Clave said.

"Let's not." Nicholas took the remote control from the console. "Are you sure this will do the trick?"

"It better," Clave said. "We have no other tricks to try."

"How close do we have to get?" Nicholas didn't like the idea of moving too near the devouring singularity. Neither of those two words sounded very inviting.

"No idea," Clave said. "We'll just have to keep trying. Slowly. If we get too close, we might get trapped."

Nicholas pointed the remote at the singularity and pushed the ON/OFF toggle. A tiny light at the top of the switch, which is another nearly universal feature of remotes, whether or not the remote itself is of the universal sort, showed that it was working. But ahead of them, nothing changed. Nicholas released pressure and the toggle sprang back to the neutral position.

They drifted closer. Nicholas kept trying, without success, to turn off the power core. The singularity grew in the viewport until its edges reached the top and bottom of the screen. The peak that had once been the home of the atomizer was now a depression on the surface of Zeng.

"I can see something shimmering." Nicholas squinted, but couldn't make out any details. The light also seemed to pulse, as if it were being partially and repeatedly blocked.

"I'll zoom in." Clave swiped the viewport. The image expanded, enveloping the entire screen. As it grew even larger, Nicholas said, "Hold it there. See that?"

"Yes," Clave said. "Just one blade left."

Nicholas watched the single enormous blade as it spun in lopsided circles at the center of the opening, making the light beneath it pulse. To either side, he could see torn, warped, and mangled blades that had been destroyed by the gold. And beyond the blade, dead center and anchored to the sides of the opening with bolts of light, sending other bolts into the depths, the mangled power core absorbed the scattered emissions and reflected energy from the various layers of the atomizer, and slowly destroyed the universe.

Nicholas tried the remote again.

The ship lurched forward. Nicholas screamed as the spinning blade filled the entire viewport. He dropped the

remote, threw his arms in front of his face, and braced for destruction as the ship was cleaved in half.

Henrietta leaped from his shoulder to the top of the viewport. As she slid down, the scene shrank back to normal. The opening was still far enough away that the blade was no threat.

"Roach brains!" Nicholas shouted. "I thought we were about to get cut in half."

"We will be, soon, if we can't get this power core shut off and make our escape," Clave said.

The ship lurched again.

"We're getting caught in the field," Clave said.

"Can you back off?" Nicholas asked.

"Sure. But that won't get us where we need to be. We have to get within range."

"And we have no idea where that will be. How much closer can we get before there's no escape?" Nicholas asked.

Clave went to the console and put his hands in the nav field. "Not much. There's already a strong pull. We're moving forward without using any thrust. Pretty soon, we'll have to thrust against the pull, just to slow our approach."

Nicholas waited for Clave to say more. Clave stared at

him. Nicholas stared back. Neither wanted to explore their options.

Clave finally broke the silence. "We've got to take the ship all the way in. We have to get right next to the power core."

"We'll never make it past the blade," Nicholas said. He'd played enough video games to know that this was the sort of challenge that killed you twenty or thirty times before you figured out the timing needed to survive, or threw the controller against the wall. The ship was too big to get past the blade easily, if at all, and there were no checkpoints or respawns. A person, on the other hand, had a good chance to slip through.

Nicholas pointed toward the lockers beyond the hatch. "Somebody has to suit up and take the remote right up to the core."

Again, they stared at each other, like two reluctant gunfighters, each waiting for the other to draw first.

"You're young," Clave said. "You have a whole life ahead of you. A barbaric life wallowing in the primitive mud of Earth, shielded from all the splendor of the universe, but still a life marginally worth living. And you have absolutely no experience moving in space or wearing a space suit. It has to be me. My courier career probably ended when all my packages got dumped. And, as much as I've gotten more fans for my sfumbles, I guess the truth is they're really your fans. Without you, they'd forget about me in a nanosecond."

"No," Nicholas said. He thought about that moment on the platform above the atomizer, when he reconciled himself with death. It looked like he had to do that again. But this time, it was his own decision, and it would save countless lives. "All of this is my fault. I'll go."

"None of it is your fault," Clave said.

"Okay. Not my fault. But my responsibility. It has to be me. I can't pilot a ship. If you go, I'm trapped here."

"You can call for help," Clave said. "You'll be a hero."

The ship jolted again. But this jolt was different. It was accompanied by a deafening thump.

"Shields at ninety percent," the ship said.

Another jolt.

"Shields at eighty-one percent."

The console display turned into a shower of violet lights.

Clave shouted a swear word that had no translation. "We're being fired at." He pulled up an inset display. Three ships were zooming toward them from behind. One was a Yewpee craft. It wasn't firing. But the other two, which were closer, didn't seem to have any hesitation.

The transceiver squawked.

"Prepare to experience Craborzi justice," a voice said.

"Menmarian vengeance is swift," another voice said.

"They're after me," Nicholas said. "If I leave the ship, they'll chase me. You'll have time to escape. They probably won't even care about you once they have me. I'm getting in that suit and turning off the singularity."

"Activation of breaching-harpoon targeting system detected," the ship said.

Nicholas wasn't sure what that was, but it didn't sound promising. He looked down at the floor by his feet for the remote. It wasn't there. He realized it must have slid across the bridge during the jolts. He dropped to his knees to search. "I need to get out there."

"But the atomizer will destroy you," Henrietta said. "Even if you turn off the power core, you'll fall the rest of the way into the depths of that thing."

"It will destroy everything, anyhow," Nicholas said.

"At least you'll be famous," Clave said. He pulled out his sfumbler. "I'll make sure the whole universe knows of your valor."

"Just make sure my parents know," Nicholas said. "Can you do that without scaring them to death?"

Clave nodded.

"And take care of Henrietta and Jeef," Nicholas said.

"Of course," Clave said.

Another jolt struck.

"Shields at seventy-two-point-nine percent. Approaching vessel nearing harpoon range."

A light far more purple than any before flashed on the console, along with a siren that echoed through the cockpit.

"Breach!" Clave shouted. "Why aren't the shields holding? Don't tell me we've been harpooned already." As he rushed to the console, the warning light went out.

"Are we okay?" Nicholas asked. He hated the thought that the ship could get destroyed before he saved his friends.

"For now," Clave said. "Are you sure you don't want me to tell the whole universe your story? It's a pretty amazing tale."

Nicholas realized how important this was to Clave. Fame was basically the only gift Clave could give him at this point, and it was his responsibility to accept that gift. "Just a quick one. Okay? Really quick."

He stood there while Clave recorded a sfumble and told the viewers, "Nicholas V. Landrew is about to save the universe."

"I really don't care about fame," Nicholas said after Clave had collapsed the sfumbler. He reached up and stroked Henrietta, who was still perched at the base of the viewport. "I care about saving everyone. Especially my friends. You understand, don't you, Jeef?" he asked as he looked around for the cart.

There was no answer. And no sign of the cart.

"Roach brains!" Nicholas ran out to the corridor. The lower locker was open. He realized the ship hadn't been breached. Jeef had taken the remote, then managed to strap on a jet pack. She'd gone outside the ship from the cargo hold and launched herself toward the singularity.

"Come here," Clave called.

Nicholas joined Clave and Henrietta by the viewport. "Jeef! No!" he screamed.

As he watched, the image shifted from a package of ground beef jetting a wheeled cart and clutching a remote control into a space-suited boy roughly the size of the notorious assassin and destroyer of worlds, Nicholas V. Landrew.

"Brilliant," Clave said.

Thank you for treating me like I mattered, Jeef said. She entered the opening of the devouring singularity. Bits of vapor wisped from the image, then glittered as the water formed ice crystals.

"She's freezing," Nicholas said. He realized Jeef had not only sacrificed herself, but she'd jumped into one of her worst nightmares—a place far colder than any freezer on earth. He held his breath as Jeef jetted past the enormous blade. The two ships that had been firing at Clave's ship shot by it, pursuing Jeef. Both were small, fast, and skillfully piloted. Both managed to avoid the blade. Both did so by jetting to the same safe spot where they could slip past the obstacle unharmed. Both tried to occupy exactly the same spot at exactly the same time. Not being massless thoughts, this proved to be impossible. Hence, both exploded in one merged, strangely beautiful fireball. That didn't seem to dissuade the Yewpee ship, which was seeking its own safe path past the blade.

"Jeef . . ." Nicholas said. Beyond the blade, the power core flickered, and then faded toward darkness. Nicholas's heart shattered as he watched Jeef crash directly into the core. The bolts that had spread from the core vanished. Jeef and the core were absorbed by a blackness so dark it hurt the eyes like a thousand suns.

For another instant, the universe held its breath.

And the devouring singularity, unbalanced by the sudden loss of the power core, expanded in a flash that was the exact opposite of total darkness. It was unbearably bright. The flash, which was made of the fabric of the universe, and not bound by the limitations of light, enveloped the ship, the solar system, the galaxy, and ultimately, the universe.

And one small spot in the universe, once occupied by Jeef, became unbearably empty.

Unless . . .

"Do you think she could have survived?" Nicholas turned to Clave with the same blind faith and bottomless hope he'd had when he'd turned to his parents as a

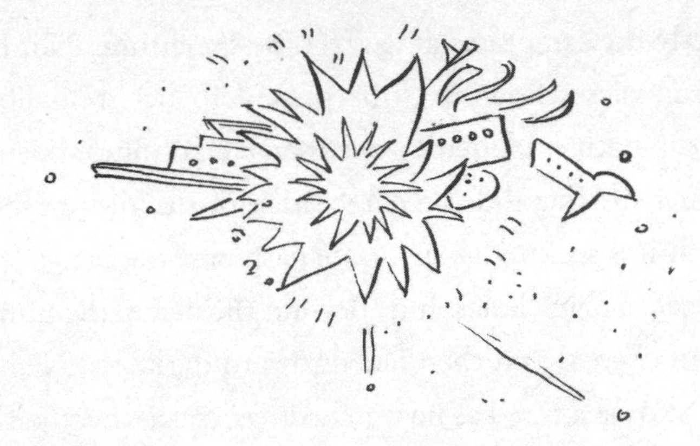

toddler and asked whether his dying goldfish could maybe get better.

"I'm sorry," Clave said. "Between the collision, the explosion, the cold vacuum, and whatever other horrors lay beneath the blades . . ." He let it go at that.

Nicholas blinked, still dazed by the flash, still numbed by the loss. He realized he'd scooped Henrietta up and was clutching her to his chest. "Are you okay?"

"I think so," Henrietta said.

"You?" Nicholas asked Clave, who looked equally stunned.

"I guess."

"Aren't you going to post about this?" Nicholas asked, wiping a tear from the corner of one eye.

Clave looked at the sfumbler dangling from his hand.

He seemed surprised he'd even pulled it out. "Maybe later . . ."

Nicholas inventoried his own body and mind. He was alive. He was unharmed, except for an aching sadness from his loss, which was somewhat eased by the knowledge that countless others, including Beradaxians and Earthlings, had survived, as had he and his friends.

"It's over," Clave said. "The universe can continue to exist for far longer than three years."

AND THEN...

It was hardly over.

AND STILL PRETTY MUCH THEN...

In some ways, it had just begun.

YOU'RE ELECTED

I guess we can head to Earth," Clave said. "You're finally going home."

"We're going home," Nicholas said, picking up Henrietta. He remembered the discussion he'd had with her about Jeef. "When we get back to Earth, will Henrietta still be able to speak?"

"I doubt it," Clave said. "Not with the Ubiquitous Matrix shielded."

"That's okay," Henrietta said. "We got along just fine before I could speak."

"We'll always understand each other," Nicholas said.

"Whatever happens, we can still watch movies together," Henrietta said.

"I don't think they're going to be as exciting anymore."

Nicholas turned toward the viewport and leaned against it, staring at the spot where the devouring singularity had been. "I feel terrible about the Yewpees. They were just doing their job. It's like one last way the universe is telling me I'm bad news for everyone I meet."

Stella popped up. "And now for our top, and only, story of the moment. In breaking news of interest to all, physicists believe the devouring singularity has ceased to exist, and the universe is no longer in danger of imminent collapse."

As Stella vanished, an object at the side of the viewport caught Nicholas's eye. "It can't be . . ." he whispered. He watched the tiny dot move closer. It seemed to be heading for the ship.

"Jeef?" Nicholas called. Maybe the explosion had blown her clear of the singularity.

"Yewpees," Clave said as he magnified the image. "You can start feeling better about their fate, and bad for us. It looks like they managed to avoid the blade and survive the blast."

The Yewpee ship was racing toward them.

A demand came over the transceiver: "Nicholas V. Landrew, you are wanted for crimes against Craborz, Menmar, Zefinora, and Zeng. Clavesnout Kittywhimper, you are wanted for harboring the fugitive Nicholas V.

Landrew. Prepare to be boarded. Any resistance will be met with lethal force."

"Do you want to run for it?" Nicholas asked.

"I'm tired," Clave said. "And I suspect running might fall into the category of resistance. They'd be free to fire at us. We'd never reach the jump node."

"I'm tired, too," Nicholas said. "Henrietta?"

"Very tired," she said. "I just hope alien prisons have cedar shavings."

They watched the approaching Yewpee ship.

"Kittywhimper?" Nicholas asked.

"You can't choose your name," Clave said. "But you can choose your friends, who will mock your name." He draped his arm across Nicholas's shoulders.

"No slap on the nose?" Nicholas asked, remembering his first encounter with Menmarian signs of affection and farewell. "Or finger up the nostril?"

"I've been studying your world," Clave said.

Nicholas draped his own arm across Clave's shoulders. "I hope we get to share a cell."

The Yewpee ship stopped. The transceiver pinged. "All charges have been dismissed. You are free to go. Please obey the speed limits and avoid littering. Have a nice day." The ship flew off.

"What in the world . . . ?" Clave said. "Oh . . ." He pointed to the inset images on the view screen.

Seven enormous ships had converged from behind. The transceiver pinged again, and a message emerged:

"Nicholas V. Landrew, you have been summoned to the center of the universe by the Syndics."

"What if I refuse?" Nicholas asked. He had no idea who the Syndics were, but he was tired of being summoned, and ready to go home.

"Only the emperor can refuse the Syndics."

This pronouncement was followed by a laugh that made no sense to Nicholas until later.

As he soon learned, universal euphoria at the destruction of the devouring singularity quickly turned into a universal call for Nicholas, who by now was almost universally known, universally adored, and universally believed to have single-handedly saved the day, to be put in charge of everything. Conveniently, there was a current vacancy in that "in charge of everything" job category. And everyone had always felt there was something not quite right about the previous emperor, though they couldn't put their finger, or feeler, on it.

Thus the summons from the Syndics, whose role it was to select and inaugurate an emperor whenever the need arose. Ironically, only the emperor could refuse to follow such an order. But Nicholas wasn't emperor quite yet. Thus, the laughter.

Clave's ship was loaded into the imperial transport. Clave, Nicholas, and Henrietta were brought to the emperor's palace at the center of the universe. By Nicholas's count, which he'd be the first to admit got a bit inaccurate toward the end, the trip required thirty-five jumps.

When Nicholas entered the Great Hall, all of the 128 Syndics who possessed at least two arms raised one and slapped the other hand into their exposed armpit. (Historians believe the motion is a tribute to an early emperor, Pitreek Armbeard, whose head was nestled in that fragrant location.)

"Emperor!" they shouted, as the sixteen first-tier Syndics touched Nicholas with their staffs, which had been dipped, as demanded by a tradition nobody understood, in a rare, exotic mix of fermented slime-gibbon dung and crushed corpsefly larva. Now, having been hailed and anointed, he was officially Emperor of the Universe.

"What?" In his life so far, Nicholas had been amazed, astounded, nonplussed (though that word was not yet part of his vocabulary), startled, surprised, and nearly gobsmacked. But he had never, until this moment, been truly flabbergasted. Right now, his gast was definitely flabbered.

"I can't . . . I mean . . . But . . ."

He looked over at Clave, who had regained his enthusiasm for sfumbling and was recording everything. "Royal robes provide a far better ride than coattails," Clave said.

Nicholas looked down at Henrietta. "I share your surprise," she said.

Despite the chaos running wild in his brain, Nicholas smiled at the familiar words from the first moments of their adventure.

"We await your orders," the Prime Syndic said.

"I can't do this," Nicholas said.

"All hail Nicholas," they said, as if they were incapable of hearing any sort of abdication from their brand-spanking-new flabbergasted and dung-scented emperor.

"No. Listen to me. I can't do this," he said. He thought

about all the destruction he'd brought about when he didn't even have any power. He could barely imagine how much damage he'd do as emperor. He'd already nearly destroyed the whole universe once. He really didn't want a second chance. "Seriously, I cannot be your emperor. I can't possibly do the job."

Yes, you can.

Nicholas's shattered heart, which hadn't even begun to heal from the tragic loss of a friend, jammed back together, jolting him with the force of a miniature fusion explosion, or a collision between matter and antimatter. He stared around desperately, afraid to invest too much belief in the unbelievable, and shouted a name.

"Jeef?"

It was a question, a prayer, and a hope, all in one. Maybe, in a large enough universe, the impossible could become possible. The lost could be regained. The shattered heart could be made whole.

The Syndics screamed back "Jeef" in unison, eager to echo the exclamations of their glorious emperor, even if they didn't understand them. It would not be the first time this had happened. Or the thousand and first.

I'll be with you, always.

"You're alive?" Nicholas said. "Henrietta, Jeef is alive!"

"I heard," she said. She let out a joyful squeak and sniffed the air, as if searching for the location of the voice.

Nicholas scanned the chamber. "Where are you?"

Everywhere.

"And nowhere to be seen," Clave said. "What a shame. This would make a great sfumble."

"You're okay?" Nicholas asked.

I believe I am.

"And in one piece?"

Quite the opposite.

"Holy cow!" Henrietta said.

Not exactly. Just wholly present.

It seems the Zeng had the right idea with their Fragmentation Cult. They just had no means to carry out a total, universal dispersion. Jeef, who had already been ground, was overlaid by the dying singularity and the remains of the atomizer onto the Ubiquitous Matrix. Essentially, thanks to the sonic pulses, high-frequency polarized rays, magnetic inversion, absolute-zero shattering, and quantum fragmentation, enhanced by the energy of the antimatter power core, Jeef had become one with the universe.

"So you're everywhere?"

As far as I can tell, Jeef said. *As a certain newly self-aware gerbil once said, there's a lot to sort out.*

"I think I said a lot of other things," Henrietta whispered to Nicholas. Louder, looking up toward the sky, she said, "I never meant a word of any of those nasty comments."

Yes, you did, Jeef said. *But I still love you. And don't bother looking up, or whispering. I really am everywhere.*

"Can everyone hear you?" Nicholas asked.

Only if I want them to, Jeef said.

There was one more thing Nicholas needed to say. "If this whole thing hadn't happened, I would have fried you."

I know, Jeef said. *I still love you.*

Nicholas couldn't quite manage to say *I love you, too.* But he was pretty sure Jeef knew what was in his heart.

We can talk about all of that, and many other things, later, Jeef said. *Right now, you have some emperoring to do.*

"Emperor Nicholas," Nicholas said, trying to make his position seem less absurd by putting it into words.

The Syndics outlined the few basic powers and responsibilities that were essential to the job, finishing with the three most crucial ones.

"Do you swear to defend the universe from all attacks?" the head Syndic asked.

Nicholas took a moment to puzzle over how such a

thing could happen, and then decided it was safe to say, "Uh, yeah. Sure."

The head Syndic asked the second question: "Will you solve that which cannot be solved?"

"I'll try. As long as it's not algebra," Nicholas said. "Or in French."

That seemed to satisfy everyone.

The head Syndic asked the final question. "Will you accept blame for all things for which there is no blame?"

Clave laughed, jabbed Nicholas in the back, and said, "You were born for this job."

"I doubt that," Nicholas told Clave. "But maybe I can grow into it. Starting now."

If he had to do the job, he planned to do it right. "I will accept that blame," he said. He waited to see if there was anything else, but the Syndics were finished.

"Give us some privacy," he told them, as several nearly unimaginable ideas came to mind. "I need to speak with my inner council."

He explained his ideas to Clave, Henrietta, and Jeef, got their approval—which, while unnecessary for any Emperor of the Universe, was pretty important to Nicholas of Yelm—and then summoned the Syndics back in. "I want to establish my reign with an unforgettable act," Nicholas said. "We need to end as many wars as possible. Especially those that have gone on for far too long, and for far too little reason." He ordered two planet torchers to be escorted to the planets involved in the Sagittarian war. He sent a third one to Earth, with specific instructions on where to find a deserted landing area.

His orders were immediately obeyed without question.

Emperor Nicholas was pleased.

LAST WORDS

This is nearly my last opportunity to share information, and to shed light on the story, before we reach the end. It's not enough. Not even close. There's so much about the universe I didn't have a chance to tell you. I really could use five hundred more pages, no matter what universe we're in. Or a thousand. But you're probably eager to see how all of this ended. So I'll let you get back to our emperor, and the earthshaking launch of his reign.

THE END OF LIFE AS WE KNOW IT

Nicholas dropped into his seat in algebra. It was his first class after spring break. His two-week suspension was over. His new punishment had just begun. While he'd arrived back home on Friday just moments before his parents, he'd stepped out of his bedroom into a stomach-wrenching stench that made him yearn for the scent of tacos or the gentle aroma of slime-gibbon sweat-gland stew. A mad dash to the kitchen revealed his vague suspicion was actually a harsh reality. He'd left the fridge door open.

He'd slammed the fridge door shut, but that didn't help. The air dripped with the putrid smell of rotting food. His frantic thoughts about the best way to deal with the situation were almost immediately interrupted by the last thing he needed to hear. The sound of the front door opening was followed by a cheerful *we're home* from his mom, which was immediately followed by shrieks of disgust as his parents entered the reeking house. A brief interrogation led to the inevitable confession about his deception, though he decided not to share any details of his off-planet adventure. His parents slapped him with a one-month grounding. That seemed fair to him.

To soften the blow, since Mr. and Mrs. Landrew were softies at heart, they'd let him keep the gifts they'd brought—an authentic boomerang and a Krazy Kool Kangarule T-shirt with an enormous pocket. He knew better than to take the boomerang to school. But he did wear the shirt. It was a perfect fit, in more ways than one.

"Welcome back, you eager young scholars," Miss Galendrea said after the bell rang. "And brace yourselves. This is going to be the toughest challenge you've ever faced in your lives, but by the end of the month, you'll be able to solve it."

She wrote an equation on the board. It looked like gibberish to Nicholas.

Jeef explained the solution in a way that made sense.

Nicholas smiled and settled into his seat. "It's good to be emperor," he whispered in the direction of his shirt pocket.

"Very good," Henrietta whispered back.

Much to his relief, his plan to end the Sagittarian war had worked perfectly. The planet torchers, which could selectively target any specified molecule, had extracted all the petroleum from both planets and teleported it to waiting disposal ships. Each of the two battling sides now heard the other use the proper length for a year. So each thought the other had finally conceded and admitted they'd been wrong all along. Which was all anybody ever wanted. That ended the war, and marked the beginning of Nicholas's reign. The universe rejoiced at having a peacemaker as emperor.

That was actually his second act as emperor. But he would never have agreed to retain the title if the Syndics hadn't agreed to his first act. The emperor ruled from the center of the universe. Nicholas declared Earth the center. And then, he had all the petroleum removed from Earth, preparing his fellow Earthlings to eventually become citizens of the universe, and putting an end to vanishing socks, since tourists were only allowed to mess with petro-cloaked worlds. (He was also putting an end to mysteriously appearing crop circles and inexplicable spontaneous traffic jams, among other things, though he was not yet aware of this.)

But, to balance this loss of a major fuel source, he posted the plans for the electron harvester on the internet, giving every country free energy. The wealth of nations would rise or fall because of this, and the balance of power would shift in small and large ways, but all in all, life would become better for most people. And, as a bonus, now that everyone could understand each other, French class was a piece of cake. Or *gateau.*

Each evening, Nicholas would step into Henrietta's cage at the selected time, and his advisor, publicist, chronicler, and friend, Crazy Clave, one of the most popular and beloved sfumblers in the universe, would teleport him and Henrietta to his ship, *The Nick of Space,* where they would deal with official emperor tasks and reminisce about the good old days. At least once a week, while his parents were out at an auditorium or birthday party, entertaining infants, they'd jump somewhere amazing and slightly dangerous, because it's a big universe and there's a lot to see.

And they never missed one of Spott's concerts.

But let's get back to class, to observe one more incident

in the increasingly amazing life of Nicholas V. Landrew, Emperor of the Universe, and enjoy the wonderful moment that he experienced toward the end of algebra.

"Class, please welcome our new student," Miss Galendrea said. "Come on in, Stella."

Nicholas's head snapped around so fast, he almost ended his reign with a broken neck. Then his jaw dropped, falling slightly farther than it had ever dropped before—though with good reason—and his eyebrows rose high enough to prove, beyond any doubt, that he was not a Menmarian.

It was her!

"This is my cousin," Miss Galendrea said. "Please make her feel welcome."

Nicholas managed to send a smile toward Stella. She smiled back, as if he mattered. Which, he realized, he did.

And so, you now know the story of how Nicholas V. Landrew, a seventh grader from Yelm, Washington, became Emperor of the Universe. And how I, your narrator, became one with it.

Moo.

READ ON FOR A SNEAK PEEK AT

THE CLONE CONSPIRACY

THE SECOND BOOK IN THE EMPEROR OF THE UNIVERSE TRILOGY!

JAMMED UP

When Cloud Mansion Intergalactic, the massive spacecraft that served as his home and base of his operations, self-destructed, Morglob Sputum, the universally famous talent agent, was in his office, near the center of the complex. Thus, he wasn't ejected into the bleak vacuum of space at a high velocity. It was more of a nudge. Four days later, he was still traveling at pretty much the same speed, since Isaac Newton had nailed it when he observed that a body in motion tends to stay in motion unless acted upon by an external force.

Morglob was basically coasting.

The pirate ship he encountered was another matter. It was moving fast, running toward a rumored incapacitated freighter carrying a precious cargo of Swerdlian tongue swords. Morglob met the ship head on, splorking into it with enough force to smear himself into a thin jelly across several dozen square meters of the outer hull. While this did him no harm, it also did nothing to improve his mood.

The ship's captain noticed a glitch in the instrument readout, indicating a minor collision. He ordered a crew member to suit up and examine the hull.

While the crew member was pushing herself into a spacesuit, Morglob was pulling himself back into a thicker form. When the crew member entered the airlock, Morglob was in the process of flowing toward the small hatch on the outside of the airlock. When the outer hatch cycled open, he splashed inside, startling the crew member, who was in the process of attaching her safety line. She lost her footing and stumbled into space, untethered.

By the time someone thought to check on the crew member, it was far too late to try to find her. Not that they would have, even if they'd seen her drift past the viewport, waving frantically and trailing her safety line like an umbilical cord.

When the pirates eventually cycled the airlock and admitted Morglob, they formed a circle and stared down at the slimy, glistening creature.

"What is it?" the first mate asked. He prodded Morglob with his foot.

"Jelly?' the second mate suggested.

"I like jelly," another crew member said.

As they stood there, discussing the virtue of jelly and daring one another to give the currently available jelly a taste, Morglob glorped across the room to an air duct. It wouldn't work as well as his normal speaking tube, but it would have to do for now. He flowed around it and said, "Bring your captain here."

The pirates stared at one another. The captain hated them as much as they hated him, and he generally stayed in his quarters unless there were vulnerable ships to attack.

"Now!" Morglob shouted.

Losing his home had made him cranky. As had being snubbed. He'd offered to make the Earthling a star, and was rewarded with treachery. The long drift through space afterward had not improved his mood. It had, however, given him ample time to contemplate various means of revenge against the monsters who had destroyed his home. They would pay. And they would suffer.

He did not know, yet, of the events that had transpired after he was booted into space. He had no idea

Nicholas was now the Emperor of the Universe. He would learn this soon enough, since Nicholas seemed to be a favorite subject of newscasts, sfumbles, and reality series. That information would only make his task easier, since an emperor would not be hard to find. Nor would his companions.

And it would make their eventual destruction all that much more enjoyable, since they would fall from great heights. Morglob issued a small glorble of happiness as he pulled free of the register and awaited the captain—who, if all went according to Morglob's rapidly forming plan, would soon be his servant. "They will suffer," he said. "And then they will die."

He was not the only one with plans of vengeance.

STARSCAPE READING AND ACTIVITY GUIDE TO

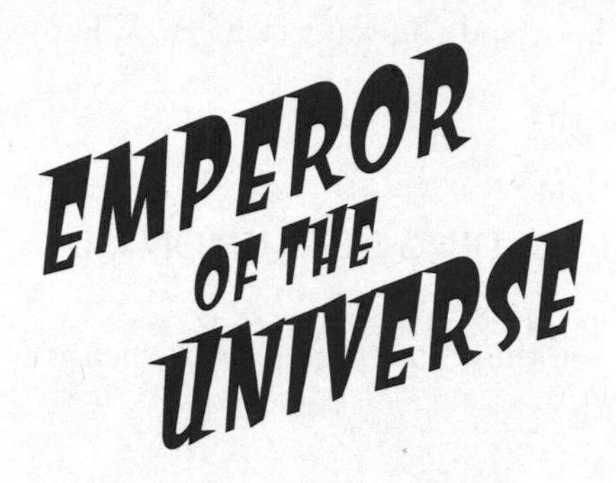

BY DAVID LUBAR
Ages 9–12; Grades 4–7

PRE-READING DISCUSSION QUESTIONS

1. What are the first questions or reactions this book's title brings to your mind? Does the title make you think the story is going to be funny, sarcastic, dramatic, silly, serious, or a combination of those things? Author David Lubar subtitles this book: "A Fable with Spaceships and Aliens." Have you read or heard a fable? What was it about? A fable usually has a moral—a meaningful message or lesson—the author hopes to pass along to the reader. Why do you think the author might want you to know *Emperor of the Universe* is a fable from the moment you see the title?

2. In *Emperor of the Universe*, middle-schooler Nicholas V. Landrew finds himself on a wacky interplanetary adventure when circumstances (and some sneakiness on his part) land him on his own for three weeks. If you had three weeks on your own, with no school, parents, or plans, and could go on an adventure—unrestricted by real-world limitations like money, age, or the rules

of school, parents, or even nature—where would you want to go and why? Who would you want to meet? What would you want to do?

POST-READING DISCUSSION QUESTIONS

1. Who did you think the narrator was when you began to read the story?

2. Other than brief mentions or appearances, and a few texts and phone calls, the grown-ups in Nicholas's life (his parents, Uncle Bruce, Aunt Lucy) are given very small roles in the story. Why do you think the author chose to do this?

3. Nicholas makes the decision to step into the gerbil cage after he witnesses his gerbil, Henrietta, and the "test" package of ground beef disappear in a flash of purple light. Would you have chosen to do the same thing if you found yourself in Nicholas's situation? Why or why not?

4. In chapter three, "A Brief, but Useful, Morsel of History," we learn: "From the moment that one race ventured off their home planet and stumbled across another inhabited world, there has always been an Emperor of the Universe." How do you think these two ideas—races from different planets meeting and the need for a universal leader—are related? Do you think the Emperor of the Universe compares to the concept of a God or God-like figure from religion or mythology? Why or why not?

5. From the outset of the novel, author David Lubar intertwines chapters that focus on Nicholas V. Landrew's specific story with

chapters that take a much broader view—as broad as all of time and space—almost like a telescope zooming in and out. Why do you think the author chose to structure the book this way?

6. Author David Lubar is a master of word play. Can you cite chapter titles or quotes where the author uses puns or a twist on a common phrase or famous work to foreshadow or emphasize specific plot points or themes?

7. How does Nicholas's encounter with the Craborzi lead to the "Flamenco Dance of Death"? What is the GollyGosh! and how does it relate to the "amazing thing that didn't happen next"?

8. How do Stella Astrallis and her newsflashes develop and connect parts of the story?

9. In chapter ten, "All Aboard!" Nicholas meets freelance space courier Clave. How does his use of terms like "barbarians" and "backwater planet" reveal Clave's view of Earth and Earthlings? Clave says to Nicholas: "I'm sure you're a little dazzled by learning how small your place in the universe is." Should we be careful about making assumptions about what an advanced, intelligent, significant race we human beings are? How does the author use Clave and other characters to help Nicholas (and the reader) see that everything is a matter of perspective, and that there might be many perspectives that differ from the Earthbound point of view?

10. What does Clave explain to Nicholas about the Ubiquitous Matrix and Earth being a "petro-cloaked" planet? Do you think the Ubiquitous Matrix is like a universal internet? Or do you think it's more a spiritual than technological system? Why do you think the Ubiquitous Matrix is compromised on petro-cloaked

planets? Do you think the author is flagging issues like poor environmental stewardship of planet Earth, pollution, climate change, and our society's priorities being out of sync with nature?

11. Can you discuss how Clave's obsession with "sfumbles" is a spoof on cellphones, texting, blogging, or posting constantly, as people of all ages tend to do these days? Later, the author comments on things going "univiral." How does this spoof the modern phenomenon of silly, trivial things "going viral" in our chronically plugged-in society?

12. How does Nicholas's diplomatic advice to Menmar's President Nixon get misinterpreted and lead to disaster? "Planet torchers" sound like the stuff of science fiction, but how are they similar to real-world nuclear bombs?

13. How do Henrietta and Nicholas figure out that Jeef is a "holy cow"? Do you think Jeef, who often uses Bible phrases, represents a religious or spiritual perspective in this story? Why or why not?

14. How does the expansion of Thinkerator technology compare to the proliferation of personal computing, cellphones, and online commerce in our society? Can you think of real-world counterparts for companies like Hyperjump Unlimited?

15. Why is Morglob Sputum interested in Nicholas? Why does Spott want to escape? What happens to Cloud Mansion Intergalactic?

16. What happens on Zeng, and how does Spott save the day? Why is Nicholas afraid to go to Spott's home planet, Beradaxia? Why does Nicholas decide to return to Zeng to fix the "devour-

ing singularity"? How does this show how he has grown, or changed, in the course of the story?

17. Do you agree with the first acts Nicholas takes after the Syndics inform him he is the new Emperor of the Universe? Would you have made the same or different choices?

18. Though he highlights some positives (including friendships that transcend huge differences), author David Lubar's interplanetary citizens struggle with many of the challenges that plague Earthlings—consumerism; materialism; war and conflict; pettiness; obsession with celebrity and style over substance; money, rather than morals, driving "progress" and proliferation of technology. Does he fill his universe with these flaws and perils so we can reconsider the havoc they are wreaking in our own (real) time and place? Nicholas gets the unique responsibility and opportunity to make a difference as Emperor of the Universe, but shouldn't each of us do our part?

COMMON CORE–ALIGNED READING, WRITING, AND RESEARCH ACTIVITIES

These Common Core–aligned activities may be used in conjunction with the pre- and post-reading discussion questions above.

1. MEAT YOUR NARRATOR (POINT OF VIEW). Philosophical Jeef is the omniscient narrator of *Emperor of the Universe*. Having gone from content cow to ground beef to her current (almost) all-knowing state of "one with the universe," she has a very unique, fluid view of time and space and how and when Nicholas Landrew's story unfolds within it. Invite students to consider how

the story might be different if it were told from another character's perspective. Have students choose a key event from the story and write a 2–3 paragraph description of it from another character's first-person point of view (such as Nicholas's, Henrietta's, or Clave's). Students can write an additional 1–2 paragraphs comparing and contrasting the omniscient viewpoint to the first-person viewpoint. What challenges or opportunities does each point of view create for the author, the reader, and the characters?

2. HOW ON (OR OFF!) EARTH IS THAT POSSIBLE? (TEXT TYPE: OPINION PIECE) In chapter five, "What Didn't Happen Next," the narrator (Jeef) observes: "Many physicists believe our observations help determine the nature of reality, and our decisions create parallel universes." This suggests that a single person's perceptions and decisions have an enormous amount of power, as well as the mind-boggling idea that there can be more than one reality, or multiple dimensions or versions of reality. Write a 1–2 page essay explaining why you agree or disagree with this idea.

3. ALIEN ALERT! (TEXT TYPE: NARRATIVE) In *Emperor of the Universe,* Nicholas V. Landrew goes on a mind-blowing, life-changing three-week intergalactic journey. Can you reverse the circumstances and write a detailed, action-packed 3–4 page story imagining what would happen if an alien beamed down into your bedroom, rather than beaming you up onto a ship like Nicholas experienced? What is the series of events that unfolds when the alien visits you? How does the alien affect your life at school and at home? What adventures or misadventures do you have together? What do you learn from each other?

4. SLIME AND PUNISHMENT (TEXT TYPE: ARGUMENTS). In *Emperor of the Universe,* Nicholas seems to wreak havoc wherever he goes on his unexpected and chaotic journey through the universe. (There was also the "exploding roach brains" incident at the science fair back on planet Earth.) Ask students to review the "roster" of incriminating incidents: the stomping of Craborzi scientists; the mutual destruction of the Menmarian and Zefinoran planets; the self-destruction of Morglob Sputum's headquarters; the escape from Zeng (to avoid becoming human sacrifices), which causes Zeng to start imploding, creating a "devouring singularity" that threatens to end the entire universe. Invite students to select an incident, decide if they think Nicholas is innocent or guilty, and write a 1–3 paragraph argument supporting their position with relevant evidence drawn from *Emperor of the Universe.* (If desired, students may write arguments for or against more than one of Nicholas's unwitting "crimes.")

5. DEEP THOUGHTS IN DEEP SPACE (THEMES). In *Emperor of the Universe,* author David Lubar explores many timely and philosophical themes and ideas. (For example: the nature of self-awareness, the possibility of alternate realities, the irony and futility of war, the consequences—both humorous and dangerous—of individual or cultural assumptions, the power of media to shape or mislead public perception; the concepts of mortality and immortality, the unchecked proliferation of technology.) Ask students to select a theme and write a 1–2 page essay examining how that theme is developed throughout *Emperor of the Universe,* making sure to include relevant quotes and references from the story. Or you can focus on themes in small groups or class discussions and debates.

6. BUILDING CHARACTER (COMPARE AND CONTRAST). In a short essay, compare and contrast the characters of Nicholas V. Landrew and Clave the Menmarian. Consider physical and emotional differences. Be sure to discuss their *philosophical* differences, too—analyzing how these characters view and understand the world, or the universe, and their role in it—something which author David Lubar has humorously and thoughtfully emphasized in characters, situations, and narration throughout *Emperor of the Universe*. How does Mr. Lubar explore and develop the relationship between Nicholas and Clave over the course of the story? How do these characters discover and overcome their "cultural" differences? How and where do Clave and Nicholas, citizens of entirely different planets, find common ground? Use relevant details, examples, and quotes from the text to examine how Clave and Nicholas act and interact in different situations throughout their complicated journey. Do they see themselves, and each other, differently at the end of the story than they did at the beginning? Explain how and why.

7. FACT AND (SCIENCE) FICTION (RESEARCH AND PRESENT). Invite students to work in pairs or small groups to do online and library research to inform a presentation on one of the subjects listed below. Use the research to create a PowerPoint or other multimedia presentation to share findings with classmates. Invite students to discuss how the factual information presented relates to the fictional *Emperor of the Universe.*

- Douglas Noel Adams. (David Lubar dedicated *Emperor of the Universe* to this English essayist, humorist, and satirist, who authored *The Hitchhiker's Guide to the Galaxy.*)

- French philosopher and mathematician René Descartes. (David Lubar revisits Descartes's famous quote "I think, therefore I am" with Henrietta the gerbil's remark after gaining self-awareness and the ability to speak: "I am. Therefore I think.")

- Studies or statistics exploring the impact the proliferation of cellphones, social media, and digital devices is having on youth (or overall) culture.

- Brief history of World War I (1914–1918) and why it was dubbed "The War to End War" or "The War to End All Wars." (The *Emperor of the Universe* chapter title "An End to All Wars" seems to echo this sentiment, but is it ultimately a hopeful or hollow promise?)

- NASA's recent mission to Mars. (How might some of the scenarios in *Emperor of the Universe* be a cautionary tale for how one species thinks about and pursues interplanetary exploration?)

ENGLISH LANGUAGE ARTS COMMON CORE READING AND WRITING STANDARDS

RL.4.1-3, RL.4.6, RL.5.1-3, RL.5.6, RL.6.1-3, RL.6.6, RL.7.1-3, RL.7.6; W.4.1-2A, 4.3, 4.7, W.5.1-2A, 5.3, 5.7, 5.9 W.6.2A, 6.3, 6.7, 6.9 W.7.1-2A, 7.3, 7.7, 7.9; SL.4.1, 4.4; SL.5.1, 5.4; SL.6.1, 6.4; SL.7.1, 7.4.

ABOUT THE AUTHOR

© Joelle Lubar

Ever since DAVID LUBAR was little, he has traveled to alien planets, fantasy realms, and earthly wonders by means of books. He's thrilled he can help launch others on this journey through his own novels and short stories. In the past twenty-five years, he's written fifty books for young readers, including *Hidden Talents* (an American Library Association Best Book for Young Adults); *My Rotten Life,* which is currently under development for a cartoon series; and the Weenies Tales short story collections, which have sold more than 2.7 million copies. He grew up in Morristown, New Jersey, and currently lives in Nazareth, Pennsylvania, with his awesome wife, and not far from his amazing daughter. In his spare time, he takes naps on the couch.

www.davidlubar.com